BECAUSE OF YOU

SWANSON COURT SERIES #5

SERENA GREY

SWEET ACACIA PRESS

Copyright © 2020 Serena Grey
All rights reserved.
ISBN-13: 978-1-7336286-5-5
Sweet Acacia Press

Because of you
In gardens of blossoming flowers
I long for the sweet perfumes of spring.
- Pablo Neruda.

To second chances.

CHAPTER ONE

LIZ

*I*n a matter of moments, I'll be face to face with Aidan Court.

For the first time in seven years.

I swallow the tension tightening in my throat and try to dampen the nervousness building in my chest.

Aidan.

He hates me.

He detests me.

And I don't blame him.

Not when I've spent years hating myself for what I did to him.

In front of me, slanting brass script on a white door spells out the number of actress Celeste Granger's Park Avenue apartment. The lively sounds of a party—music, laughter, and gossip—filter through the doors and walls and into my ears, pulling at my fluttery nerves.

"You should show up at Celeste Granger's soiree," Natalia had suggested yesterday.

"Why on earth would I?" After abandoning my debut play on Broadway seven years ago to chase Hollywood stardom, hanging out with the theatre crowd wasn't high on my list of preferred activities to occupy my time in New York city.

"Aidan will be there," Natalia replied with a shrug. She's my father's longtime assistant, sometime lover, and now manager of McKay Theatre productions, and she always has a solid reason for everything. "The sooner you two get your...reunion out of the way, the better for the new play."

The new play. My pretext for being in New York at all.

Now, with my inevitable confrontation with Aidan only moments away, I take a deep breath and push the door open.

The hushed whispering starts from the people standing closest to the entrance.

Liz McKay.

Liz McKay.

When you're a box office sensation and multiple time sexiest woman of the year, you get used to stopping conversation when you walk into a room.

I ignore the murmurs of my name and look around, searching for the one face I'm here to see.

Aidan.

My eyes lock on his, drawn toward him, almost as if I've heard him call my name.

Seeing him knocks the breath out of my lungs.

He's standing at the bar, glass in hand. Dressed in an inky black jacket, dark pants and a dark gray shirt, he's an improbable mixture of a bad-boy and a prep school prince. From across the room, his vivid blue eyes blaze daggers at me from a face that's perfection personified—A face filled with emotions so intense, they almost knock me off my feet.

I take a step forward, drawn to him despite the animosity I can feel coming off him in waves. He turns away, tossing back his drink like he's not aware the whole room is looking at us...waiting for us.

Someone vaguely familiar comes over to my side and starts to talk to me, and I smile in response, my eyes still on Aidan. He's facing me again, glass now empty, the fierce burning in his eyes filling me with memories I've tried to ignore for seven years.

No more.

Cutting across the room, I make straight for him. I feel like he could devour me with his intensity alone, right here, in front of all these people, he would claim me and burn me to ashes, along with every single heartache of the years I've spent apart from him.

He doesn't move until I'm right in front of him. I open my mouth to say his name, and right then, he strides past me, leaving me standing alone, open-mouthed, staring at his empty, abandoned glass.

FOUR DAYS EARLIER.

It's evening when we land in New York. The plane, a sleek jet with plush leather seats and thick carpeting is gliding through gold-hued clouds when the pretty stewardess appears and reminds me to fasten my seatbelt. After we land, she returns to ask for my autograph. I oblige, signing my name on the cover of a glossy fashion magazine adorned with a picture of me wearing bright lipstick and a careless smile.

Outside, a faint breeze stirs my hair and teases my cheeks. My sunglasses are already in place—black, oversized designer shades. With my high heels and straight-from-the-runway dress, I look every inch the glamorous movie star.

Two cars are waiting on the tarmac—one to transport my luggage to my rarely used apartment in the village, and a black SUV with tinted windows, to take me to my father's home.

My gaze sweeps across the Manhattan skyscape visible across the river and longing fills my chest.

Home.

I've missed this place.

The sudden burst of music from my phone snaps me out of my nostalgia.

It's Jenny, my assistant. "What's up?"

"Nothing," she replies, her voice bright and chirpy, as usual. "Just checking to see you've landed. Marvin's been blowing up my phone all day. He's trying to reach you."

I groan at the thought of my manager. "He's the last person I want to talk to. He's determined to make me change my mind about the movie."

"Well..." Jenny draws out the word. "A guaranteed box office hit with one of Hollywood's biggest stars who also happens to be your ex? Think of the free publicity. He'd be a horrible manager if he didn't try to change your mind."

"Well, I'm not going to, Jenny, and you know why."

She sighs. "Maybe if you told him why you had to leave, about your father... he'd understand..."

"No." My voice is sharp. I trust Marvin Steeps with my career, but privacy in my personal issues is something I need to work harder than most people to attain and it's something I guard closely. "Marvin might reveal something to the press," I continue, my tone softer. "The *Liz McKay* brand is more important to him than discretion about my father's condition."

"You're right," Jenny sighs. "I'm sorry, Liz."

"It's fine." At this point I just want to see my father. His illness is a shocking surprise. I didn't know he was sick until his former assistant Natalia Barrow called me a week ago.

"You need to come down and spend some time with your father," she'd said without mincing words. Instantly, I knew something was wrong, that my twice monthly phone calls with my father had not nearly been enough.

His housekeeper, Gertie, confessed the rest to me. My dad's health has been failing for a while.

And I had been oblivious.

Guilt floods my body once again and I hurry toward Percy, my father's long-time driver, who is waiting by the SUV. He opens the rear door as I approach.

I greet him with a smile. "How's it going Percy?"

He shrugs powerful shoulders, his face creasing with a fond expression that amplifies my nostalgia. "So, so, Lizzie-bean. How are you?"

"Hanging on."

"Aren't we all?"

With a chuckle, I slide into the back seat. During the drive, I fiddle with my phone. I don't tweet anymore, or do Facebook, but I have an Instagram account where I post things that interest and inspire me—books, art, images from the sets where I work and little snippets about my life.

My last post is a picture I took in an obscure art gallery I found close to my last movie set. *"Don't hesitate to reach for your dreams,"* I'd typed under the colorful painting of a figure reaching for the sky. Now, I scroll through the comments, smiling at the sweetest ones.

If only I didn't feel like such a hypocrite.

Once, I thought I knew what it meant to reach for my dreams, but now I know my dreams will remain incomplete until I reach into my past, toward the one person who has haunted me for seven years.

Aidan Court.

Just thinking about him fills me with an acute and painful longing. For so long, I've buried that longing under a pile of work and events, but something about my father's illness has hollowed me out, and now, I'm swiftly succumbing to the tender ache that has never gone away.

Once again, I'm in the same city, breathing the same air as him. But this will not be like all the other times. This time, I will see him. I will talk to him.

"Aidan," I whisper his name under my breath.

"Did you want something?" Percy asks.

"No." I shake my head and turn my gaze outside the window. Soon, we're in Manhattan, and I drink in the familiar sights and the memories that jump out at me like fireworks. No matter how long I stay away or how far I go, this city is where I feel like I am home. Not my much-too-large house in the Hollywood hills with the pool, the magnificent patio and the private cinema. This place, with the noise, the people, and the traffic—it's where my spirit lives.

The car stops at the entrance to a classic art deco building. It's very old New York—home to at least two billionaires and other wealthy people. Outside, there's no mob of paparazzi, no cameras, only a doorman dressed in uniform standing under the ancient awning at the entrance. He approaches the car and opens the door, inclining his head as I step out.

"Nice to see you again, Ms. McKay."

"Thank you..." I try to remember his name. I met him a year ago, the last time I visited my father.

"Jeffrey," he reminds me, still smiling.

"Thank you, Jeffrey." There's an apologetic note in my voice, and I hope he's not offended enough to write an anonymous post trashing me on the internet. Sighing, I adjust my shades and hurry into the building.

On my way to the elevators, my heels click on polished marble. An elegant woman in a faux-fur coat glides past me, leading two beautiful terriers on gold threaded leashes. She neither looks in my direction or registers recognition of my face.

"God, I love this city," I say under my breath.

The elevator deposits me in front of my father's apartment. Inside the entrance foyer, my feet sink into the thick carpet, my eager gaze taking in the familiar room, the framed mirrors, paintings and pieces of baroque furniture. The decor is from a time before it was fashionable to be minimalist, and it fills me with heart-tightening nostalgia.

The door to the living room opens, revealing a stern face that has softened with age.

"Darling!" Gertie's voice is deep, firm and familiar. "My beautiful darling Lizzie-bean."

"Hi Gertie," I murmur, walking into the comfort of her embrace. Gertie has been with my father since I was twelve. She's family, and I love her dearly.

She peers at me with sharp gray eyes. "You look tired. Have you been working too hard? Those weeks and weeks on set..." she shudders. "You should slow down."

"I will." I follow her into the living room. It's decorated like the foyer, with ornate furniture and large windows that frame a spectacular view of the park.

"I'm glad you're here," Gertie is saying. "It feels like forever since we last saw you."

"Just a little more than a year."

"You had that premiere, and you came to visit us for a minute."

"A day."

"It felt like a minute." She sighs, watching as I walk over to the grand piano in a corner of the room. "Nobody plays that now."

I have a sudden memory of a famous actress playing the instrument at one of my father's parties and my nostalgia intensifies. "How bad is he?" My voice is strained. My father was diagnosed with cancer. For a year, he underwent the treatments without telling me anything about it.

Days ago, after I'd spoken to Natalia and Gertie, he confessed everything to me, leaving me heartbroken for a whole number of reasons—the pain he's going through and the knowledge that he waited so long to confide in me. I'm also afraid, because I don't want to lose him.

"He was very sick for a while, what with the chemo and all." Gertie sniffs. "He's been better these past few weeks. Stronger. He can't wait to see you."

"And I can't wait to see him." I imagine the physical toll this sickness would have taken on him, and a cold hand of fear grips my stomach, but I steel myself. No matter what, I'm determined to be strong. "Where is he?"

"The patio. He likes to sit out there these days."

Outside, there's a faint breeze stirring the leaves of a few potted plants that line the patio. My father is lying on a recliner, his body covered by a thick blanket. Beside him, there's a recent bestselling novel with an old tasseled bookmark sticking out of the pages. His eyes are closed, so he can't see me, but I see him. I see his drawn face and his thin hair. I see the hollows that were once his cheeks and I choke back a sob.

His eyes flutter open and come alive when they land on me. His face brightens, and he starts to rise from the recliner.

"Dad!" I rush over to him, "You don't have to get up."

He ignores me and pushes his blanket away, rising to his feet with some effort. "Nonsense." His voice is firm, and he pulls me into his arms for a hug. "As if I would lie here like an invalid instead of giving my princess a proper welcome."

He's thinner than I remember, and even his voice has changed. How did I never notice on the phone that his commanding baritone had given way to something weaker and more strained? My eyes water, and I relax into the warm comfort of his hug. There's a faint odor of medications, but I don't care. "I've missed you, Dad."

"Missed you too, sweet-pea." He cradles my face in his hands. "You look good." There's a note of approval and satisfaction in his voice. "How was your flight?"

I shrug. "Smooth."

He nods, then glances at the recliner with distaste. "Let's go inside. We can sit in my study and drink tea while you tell me everything that's been going on. This old man has no idea what's happening outside this apartment."

"You're not old," I protest, taking his arm so he can lean on me as we walk. It hurts to see how fragile he is. He's only sixty-five and has always looked young for his age. Now, he looks at least ten years older.

The study is warm, cozy, and still furnished with the thick carpet, dark mahogany bookshelves, solid desk, and the plush settee where, as a teenager, I'd often curled up to read. Battling another wave of longing for days gone by, I wait until my dad settles into his favorite stuffed-leather winged armchair, then I curl up on a corner of the settee. Gertie appears with tea, green for my father, and Earl Grey with a splash of lemon for me.

"I read somewhere that you were planning to film an action flick in Spain," my father says, raising his cup to his lips. There's no disapproval in his voice, but I've always known, somehow, that he's not very impressed with the movies I've done in the last seven years. Movies that have done little to showcase my dramatic talent but have made my face and name recognizable everywhere in the world.

"I pulled out of that project." I sip my tea and give him a smile. "I've been working too hard...I needed some time off."

His face tells me he's not buying the lie. "Liz, I don't want you to put your work on hold because of me."

"Is that why you didn't tell me you were sick?" Dropping my mask, I let him see the hurt I've been hiding. "Because you think my work is more important to me than you are?"

He looks away.

"Dad..."

"I thought I could beat it." He shrugs, and there's a bitter note in his voice. "I wanted to tell you good news. That I'd been sick, and I wasn't anymore."

"But you aren't." My voice rises. "The treatment..."

He shakes his head. "I'm still sick, Liz. There'll be a second course of treatment."

Panic races through my chest. "But then you'll get better."

"Maybe." His voice is soft, his eyes earnest as they hold mine. "Maybe not."

Tears sting at my eyes and I will them not to fall. I'm not here because he needs my strength or support. I'm here so he can prepare me for an eventuality he thinks he can no longer avoid.

You need to come down and spend some time with your father. Natalia had said.

Before it's too late.

"I'm sorry, Liz."

"No, I'm sorry, dad." My eyes are stinging. "I'm sorry I wasn't here. I should have been here from the beginning."

"No. No. Sweet-pea. I don't want that. I never have. I don't want you locked up in this old apartment with me just because I'm sick. I've lived, Liz. I've had a great life, and I want you to live yours. That's what I've always wanted." He sighs. "And let's face it, you're not just my daughter anymore. You're Liz McKay. What will you tell your public? How will you explain an extended absence from your work?"

He's right. I don't want people—the tabloids, forums and fans—to speculate about his health and tie it to when I would be free to work again. He deserves more than that. "I hate when people say that," I reply in a small voice. "*You're Liz McKay.* Like I'm a product."

He chuckles. "A very valuable product."

I can't argue with that. "I spoke to Natalia before I came to town." Natalia has been managing the McKay theater company since Dad's retirement two years ago. "There is a play..."

"The Break of Day." He nods. "Natalia's been working hard to get it off the ground. Difficult sponsors..." He shudders, though a sad softness enters his voice when he says Natalia's name. "You're considering playing Lillie? Are you sure? It's a big part, and you haven't worked in theatre for years."

I try not to be offended. "I've not forgotten how to act just because I've been doing action movies and romantic comedies. With the play, I'd have a perfect reason for being in the city, and it could advance my career too, so you don't have to worry about my life being on hold."

"It's not a bad plan." His eyes close and I realize he's tired.

"Why don't you rest?" I suggest. "We'll continue talking later."

He releases a soft breath, already asleep. I leave the study, and once I'm outside the door, I allow myself to cry. Out in the patio, my vision blurs as I ball my father's blanket in my arms and bury my face in the soft wool, feeling more helpless than I've ever felt in my life.

I take a few moments to compose myself. Back in the study, my father is still asleep, so I cover him with the blanket and go around the desk to the window.

The drapes are drawn, but I peer out through a gap in the hanging fabrics at the people on the sidewalks, the trees, the cars that never stop...

There's so much life everywhere, and yet its very essence is out of anyone's control. We can't even prevent our loved ones from falling sick.

The wall to one side of the desk is lined with bookshelves. Walking over, I trace my fingers over thick volumes—memoirs, business guides, insider stories about famous plays and the legends that starred in them. I spent my childhood poring over the pictures in these books, long before I read any of the words.

One shelf holds the awards my father has collected over the years. Two awards for best producer occupy pride of place, next to a picture of my mother who died when I was seven. She's bowing on the stage of her last musical. There's also a framed letter in my childish teenage scrawl. *"To the most loving father in the world,"* it begins. I smile at the familiar words before moving on to the pictures of my father with playwrights, theater owners, and politicians. There's a picture of me on-stage, and another, with me, my father and Aidan.

My heart catches and I close my eyes, stunned by the clarity of my memories. It was the opening night of my first play, and after the standing ovation at the end, I'd felt almost drunk with triumph. That night was magical, and Aidan...

Aidan...

The familiar ache of loss blooms in my belly. I

haven't seen him in years. Seven years to be exact. I've read about him and followed his career, the award-winning plays, the two acclaimed movies... I've seen all his plays, in what Jenny calls my stealth mode, but in the flesh—though I have hungered, thirsted for him, it has been seven years.

There's a familiar ache in the tips of my fingers— longing, the desire to feel someone else's warmth, someone else's love. Reaching out, I touch his face and my fingers find glass. I release a slow breath. He's smiling in the picture, a lighthearted, carefree smile, his sensuous lips perpetually upturned in one corner, his thick dark hair reaching almost to his shoulders with the stubborn forelock spilling forward onto his face. I remember my fingers in that hair, those lips kissing me, his mesmerizing blue eyes boring deep into mine as we pledged our bodies to each other, found pleasure and made promises...

Promises you broke.

I suppress the accusing voice, keeping my gaze on Aidan's face. He no longer looks like he did the night the picture was taken. He was twenty-four then. Now, he's thirty-one. The hair is shorter, the eyes less carefree, the smile is now a wry smirk, and sometimes I wonder how much of that is my fault.

"That was a wonderful night." My father's voice startles me, and I turn around. He's still in his chair, but his eyes are on the picture.

"It was perfect," I agree, my voice soft. "You, me and Aidan." Saying his name out loud has a strange effect on me. My voice catches, and my stomach suddenly feels light. I close my eyes and repeat it silently to myself. Aidan. Aidan. Aidan.

My father is studying my face. "He's one of the best. He'd coax an award-winning performance from anyone. I always hoped you two would resolve all the..." He stops and sighs. "Natalia wants him to direct the play. She's been trying to lock him down for ages. She hoped he would be a draw for investors."

I frown. "I wasn't aware of that."

"I know." He shrugs. "Although, with you both on the project..."

My laugh is bitter. "With our history together, it will become a carnival. An investor's dream come true, for sure. The tabloids would speculate to death about us. It won't happen, though. Aidan will never agree to work with me. Once he discovers there's a chance I'll be in the play, he will never sign on to do it."

"And if he does..." My father gives me a piercing look. "Would you work with him?"

The possibility causes something to tighten low in my belly. I close my eyes. *Reach for your dreams.* I'd come for my father, but I also came for Aidan. "Yes." My voice is soft but firm. "Yes, of course."

"Maybe he feels the same."

My lips curve in a sad smile and I shake my head. "I broke his heart, dad. He hates me. If I were him, I wouldn't want to work with me either."

My father shrugs. "You might be surprised."

I know he's wrong, but still, the words give me hope.

CHAPTER TWO

AIDAN

"Fuck me," I mutter under my breath before scrawling my signature on the dotted line.

"This is a great project," Debra reminds me with an elaborate eye-roll. "I know you're excited."

I ignore the eye-roll and watch her gather up the contracts. She has a quiet efficiency that's invaluable in an assistant, and she is right. I am excited, but I know the feeling will only last until I enter the theater and face the stage, and it would feel as though Liz was standing right there, eyes dancing, watching me with that trademark Liz McKay expression that is both challenge and capitulation.

Then for the next few months, I would drive myself and my actors, demanding their best performances, trying to forget the one woman I don't want to think about, the one woman I can't stop thinking about.

Liz.

It doesn't help that when I walk out of the theater there'd be a twenty-foot billboard in Times Square with her face smiling slyly down at me. It doesn't help that the critics can't stop comparing any new play I direct with that first play. She's like the poet's *voiceless ghost*, facing round about me everywhere.

"So, I'll get these back to Natalia ASAP," Debra announces, interrupting my thoughts. "Don't forget, you're attending Celeste Granger's party later this evening."

I grimace. "That's today?"

She gives me an exasperated frown. "Yes."

I respect Celeste Granger. She's a talented performer, and her soirees are legendary—a way for industry heavyweights to socialize and make deals over cocktails and aperitifs. She always invites me, and I'd agreed to attend this one, though I'm already regretting that decision.

"Everybody who's anybody will be there," Debra tells me, "and it wouldn't hurt you to socialize a little."

"I wouldn't be too sure about that." I drum my fingers on the surface of my desk, pensive, and unsure why. It feels like there's a storm cloud in the air, about to burst.

My eyes go to the documents now tucked under Debra's arm. I never sign contracts without a thorough vetting by my lawyers and myself. I've also met with Natalia Barrow, the producer, over the last few weeks, to discuss the play, logistics, auditions, everything...and yet now that I've signed the contract I feel like there's something I've missed, something significant that I won't like.

"Do you need anything else?" Debra asks, no doubt eager to run off to her boyfriend in Brooklyn and indulge in a few hours of eye-rolling about her privileged yet bad-tempered boss. Not that I blame her.

Just then, the door to my bedroom opens. I don't turn to look, but Debra's eyes follow Claire as she emerges fully dressed and walks over to my chair.

"Hi, Claire," Debra's voice is dry. She doesn't like Claire. Hell, it's not even settled that she likes me.

"Hey." Claire acknowledges her, then kisses me on the lips. After our lunch *date*, which occurred mostly in my bed, she's ready to get back to work at the reputable art gallery where she's a curator. "See you tonight?" Her eyes are questioning.

I shake my head. "I have a thing."

"Oh." Her smile stays on and she looks from me to Debra. "Call me, then."

As soon as the door closes behind her, Debra makes a sound in her throat. "She lives here now?"

"You know she doesn't."

She smirks. "You should give her a key. She looks like she wants a key."

"Maybe, I will," I reply, glaring at my assistant. In the seven years since Liz, there have been a few women. Like me, they soon realized there would be no one else for me, and that to me, love, commitment, and all that forever stuff would always be little more than bullshit. Claire is the most recent, and she knows that anything more than sex is off the table.

"That will be the day."

"It's none of your business, Deb, but we're just casual and it's fine."

"Does she know?" Debra sings under her breath, then grins and taps the folder she's holding. "I'll take care of this...and don't forget...Celeste Granger."

I wave her away. "I'll be there."

After she's gone, I leave my desk, walking barefoot across the large space that is both living room, kitchen and office. There's coffee brewing on the counter, and I pour a large amount into a plain white mug.

Why am I on edge?

Maybe because *she* is in town. It's impossible to be unaware when one of the biggest Hollywood stars is in your city. Social media, magazine headlines, even news websites all conspire to feed people information they don't need, like the fact that Liz McKay has set her dainty little feet in Manhattan.

Her dainty little lying and betraying feet.

I hate that I care. I hate that I pored over the articles speculating about her reasons for being in the city. I hate the longing that gripped me when I saw the pictures of her emerging from the building on Fifth Avenue where her dad, Dennis McKay has lived for years.

What is she doing here?

There are unconfirmed rumors that she pulled out of her latest project, an action blockbuster starring her ex-fiancé. I've tried not to care, but I can't stop wondering why she's been in town for almost a week now.

"I don't care." I say the words out loud, as if that will make them true.

I don't care.

Except, I do.

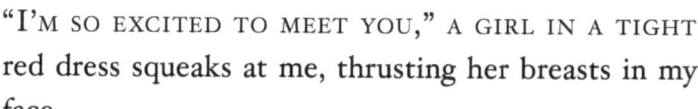

"I'M SO EXCITED TO MEET YOU," A GIRL IN A TIGHT red dress squeaks at me, thrusting her breasts in my face.

The living room of Celeste Granger's spacious apartment is buzzing with people and conversation. Soft music flows out from hidden speakers, and servers weave through the guests with trays of champagne. I smile drily at the girl in front of me. "Of course, you are."

Undeterred by my lack of interest, she tries again. "I love your work!"

"Oh, you do?" I lean close. She smells like antiperspirant and heavy perfume. "Tell me, which of my *plays* do you just *love* the most?"

"All of them," she breathes. "I'm an actress." She thrusts out the breasts again, more vehemently this time. "I've always wanted to work with you. You're an icon."

I am bored. "You're trying too hard, and yet not hard enough." I walk away, taking only a few steps before I feel a hand on my arm.

"Aidan!" It's Celeste, resplendent in a glittery black dress. She looks gorgeous, and she knows it.

With a delighted laugh, she kisses both my cheeks. "I think someone is unhappy with you," she declares, her eyes on the girl I've just abandoned. "You're not nice to anyone, Aidan. Not the starlets, not the producers, not even the investors. Why?"

"I am nice to you."

"Not as nice as I'd like." She winks and raises a finger to stroke my face. "Why don't you stay after the party? Let's have a party of our own."

It's not the first time she's propositioned me, and even though she is older by a couple of decades, she's still one of the sexiest actresses on the stage. I'm not tempted to take her up on her offer though. After Liz, there have been no more actresses.

"Celeste," I give her a gentle smile. "I'm working tonight."

She sighs and motions for a waiter to bring refills for both our drinks. Someone shouts her name from across the room and she waves at him, then turns back to me and leans close. "So..." she whispers. "A little bird told me you've agreed to direct Break of Day."

I raise my brows, impressed. "Why am I surprised at how fast word gets around in this town?"

"Not around." She shrugs. "You know me, Aidan. I have my sources."

"Your sources are right."

"You haven't cast Lillie, have you?" She gives me a mischievous look. "I'm almost too old, but I could pull it off."

My expression is incredulous. "Old? You?"

She laughs. "Flatterer. I wouldn't play Lillie for the world. While my peers are trying to get parts meant for ingénues, I've cornered the market on the mature roles. Better to be the sexy older woman than the stiff arthritic ingénue, don't you think?"

"What can I say, Celeste? You're always miles ahead of the rest of us."

"And you're always so charming." She chuckles.

"Anyhow, what's this I hear about the investor's choice for the role."

I frown and sip my scotch. "What do you mean?"

"I hear they are pushing for someone big. Liz McKay kind of big. Although why they would trust her with such a part with her limited experience on the stage...and after what happened the last time..."

Celeste keeps talking, but I can't hear a word. My blood is pounding through my veins in a deafening rush. It's not possible. It can't be.

But deep down, I know it's true.

My vision fills with her face, my mind with her name. Regret, fury, longing and loss race uninhibited through my system. *Fuck her!* My fingers tighten around my glass and I take a deep breath, loosening my grip and downing the contents in one gulp.

Celeste is still waiting for me to confirm the rumor. I shrug, injecting my action with a nonchalance I don't feel. "I suppose it's possible."

She arches an eyebrow. "Given your history, I would have thought..." She doesn't finish. A noted theater critic joins us and I half-listen as he goes on about a piece of gossip in which I have zero interest.

I am fuming. My mind is churning. Fuck Natalia for trying to blindside me and fuck Liz. I'd swallow an anaconda on live television before I ever work with her again. In fact, I'd let the anaconda swallow me, if it meant never ever seeing her face again.

Screw her and the jet she arrived in.

Someone else joins us, then another. An actor says something to me about one of my plays. I give him a mechanical reply and move away from the crowd, going to the temporary bar set up in one corner of the room. The barman pours me another scotch and I cradle the glass, wondering how many I'll need to wipe the thought of Liz from my mind.

The sounds of the party continue around me— the chink of glasses, laughter, someone tinkering out a tune on the piano—they've suddenly become unbearable. I feel like I can hear her name above it all, over and over, echoing across the room. Liz McKay. Liz McKay.

Liz McKay.

I start, almost dropping the glass as I realize that someone has said the words out loud, as if reading them aloud from my thoughts. My body stiffens, and a tingling warmth floods up the back of my neck.

Don't turn around.

Don't turn around.

I turn, drink still in my hand and there she is across the room.

My breath stops.

Dressed in a silky top and white pants, she is stunning, and not for the first time, looking at her makes me feel lightheaded. Lustrous auburn hair falls around her creamy, smooth shoulders in thick waves, accentuating the clean, perfect lines of her face. Her luminous green eyes are full of the kind of promises her full sensuous lips were made to keep. After all this time, she's still the sexiest woman I've ever seen.

"Liz." Her name escapes my lips in a whisper. My entire body strains toward her with an uncontrollable pull of desire combined with the painful ache of longing.

She's scanning the room, and almost as if she heard me whisper her name, she looks in my direction.

Her eyes widen as our gazes meet and hold.

Damn!

Years pass as I drown in those eyes. I remember pain, intense pain. I remember trying and failing to forget. I remember watching from afar as she became the star she was always meant to be. I remember the high-profile relationships that broke my heart all over again, the celebrity engagement I avoided thinking about by drowning myself in alcohol...and my life, filled with work, women, and more work, yet empty, because it lacked her.

I pull my gaze from hers, and the party— everybody that disappeared in that one moment when our eyes met—reappears. I feel sick with desire and infuriated because she can still twist my insides around with just one look.

The air crackles with excitement. I feel the pricks

of eyes on me, waiting for my reaction. They know, of course, they know they are witnessing the confrontation of a Hollywood star and the man she tossed away for bigger, brighter things.

I want to curse. I wish I was anywhere else. I down my scotch and place my glass on the bar. When I look in her direction again, there's an actor I vaguely recognize talking to her. She smiles at whatever he's saying, but her eyes find me again and then she's walking, cutting across the room, through the stares, coming straight toward me.

Our eyes hold, and there's something hopeful in her gaze that inflames and enrages me. It makes me want to put my arms around her, to get on my knees and beg her for forgiveness even though she's the one who ruined everything we had. It makes me want to rage and confront her, the way I never had a chance to do. It makes me want to crush her lips with mine, regardless of who is watching.

I wait until she's a few steps from me, then just as she opens her mouth to speak, I move, striding right past her, through the crowd of titillated guests and out of the apartment.

PAST

CHAPTER THREE

LIZ

The thick, musty smell of the old building envelopes me as soon as I enter the theater, but I don't mind it at all. I've been in and out of theaters since I was a child, and I'm addicted to everything about them, the performances, the frenetic energy backstage, the costumes, the audiences... everything.

"Hey Liz," Freddy, the security guy on duty grins from behind his desk as the stage door clicks shut behind me. "Come to see your pops?"

My *pops* is Dennis McKay, award-winning producer and best dad ever. I return Freddy's smile. "Maybe. Maybe someone else."

He gives me a measuring look from under arched and tweezed eyebrows. "Whatever it is, it better be good."

"It will be," I declare, sounding more hopeful than confident as I leave Freddy and make my way past the entrance lobby, the newly installed elevator and the serpentine stairs that lead to the basement.

Trembling with excitement, I reach a door with a small white sign that reads *Edge of Madness. Producer. Dennis McKay* in bold script.

The door is unlocked, and I step inside to find my father at his desk. He's having a heated conversation on the phone, and his deep voice booms and reverberates around the small room.

"I expect you to be reasonable," he says to the person on the other end. "I've gone over and beyond on this..." When he sees me at the door, he stops talking and his face breaks into a smile.

I wave. "Hey, Dad."

"Hey," he mouths, pointing to the phone at his ear before gesturing for me to sit. I shake my head. He's a busy man, and I know from experience that he could be on the phone for a long time.

Back in the corridor, I almost bump into a group of technicians. They ignore me and keep walking, arguing about lighting while I wonder what to do with myself. I have about an hour to spare. As I hinted to Freddy at the stage door, I'm not at the theater to see my dad. I'm here for an audition with Aidan Court, the director of my dad's new play.

I've been looking forward to meeting Aidan

Court. He's the latest and hottest thing to hit the New York Theater circuit. A talented twenty-four-year-old who has already directed a few acclaimed productions off-Broadway. He's clever, irreverent, and also incredibly hot.

I've read every article written about him and pored over his profiles in the industry magazines, and now...I'm going to work with him.

Excitement courses through me and I take a deep breath.

Relax, Liz. You still have to get the part.

I'm confident that I will. In my second year studying drama at one of the most acclaimed theater programs in the country, it's not news to me that I have enough talent to knock some of the best performers off the stage. In a way, I'll be saving the play. The top-billed actress who rehearsed for the starring role pulled out because of a scheduling conflict, the same week her standby left to take another role.

I've never performed in a paying, public role, but I know this play like the back of my hand. Aidan Court can either pick a less talented person from the earlier auditions, give his understudy top-billing, or he can give me a chance to show him what I can do.

Another surge of excitement mingles with anxiety in my stomach until I'm sure I'll be sick. To be truthful, I'm more nervous about meeting Aidan than

I am about the audition. I'm a little too obsessed with him—his looks, his talent. Will he be able to tell? Will he be as impressed with me?

I turn a corner and find myself at the back of the stage. There are no workers around, only boxes and parts of the set stacked among dark velour drapes hanging from the suspended battens. Navigating past the paraphernalia, I end up in the middle of the stage.

The auditorium is barely lit. A single work light illuminates the part of the stage where I'm standing, showing me only the dark outlines of the seats. I imagine those seats filled with a rapt, admiring audience. I imagine the thunderous applause that would follow my future performances, the appreciative shouts of my name. It feels so real that, unable to resist, I perform a small bow.

Just then, a door at the gallery end of the auditorium opens, spilling bright light across the seats. Feeling ridiculous, I skitter away from the light. From the open doorway, the long-legged figure of a man I instantly recognize as Aidan Court strides into the auditorium, followed by a woman in high heels.

She looks around the empty seats for less than a millisecond before walking into his arms.

He backs away. "You wanted to see the empty theater," he says, sounding amused. I can't get enough of the deep, husky timbre of his voice. I've never considered that a voice can be sexy, but now I want to close my eyes and burrow into the sound.

His companion giggles and leans into him. "I did."

"Well, now you have."

Even I can tell he's dismissing her. Is she too blind to see it, or does she just not want to leave?

"I should get back to work," she says, her tone regretful.

"Me too." He sounds relieved. Too relieved for her not to notice. After a pause, he adds. "I'll call you."

"You don't have my number."

From where I'm standing, I can't see his expression. She holds out her hand for his phone and enters a number. I hear the muted sounds of a phone ringing from her purse.

"Now you can call me."

I've got news for you, lady. He won't.

She walks back to the open door, hips swaying. He watches her go, silent. Another man enters the auditorium just as she leaves. He's as tall as Aidan, well-built, with luxurious brown locs in a ponytail.

"How was lunch?" The new arrival asks, amusement in his voice.

Aidan chuckles and inclines his head toward the door and the woman who just left. "That was lunch."

"Lucky you."

"We can't all have the love of our life waiting at home for us after a long day at work, can we?"

The other man laughs. "Can't, or won't?" There's a pause, when Aidan doesn't respond, he continues. "So, are you ready for this audition?"

"Don't remind me," Aidan groans, running one hand through his thick, wavy hair. "It's unnecessary and frankly, a waste of my time."

The second man chuckles. "I hear she's good."

"Good is relative, isn't it? His nineteen-year-old daughter for the lead? For fuck's sake...It's a Broadway production, not a kiddie special for Disney junior."

It takes a moment for me to realize he's talking about me. My face heats with shock and embarrassment. They keep talking, but I'm not listening anymore. I was so excited to meet him, meanwhile, he had already made up his mind about me.

Without even giving me a chance to prove myself.

"I'm exhausted," he continues. "Let's just get it over with so I can cast a new lead actress."

There's a sound, and a moment later, the auditorium is flooded with light. For the first time, the men notice me standing in the wings. I barely notice the other man as Aidan Court spears me with his intense blue gaze.

The initial shock of that gaze almost knocks me

off my feet. Our eyes hold, and my throat goes dry. My anger disappears, replaced by a burst of awareness that I can see mirrored in his eyes.

He is cute.

No. That word is too bland, too banal.

He's gorgeous, more gorgeous than any pictures of him have been able to capture. His masterfully chiseled face would make any actor proud. His tousled dark hair is just slightly too long and frames his face in waves that make my heart ache. His blue eyes are hypnotic and beautiful. His clothes—jeans, a t-shirt and a black jacket accentuate his broad shoulders and a lean body that barely contains the energy radiating from within it.

I'm staring at him, rooted, unable to look away. The theater, the stage, the seats, his companion... everything suddenly disappears, leaving just the two of us.

It's only for a few seconds, then he looks away and my heart starts to beat again. He turns first to his companion, and when the other man shakes his head, Aidan turns back to me.

"Hey." The intense expression on his face relaxes into mild curiosity. He's clearly wondering who I am, unaware that I'm the subject of his disparaging comments from a moment ago.

I'm still feeling unsteady, and I breathe, reminding myself of what he'd said about me, and willing my anger and resentment to return. Just who does he think he is?

He takes a few steps forward, descending toward the stage with long graceful strides. "I'm Aidan," he says. One eyebrow quirks as he waits for me to respond.

I lift my chin. "I'm Liz McKay."

I watch with satisfaction as realization hits him, then I turn around and walk away.

Backstage, a few workmen give me puzzled glances as I hurry past them. I'm disappointed, angry, humiliated, and hurt. I don't even want to audition for Aidan Court's stupid play anymore. I'd rather lose my nose than work with him.

I'm heading toward the stage door when I run into my dad.

"I was just looking for you. Are you ready for your big audition?" He sounds almost as excited as I'd been thirty minutes ago.

I walk past him without a word. I hate Aidan Court and I'm going home. He can go ahead and *cast a new lead actress* worthy of being in his play.

"What's wrong?" My dad catches up with me. He sees my expression and his face softens. "Are you nervous? It's only an audition. It's not a big deal."

"I want to go home." I almost say the words, then I stop myself. I'm being stupid, and weak. This is my chance to start my career. Why should I throw it away because of an asshole like Aidan Court?

Why should I be the one to run away?

No, I'll prove I'm the best actress for this role. I'll show him how wrong he is about me and make him wish that he'd never dismissed me without giving me a chance.

CHAPTER FOUR

"*A*wkward."

Cruz is vibrating with merriment, but I'm not amused. I try to remember my exact words. Something about Disney specials and her audition being a waste of my time.

Damn. What was she doing here, anyway? The audition isn't for another thirty minutes.

After spending the past hour reuniting with an acquaintance from college I barely recognized, but who had been almost too eager to cut short her lunch and spend the afternoon in bed with me, I'm supposed to be in a good mood.

Not anymore.

I'm Liz McKay.

The hurt pride I'd seen on her face flashes in my memories and I grimace, feeling guilty.

Why do I care?

She's just another actress.

"Looks like you've made an enemy," Cruz says, still laughing. "What's a play without a little drama?"

He looks very pleased with himself at the pun. I scowl at him, but he's unbothered.

"She hasn't got the part yet," I mutter, dismissing Liz from my mind. She won't be my first enemy of the female variety. I've made plenty of those since prep school days. "What's she going to do? Tell daddy to kick me off the project?"

Cruz holds up his palms and climbs onto the stage, disappearing into the wings. I'm still frowning. I wasn't looking forward to the audition before, but now I have mixed feelings. While I was dismissive before, now, I'm curious. I'm interested and strangely disconcerted.

I'm Liz McKay.

That voice...low and throaty and...arresting. The kind of voice an audience would remember...A voice I want to hear again.

I shut down the thought. She's just an actress. One of the many angling for the role.

Except, when our eyes met, I'd felt the earth lurch. I'd felt as if I had to reach for her to find my balance again.

It's ridiculous.

She's just an entitled little girl using her father's influence to advance her career.

The sooner she flubs her audition and leaves, the better for all concerned.

∼

SHE DOESN'T FLUB THE AUDITION.

I remain in the auditorium until Cruz returns. Dennis Mckay arrives after a while, looking nervous and proud at the same time. For a minute, I feel regretful about his inevitable disappointment when I reject his daughter for the role. However, he's a professional. He didn't get to his level of success by letting sentiment derail his work.

Arthur Bain joins us. He's a respected forty-something actor who will read with Liz. Natalia Barrow, McKay's assistant, also joins us. She's as convinced of Liz's talent as McKay is. A point in Liz's favor.

A few minutes later, Liz walks onto the stage.

I study her, telling myself that I'm a director inspecting an actress. Her hair is a shiny, rich auburn, loose around her shoulders. She's slim as a wine stem, but curvy enough in the right places. Her eyes are a wide, luminous green, set in a face that would have been classically beautiful, if not for the unexpected lushness of her full pink lips.

She's smiling, maybe nervous. "Hello," she says in the general direction of the seats.

That voice again. It's like aural temptation. Vainly, I try to stop myself from wondering what her lips taste like, what her skin smells like.

Get a grip, Aidan.

Arthur joins her on the stage. He gives her a reassuring smile, and she smiles back. She has a lovely, brilliant smile. The audience will fall in love with her.

If she can act.

Cruz reads the name of the scene. Arthur checks his notes, then starts to read.

Leaning back in my seat, I wait for her. On the first try, her voice cracks. She stops, a pained look on her face. Not that good after all, I decide, strangely disappointed.

She whispers something to Arthur, and he nods, then says his line again. After a brief pause, she responds.

She doesn't need her notes. Hell, she doesn't need anything. No costume, set, or music. Once she becomes the character, her presence fills the stage. It's like she has lived in my mind and seen the character exactly as I imagined her, or even better.

I lean forward, the director in me thrilling like an addict at the sight of his preferred poison. She's a natural, her voice, her body, her hands, her face...she was made for the stage.

The scene ends. I'm still leaning forward, intent. Cruz turns to me, waiting, but I can't tear my eyes off Liz.

She's watching me too, her face set in a proud, stubborn expression, her eyes challenging me. Leaning back, I call out another scene.

It's the same, she flows through it like it's a part of her.

Who the fuck are you, Liz McKay?

The new scene ends, and this time, everybody claps, even Cruz. Dennis McKay is beaming with pride. I can feel his eyes on me as he waits for me to say something.

I ignore him. My attention is still on *her*. She meets my gaze, chin up and shoulders high, and my own words come back to haunt me.

His nineteen-year-old daughter for the lead? For fuck's sake...It's a Broadway production, not a kiddie special for Disney junior.

I rise to my feet, still silent. Her eyes dare me to deny that her performance blew me away. That challenge... It reaches into my guts and makes me almost desperate to take back my words. It makes me wish we'd met someplace else, somewhere I wouldn't have dismissed her without seeing what she could do.

"Congratulations." My voice fills the silent expectation in the room. She breathes, something like relief causing her body to loosen. I'm still holding her gaze, and I smile, just a little.

She turns away.

Arthur shakes her hand. "Welcome to the team," I hear him say. Cruz climbs on the stage and goes to shake her hand too. McKay is saying something, but I'm not listening. I'm already leaving. I have work to do, and somehow, remembering the look of challenge in her eyes, I know my work has just got a whole lot harder.

CHAPTER FIVE

LIZ

"So, you don't like him anymore?"

"No," I snort. "He's a jackass."

"A hot jackass." Fiona leers at me from among my pillows. "I'm sure you still want to tear his clothes off. *Aidan, oh Aidan!*" She mimics my voice and rolls around my bed in mock ecstasy. "*I love you. I need you!*"

"Not even if he were the last guy on earth," I retort, annoyed. Fiona is my best friend, but sometimes, like now, she gets on my last nerve.

"If you say so." She grins. "You showed him though, and I'm proud of you. That was a Pride and Prejudice moment right there. You overhear him talking smack about you, and then you make him eat his words."

I can't help snickering at the reference. "*In vain I have struggled. This will not do...*"

Fiona joins in. *"You must allow me to tell you how ardently I love and admire you."*

We both burst into laughter.

"Would be nice if he came back begging on his knees. *I'm so sorry for the things I said, Liz. I love you too much to survive without you."*

"Don't be silly," I snap, annoyed again. Hearing Fiona describe the unlikely scenario that's so close to my fantasies is making me feel silly. "Stop infecting me with your overactive imagination. Go write a romance novel, or something."

Her lips curve. "I will." It's all she wants to do—write romance novels like the ones she loves to read. She has the imagination, and if writing chops are hereditary, well, her dad is a successful playwright.

"What will you do now?" she asks, "about school and everything."

"I'm putting school on hold as soon as rehearsals start." My drama program was always nothing more than a concession to my father, and I don't really care about finishing my degree. Experience is the only education I want now. "Dad's office is taking care of all the business aspects, union membership...all that."

"Lucky you," Fiona grins. "I can't wait for your play to open so I can tell everyone my best friend is a Broadway star."

"Well, soon you'll be a bestselling author, and I'll be the one boasting about you."

She holds up crossed fingers and I do the same.

"But seriously Liz. Even if he was the last guy on earth?"

I throw a pillow at her head. "Shut up."

❧

WALKING INTO THE THEATER AS PART OF THE CAST in a play is a whole different feeling.

"Hey you!" Freddy exclaims from his security desk. "I hear you work here now."

"I do!"

"About time too." He hands me a keycard for my dressing room. "You aren't sharing," he adds, sounding impressed. He goes through options for delivery, food, and such, and I listen patiently, though I can hardly wait to race into the elevator and go check out the room.

"You're not gonna need a tour," he tells me. "You know this place better than the rest of us put together. House manager will probably give you a mini one though."

"Can't hurt." Making for the elevator, I glance at the key, second floor. I blow out a nervous breath as the elevator ascends, then as the doors slide open, I step out and see Aidan Court.

He's walking out of an office at the end of the

corridor. One of the doors closest to him opens and a smiling girl with short fair hair steps out.

"Hey, sweet cheeks."

"Don't harass your director, Josie," Aidan replies with a laugh.

"How about I do you and you do me, so we can call it even."

He's still walking and laughing. "Rehearsals starts in half an hour." He sees me lingering by the elevator and his smile fades as those beautiful blue eyes lock onto my face.

My stomach tightens, and suddenly, it's no longer easy to breathe.

He's a jackass.

He's a jackass.

He said you belong on Disney junior, remember?

"Don't be late," he says, still looking at me.

"I don't plan to be," I shoot back.

His stride slows and one eyebrow goes up, then he disappears down the narrow stairs a few feet from where I'm standing.

The girl, Josie waves at me as I head down the corridor. I wave back, before finding my room and unlocking it. It's tiny and clean, with a window that looks out into an alley. There's a garment rack, a brightly lit dressing mirror with a vanity, a cushioned chair and in one corner, a soft looking sofa. It's perfect.

There's a knock on my door, and a moment later, Josie opens it.

"Hi." She grins. "I'm Josie."

I return her smile. "Liz."

"I know." She looks around. "Nice room. I'm playing one of the students, small speaking part. Understudied Tamsin Richards too." She grimaces. "Total diva. She couldn't believe that Aidan didn't give a fuck that she was Hollywood, or that he didn't want to fuck her."

The last thing I need to hear is who Aidan Court chooses or chooses not to have sex with. I already know more than I want to about his taste for lunchtime rendezvous with women whose numbers he doesn't bother to take.

"That can't be why she left?" The official story is there was a scheduling conflict.

Josie shrugs, but her eyes are shining with amusement. "I don't know. Maybe it was moving from the rehearsal space to the actual theater. These tiny rooms probably don't compare to the luxurious trailers she's used to. But maybe...it was Aidan not wanting to fuck her. The director should give his star anything she wants, you know. Support her, allow her to be vulnerable with him in private so she can be vulnerable to him on stage, give her everything he's packing as often as she needs it..."

We both laugh. "Well, he doesn't need to bother with all that with me."

"He won't. Aidan doesn't sleep with his actresses. Our loss." She sighs, then brightens. "I can't wait for you to meet everyone. We have a dressing room upstairs. It's a big one, can't miss it. The doors always open. We call it the dorm, because we're playing students. Come on up after the reading, then you can explain to us why you stole this part from right under our noses."

Yikes! "I...um." I'm stammering.

She bursts into laughter. "I'm kidding. You don't need to explain anything. Aidan wasn't going to offer the part to any of us anyway, or he'd have stood up to your dad. You don't need to apologize. Jeez. You're gonna have decades of people crediting your father's position for your success. Never apologize and never explain or you'll be doing it for the rest of your life."

"I...Okay."

She grins again. "See you downstairs."

Later, I make my way down to the stage. I have a week to catch up on rehearsals before we move on to tech. It will be a lot of work, but I'm not scared. On the stage, there's a new backdrop and a few more installations to house the scenery for the play. Aidan is seated alone on one side, while across the aisle, the cast members are scattered over a few rows.

I stop myself from looking in Aidan's direction and take an empty seat next to Arthur Bain. Out of the corner of my eye, I see Aidan rise to his feet. There's something beautiful about the way he moves, lithe and easy. He heads to the front and when he's just below the stage, he turns back to face us. His arms are crossed over his chest, and he looks like he's deep in thought.

I wonder if he'll introduce me to the rest of the cast.

"In a few months, people will pay a lot of money to be in these seats." His eyes land on me. "We'd better make sure we give them something worth their money."

That's it. No introduction. No welcome speech.

We go through my scenes from the top. Cruz, the friendly guy with the locs, catches me up on blocking, while Aidan remains at his seat, a copy of the play on his lap. He doesn't turn the pages, and he doesn't look up even once.

Is he even paying attention?

I try to stop stealing glances at him, to focus only on my lines, but my eyes are constantly drawn to where he's seated.

God, I hate him.

Finally, after a few hours of non-stop work, there's a break.

"Hey Liz." A tall, dark guy with short coily hair and liquid brown eyes is stretching his hand toward me. He's playing my love interest and well, he looks like a love interest. "I'm Kyle."

"Kyle Weathers, I know. I've seen your work."

He looks genuinely flattered. "That's gratifying. Welcome to the team."

"Thanks." My eyes slide back in Aidan's direction. He's already leaving. Kyle follows my gaze.

"Don't worry about him. He can be very focused, but you'll love working with him."

I give Kyle a look that says how much I doubt it. "Even when he hardly says more than two words?"

Kyle laughs. "Oh, he says a lot when he feels like it. Looking forward to working with you, Liz McKay."

"Looking forward to working with you too, Kyle Weathers."

He slings a brown saddlebag over his shoulder and heads out. One by one, I meet most of the other people in the cast. There's Kate, an older, veteran actress, Letty, Sarah, who makes a snide comment about actresses getting roles because of their connections, Lea and Dean who are a couple, and Ben, a sweet midwestern transplant with a hoop earring that makes him look like a pirate.

There are a lot of other interesting people in the cast besides Aidan Court, I tell myself. There's absolutely no reason to fixate on him, especially now that I know what an asshole he is.

I linger in the auditorium as it empties, silently listing all my reasons for disliking Aidan.

He mocked me before he even met me.

He didn't even bother to apologize.

A technical team enters the stage and starts to work. I watch for a few moments as they discuss lights and sound direction. Only mildly interested, I pick up my things and head for the door at the side of the stage.

Just as I reach it, it opens, and I almost walk flush into Aidan's wide chest.

My heart jumps and starts to race. My face heats. I have to stop running into him like this. It does things to me, things I don't want to think about.

He doesn't move, and neither do I. His eyes are such a brilliant blue up close that looking into them makes me feel hypnotized.

Snap out of it, Liz.

With an effort, I tear my gaze away from his. "Excuse me." My lips are pursed and disapproving, my face blank and free of all the screaming chemical reactions raging inside me.

He frowns, and his eyes skip to my lips, then back to my eyes.

"Liz." He says my name as if he's testing the sound on his lips. His pouty, sensual lips. I force my breaths to remain steady. "How are you settling in?"

The question surprises me. There's no way he

cares if I'm settling in or drowning in eruptions of sewer water.

"Okay," I reply, giving him a tight smile. "Though I think Disney junior has bigger dressing rooms and more snacks."

He looks taken aback, then he chuckles. "I'm sure they do," he agrees, stepping away from the door and holding it open for me.

I take one step, then turn back to face him. Reminding him of how he'd insulted me should have made him apologetic, not amused. I'm not a freaking comedian. "Aren't you going to apologize?"

"For what?" His amusement is still there. "Was I supposed to be excited about auditioning you?"

I almost stamp my foot. "You didn't have to be rude about it."

"I wasn't rude. You were eavesdropping."

"I wasn't eavesdropping."

His eyes drift over my face and rest on my lips again. My heart kicks. When his eyes lift to mine there's something impatient in their depths.

"Look. This argument has no purpose. You got the part. I don't see that I have anything to apologize for, and I can't hold this door forever."

I brace my hand on the door and glare at him. "I can hold my own fucking door."

He raises an eyebrow, then shrugs and releases the door. "Nice talk, Liz," he says, before striding into the auditorium. I hear him talking to the technical crew on the stage and from the tone of his voice, it's clear that he has already forgotten all about me.

God, I hate him!

With every inch of my heart.

CHAPTER SIX

AIDAN

*A*rguing with an inexperienced actress while wondering what her lips taste like. Check.

Feeling my dick harden every time I hear her fucking voice. Check.

I don't need anyone to tell me the whole situation is a recipe for disaster.

After only a few days of working with her, my awareness of her has skyrocketed to a point where I'm constantly looking at her, watching for her, listening for the sound of her voice.

It has got to stop.

Now rehearsing with Kyle, she's in the middle of the stage, dressed in black tights and a burgundy sweater, paired with ballet flats. I watch them go through the scene, and when it ends, I type a quick note on my tablet.

Her laughter stills my fingers. My eyes jerk to the stage. Kyle is saying something to her, and her entire body is shaking with amusement.

How can she have such a deep throaty laugh that chases everything from my mind except lingering kisses and drawn-out pleasure?

Her gaze sweeps toward me and she catches me staring. With a disdainful scowl, she turns back to Kyle.

It's like the very sight of my face annoys her.

Obviously, she's still hung up on the Disney junior remark and my refusal to apologize.

Well, good for her. She'll hear a lot worse and have to grow a strong spine if she plans to last long in this industry.

She laughs again, and my eyes go back to the stage. What the fuck is so funny?

"Kyle!" The name comes out like a growl, and Kyle turns a startled glance toward me.

Fuck! I am jealous.

I explain a few changes I want in the scene, then turn back to my notes. Why do I care if Kyle flirts with her all day? It's none of my business. I hear her voice and find myself staring at her face again.

Stop it Aidan. You will never taste those lips.

You will stop thinking about her as anything other than an actress on your play.

An annoying one at that.

I will stop thinking about her.

The scene ends, and I push up from my seat. "Good. We're done for today."

Kyle grins at me. "Sure, boss."

I can feel Liz's eyes on me as I walk away. I can feel her like she's actually touching me.

Taking a deep breath, I quicken my pace. I just needed to control my thoughts about her until the play opens and my involvement becomes minimal.

Easy.

Right?

As soon as I enter my office, I hear my phone vibrating from inside the desk drawer. I take one look at the screen and take the call.

"Sup."

"I take it you're in rehearsals." My brother Landon's measured voice fills my ear. He sounds concerned, which isn't new. He's only five years older but has been looking out for me since our mother died when I was four.

He's also almost totally uninvolved in theater, except as an occasional investor. So, it's easy to vent to him.

"You have no idea," I complain. "I have to work with this Broadway princess whose dad is producing the play." My mind fills with an image of Liz's face and I scowl. "If she wasn't so talented, I'd fire her and tell her dad to go to hell."

Landon sounds amused. "If she's so talented, what is the problem?"

"Where do I start?" Her attitude? Her barely concealed dislike? To be fair, that was because she'd heard me dismissing her, but I'm not planning to tell Landon that. "Forget about all that," I say instead. I haven't seen him since his birthday a week ago. "What's up?"

He tells me about his work, just the interesting parts. Landon manages the Swanson Court hotels that have been in our family for decades. He has big visions for the chain, and sometimes, he shares them with me, even though I have no real interest in the minutiae of luxury accommodation.

I listen to support him, just as he always supported me in my career.

"I need to know more about the girl you sent over to my apartment," he says after a few minutes.

We'd been talking about the progress of work in the new San Francisco hotel, and I don't follow the change of topic.

"What girl?"

"On my birthday," he clarifies. "The hooker."

I try to remember, genuinely puzzled. My experiences with women are rich and varied and include a few enjoyable adventures with women who'd turned out to be escorts. It's not something I ever planned to make a habit, though I respect how clear the terms are, and how they never expect anything afterwards.

I'd offered to get Landon an escort on his birthday. It was a joke, and he'd turned me down. I had since forgotten about it.

"I have no idea what you're talking about."

"The hooker you sent to my apartment as a birthday present."

"Landon, you told me you weren't interested, remember?"

"Since when have you ever listened to me." There's a note of impatience in his voice. "Stop playing around, Aidan, I need her number."

"I'm not playing around."

Landon is quiet. "So, you didn't send a hooker to my apartment."

"No!" I exclaim, even as my imagination tries to piece a story together. "Let me get this straight. Some girl showed up at your apartment and you had sex with her because you thought I sent you a hooker as a birthday present?"

His response is almost inaudible. "Yes."

I hoot with laughter, glad to get my mind off the problem I have in a dressing room a few doors away. "I don't even know if that's funny or scary. Was she cute? Did you use protection?"

"Oh, shut up," Landon growls.

I'm making up dramatic scenarios up in my mind

now. "She could have been a thief." I'm still laughing. "Or an assassin. This is precious. Why do you want to find her, anyway?"

He makes a non-committal response before ending the call, and I remind myself to tease him mercilessly when I see him face to face.

There's a knock on the door and Cruz sticks his head inside. "What's up?"

"Nothing. Come in."

"Had a drink with the cast," he tells me. "You should join us sometime."

I shrug. I'm friendly with my cast, but it's hard to let loose when one of them makes me feel as if I don't know myself anymore.

Why is it so hard to ignore her presence? Why can't I stop thinking about her?

Cruz is still talking. I catch Liz's name a few times, and I focus my attention away from whatever he's saying. On top of everything else, I don't need to hear my stage manager talk about the wonderful *princess Liz*.

Soon we're joined by the scenery design team and for the next two hours we go over last-minute changes.

When the meeting ends, it's late. I tidy my desk and leave the office, closing the door behind me. Outside, the corridor is empty. I pass a few dressing rooms before I reach Liz's door, which is ajar.

Did she forget to close it when she left?

Is she still around?

Why the fuck do I care?

I tell myself I'm not hoping she is in there, that I just want to check that the room is empty and then shut the door.

I enter the doorway and stop.

In the corner of my mind, I notice that she has added a few personal touches to the small room. Fairy lights twine around the bright bulbs on the dressing mirror, a couple of Chinese lanterns hang from the ceiling, a few motivational quotes hang on the walls along with a framed photo of a beautiful woman on a stage. On one corner of the dressing table, a large teddy is seated, smiling benignly in my direction.

Liz is standing in front of the mirror, in the same clothes she was wearing earlier, thick black tights that cling to her beautiful legs and a sweater that falls off one shoulder exposing the smooth curve.

In my mind, I kiss that shoulder and hear a low moan escape her lips. It feels real enough that I can't stop the hardening in my groin. I push my hands into my pockets.

She slides the handle of her bag over her shoulder, and looks up, startling as her eyes meet mine in the mirror.

Why does looking at her always make me feel like

I'm being punched in the gut? I curse silently as she turns around to face me.

"I was just on my way out," I tell her.

"And?" Her tone is hostile.

No surprise there.

"Your door was open." I sound lame. I am lame.

She shrugs dismissively. "You can close it if it bothers you."

"I didn't say..." I stop and cross my arms. I'm the fucking director here. If anybody should try to get on anyone's good side, it should be her. "Are you going to act like a resentful child throughout this production?"

She tilts her head back, green eyes burning in a fierce challenge. "Are you going to apologize for being a dick?"

"No."

"No?"

"Because, I wasn't being a dick. I was being frank about what I expected from you. Now you, acting like a diva who didn't get her way...making it obvious that you have some sort of *beef* with me...you're being a dick."

"I'm being a..." She chokes. "You're unbelievable!"

"And you've been mad for days because you think I should have been excited about auditioning an inexperienced actress whose only credential, to the best of my knowledge is that her father is producing the play. That's diva behavior, Liz." I shrug. "Why do you care so much what I said, anyway? You got the part. Isn't that enough?"

She looks as if she's going to cry. "I don't care," she mumbles, brushing past me. Her arm touches my chest, making me tense. Soft wisps of her hair brush against my chin. She smells intoxicating, like the first cool breeze of autumn.

And she cares what I think.

Why?

And why do I care so much if she resents me or not?

I know the answer. It's because I'm drawn to her in ways even I can't explain.

She has already swung past me and is heading down the corridor. I shut the door, my eyes going to her name printed on the nameplate.

I need to stay away from her. She is inexperienced, and she is my lead actress. I might be young, but I've seen enough to know that working relationships are better with no complications and complexities.

I will stay away from her. It's as simple as that.

CHAPTER SEVEN

"Why do you care so much what I said?"

I've asked myself that question over and over. Why do I care?

I've never been so wrong about someone. How could I have liked him, admired him for so long when he's just another arrogant asshole?

Aidan Court could be the most talented director in the world, but it doesn't change the fact that I hate him.

So much.

My phone beeps.

"What are you doing?" Fiona says when I answer. "Stewing about the nasty Aidan Court again? I'm bored."

"You're always bored..." I sigh. "And who is Aidan Court? I don't know anyone by that name."

"Ohhhhh...That's how we're playing it. I like. Let's go shopping...or let's go to a party and flirt with guys."

I like the idea of meeting guys and maybe getting Aidan out of my head.

"Which party?" Attending a regular college for her English Lit degree instead of a drama program like mine means she usually knows where the best parties are.

"Hmm?" She sounds distracted. "Forget that. My cousin has a sculpture exhibition in Brooklyn. We can meet bad guys...tortured artists guaranteed to break our hearts."

I roll my eyes. I have no interest in getting my heart broken by any pretentious artists.

Not when you're fixated on Aidan, an inner voice whispers.

I ignore it.

Anyway, knowing Fiona, she'll change her mind until we end up not going anywhere. I'm thinking of something interesting we can do when there's a knock on my door.

"Open."

My dad sticks his head inside. "Hey, Sweet Pea."

I make a face at the childhood nickname. "Hey, dad."

"You're going somewhere tonight?"

Hoping he's not planning to rope me into some

boring father-daughter bonding nightmare, I shake my head. "Not sure."

"Good. Neil Anders is in town. Many people want to see him, so he'll be here tonight for a party I'm hosting. A small one. Mostly industry people. I thought...since you're an industry person now yourself...you might want to know."

My childish scowl turns into an excited grin. Neil Anders is a movie star, Hollywood director, and a friend of my dad's. He's a big deal in industry circles, so even if the party is informal, it'll be full of heavyweights. "I'm invited?"

"Yup. You qualify. You're a working actress now."

"I'll try to act like one."

He laughs and closes the door. My notifications are full of multiple messages from Fiona. She still hasn't decided on any place.

"How about you come over," I type. "We're having a party for an actual Hollywood star."

Her response is classic Fiona. "Leonardo DiCaprio?"

"You wish."

She sends a disappointed face, then, "Okay. I'll be there."

I'VE ATTENDED A FEW OF MY FATHER'S PARTIES

before. I have memories of being trotted out as a child to meet important people and being excited for all of two minutes before I had to go back to bed.

As I grew older, I attended a few more, watched famous musicians play award winning songs on my dad's Steinway, and had short conversations with screen and stage legends, some of whom I'm sure, pretended to find me interesting for my father's sake.

This party isn't much different. It's very informal or as informal as a party with multiple award winners can be. Neil Anders is the center of attention and everyone fawns over him. A few people from the production also come, so for the first time, there are guests I know from work.

After my father introduces me to people who seem genuinely pleased to learn that I now have a professional acting role, I listen to Neil's stories about directing Hollywood projects, eat enough to make my dress feel tight, and keep my eye on the entrance waiting for the one person who hasn't shown up.

Aidan.

My father confirmed that he invited everyone from the play, and everyone includes Aidan. So, where is he?

"You look bored."

I'd wandered over to the DJ set-up. Dante is a drama major from my program who DJs as a side gig.

The music is tailored to the audience, low, muted and yes... boring.

"I'm not bored," I reply, still wondering when and if Aidan will show up. "I'm just...a little bored."

Dante's face splits in a brilliant smile. "How about I do one song for you?"

"Can I choose?"

He shakes his head. "Nope."

"Ookay."

He changes the music to an upbeat tune, a jazz remix of a popular pop song. I grin. "I like!"

"You gotta do better than just like," Dante tells me, nodding his head to the music. "Dance!"

My short, beaded dress is made for the music. Dante slides out from behind his setup and takes my hand, and we dance.

It feels awesome. The upbeat music, the excitement as older guests make space for us, watching and clapping as I shimmy, spin and laugh as Dante twirls me around.

As the song ends, he spins me around one last time and, leaving me twirling, runs back to his setup.

I come to a stop just as the song changes and find myself standing face to face with Aidan.

I'm breathless, my face flushed, and... he's looking down at me with a half-smirk on his beautiful lips. Caught in his blue gaze, I can barely hear the clapping that fills the room. I watch him raise his hands slowly and join in the applause.

Why does it feel like he's mocking me?

I take a step back. My stomach, suddenly tightly knotted. I'm wildly excited to see him, yet his presence fills me with a tension I can't even begin to explain.

"Hi Liz." His voice is deep and soft.

"Hi." I'm still breathless, still lost in his gaze. I frown, then mutter something about getting some water and hurry away from him.

He came! How long had he been standing there watching me dance? I can see his face in my mind's eye. That half-smile...and then the slow clapping. What does that mean...and why am I suddenly so nervous?

Fiona is flirting with an actor from a popular high school sitcom. She looks giddy and blissful, so I leave her and go into the kitchen where our housekeeper Gertie is supervising the people from the catering company. I find a cold bottle of water on the counter and take a long drink.

"Having fun?" Gertie asks, peering at me.

I shrug. "So so."

Her eyes soften with laughter. "I thought you'd be more excited."

My mind goes to Aidan, and the way my heart skipped when I saw him. I'm excited all right.

"You look flushed," Gertie observes. "It can't only be *so so*."

"It's okay. I was dancing." I shrug, then escape her ultra-perceptive eyes and return to the party.

Fiona is still flirting, and most people have gone back to flocking around the guest of honor. I can't find Aidan anywhere, and as my eyes travel across the length and breadth of the room, I wonder if he already left.

He's notorious for rarely attending parties and not staying for long when he does.

He probably left.

The thought fills me with something like panic.

Why do I even care about his presence or absence? He can move to Greenland for all I care.

"Hey, you good?" It's Ben, an actor from the play.

I push Aidan from my mind and force a smile. "Yeah."

"Saw you dancing earlier...you can move."

"Thanks." My mind goes back to Aidan. Crestfallen at his absence, I excuse myself and leave the party again, making my way through an adjoining sitting room and out onto the patio.

It's a cool evening, just windy enough to require a thin sweater. I step out into the quiet space and shiver when I see a familiar figure leaning on the balustrade.

I pause, waiting. I wasn't loud entering the patio,

but I'm sure he heard, or perhaps sensed me join him. As I stand by the doors, he turns around to face me.

"Are you going to stand there or are you going to join me?"

I don't reply. I should turn around and return to the party. I hate him. No one jumps at opportunities to spend solitary moments with the objects of their dislike.

Except for me, obviously.

He turns back to the view and pulls on a cigarette I hadn't noticed he was holding. I walk toward him. "I didn't know you smoked."

He holds out the e-cig and studies it for a moment, then shrugs and lifts his blue eyes to mine. "I've done far worse."

There's something haunted in his gaze, invisible demons that peek out in one quick moment, hinting at dark secrets and darker pain.

He turns back to the view.

I'm shivering again, and it's not the cold. We're standing side by side, both silent. I follow his gaze and take in the nighttime vista of the park, the city... all familiar, and all new somehow, because I'm standing so close to him.

I feel his eyes on me, and when I summon the courage to face him, he turns away. I study his face, his features, from the waves of his hair to the firm line of his jaw. He's so perfect it makes my stomach hurt to look at him. Suddenly, I don't care about the things he said about me. I don't care that I hate him. I want him to talk to me, to tell me what he's thinking. I want him to kiss me under the night sky.

"Have you ever been in love?"

The question jolts me. My skin...my whole body feels heated. "I...maybe. I don't know."

He looks amused. "Surely, you can do better than that."

I swallow. "I had a crush on a boy back in high school. He had a crush on me too and we dated for a while."

Aidan leans close to me, and I try not to faint. "A crush. So...what happened?"

"There was another guy," I shrug as if it doesn't matter. "I just...I guess I liked him so much it made my first crush seem ordinary."

He's grinning. "My! What an interesting life you've lived, Liz McKay."

His tone stings. "You're mocking me."

"No, I'm not." He shakes his head. "So how did the love triangle end?"

"I...I grew out of my first crush. He went off to college, and we broke up."

"And the new crush...Did he turn out to be the love of your life?"

I meet his gaze. His eyes are the most vibrant blue, even here in the dark. What would he say if he knew that I obsessed about him since I first saw his picture in a magazine? That I saw all his plays and read all his interviews?

He'd laugh and call me a fool, and I am a fool for not dismissing my ridiculous feelings for him even now that I know what a bastard he is.

A beautiful bastard.

I look away from his face. "No..." I murmur. "He turned out to be a disappointment."

Aidan doesn't reply. He reaches out toward my face and my heart starts to race in expectation, but he only smooths a wisp of hair behind my ear. "You know your character requires you to portray intense emotion, slightly more intense than crushes."

"My character..." For a few seconds, I'm confused, then I remember. Of course, my character. He hadn't been asking about my romantic history because he was interested. He's working, even now. While I was thinking how he was the most perfect man I knew, how much I wanted him to reach for me, to me, somehow...he was working on the blasted play.

My face falls. "I'm sure I can portray intense emotion," I snap. What had I expected? That there was some sort of connection between us? After everything? "And if you're so anal that you have to bring work into a conversation at a party," I continue. "Don't make it about my personal life. You could have just said that as my director you expect me to portray intense emotion, not ask me about my romantic history."

"You sound mad." He chuckles. "Do you regret telling me about the two great loves of your life?" His eyes are mocking. "Lighten up, Liz..." He shrugs and raises the e-cig to his lips again.

"Don't tell me what to do," I retort. "You... nicotine addict."

He raises an amused eyebrow at my lame insult. Without waiting for him to respond, I flounce back into the house.

Why do I let him piss me off so easily?

"I've been looking for you," Fiona catches me as soon as I rejoin the party. "Where were you?" Her eyes fix on a movement behind me and she grins. "Ohhhhh..."

"Ohhhh what?" I turn around and see that Aidan is behind me. For a moment, I feel actual physical pain just from looking at him. Why can't things be different? Why can't I think of him as just another guy?

I scowl and grab Fiona's hand. "This party sucks. Let's go."

She starts to protest, but one look at the infuriated expression on my face, and she follows me out of the room.

CHAPTER EIGHT

AIDAN

*L*iz stalks out of the party. Her friend follows close behind her, trying to keep up. I watch her go with regret, not sure why it takes so little to piss her off.

You're mocking me, she'd said.

The truth was, I wasn't mocking her. My laughter, my words...had been a defense against the intense jealousy that threatened to pull me under when she talked about her feelings for the nameless men in her past.

And I have no right to be jealous, no right to want to touch her so badly, no right to want to reach across the moonlight, take her in my arms, and never let her go.

"Hey, Aidan..." My thoughts are interrupted by a

familiar face. It's an actress I know from somewhere I don't remember.

"Why aren't we dancing?" Her tone is flirty.

My mind is still too focused on Liz to care about the invitation in her voice. "Because...I was just leaving."

"Me too!"

I raise an eyebrow. "I thought you wanted to dance."

"That was before." She links her arm through mine, staying by my side while I go to say goodnight to McKay and Neil Anders, who is in a friendly mood from all the wine and fawning attention.

Outside, a cool breeze teases my face and ruffles my hair. It's good weather for walking. Beside me, Amanda, if I remember her name correctly, is still holding on to my arm.

"So...the night's still young." She gives me a playful grin. "Wanna get a drink or something?"

"Not tonight." She is attractive, but I'm not in the mood for a meaningless hookup. Somehow, it doesn't hold as much allure as it should.

Because I'm thinking about Liz.

Liz, who can't even be bothered to be polite to me.

Liz, who's not just the star of my play, but also the producer's nineteen-year-old daughter.

I'm obsessed with the one girl I shouldn't even be thinking about.

My ride arrives and stops by the sidewalk, engine idling. I hold the door open for my companion. "See you tomorrow."

She looks disappointed. "You aren't coming?"

"No. I'm going to take a little walk."

"You know you could come over to my place for a nightcap."

I close the door, not bothering to give her an answer before turning in the opposite direction. I should be thinking about the play, obsessing over the minutiae and technicalities, but here I am obsessing over Liz instead.

My fingers are still tingling from touching her for that short second when I smoothed her hair.

Why did I do that?

Why couldn't I resist my insane urge to touch her?

I walk past familiar hangouts, every word of our conversation replaying in my mind. I consider, then shelve the idea of calling Landon to talk about it. What would I say? I'm obsessed with the beautiful, talented, and infuriating star of my play?

Even if she could stand to talk to me for five minutes, I'd still be crazy to think about her as anything more than a young, impressionable actress.

And considering that she hates me, well, I'm crazy to be thinking about her at all.

By the time I reach my apartment, my mind is no clearer than it was when I left her. An image of her face drifts into my thoughts, along with a memory of how desperate I'd been to reach out and touch her. I shake my head. I must have imagined the feeling...or at least, the intensity.

I just need to get through the next few weeks, and once the play opens and I'm no longer spending all day with her in rehearsals, I will forget all about her.

"I'm not going," Liz declares. Her voice is firm, with a barely perceptible tremor that betrays the vulnerability of the character. "Everybody thinks I'm lying, but I'm not." She reaches for Kyle's face. "Why can't you tell them the truth, why not tell everyone how you feel?"

Kyle steps back. He's caught between his desire for a headstrong girl on a path to self-destruction and the choices he knows he should make. "You're acting crazy. God! You've been crazy since this whole thing began."

She reaches for him again. This time, her eyes are large and wet, imploring. Kyle sighs, his resistance crumbling. "Anna," he whispers, leaning his forehead against hers, "You're so beautiful, so innocent..."

"Cut..." I call out.

Liz stops moving but doesn't look at me. I ignore her and face Kyle. "Look, you've been denying these emotions to everyone and to yourself. You're capitulating to the only other person who already knows your deepest desires. I want to see you surrender. Let go of the lies and denials and admit there's more than just an innocent relationship between you and this vulnerable girl. You're saying *I'm a liar. I seduced her, and I still want her enough to risk everything I have.*"

Kyle throws up his hands. "I get that. I'm trying to give you that. I've been trying all morning."

I ignore his outburst. Next to Liz's luminous, ephemeral talent, he's in danger of looking wooden. "You haven't succeeded."

"Maybe if you showed me what you wanted..." He gestures to Liz beside him on the stage. "Maybe you can do the scene with her and show me what you want?"

Is he trying to score a cheap point? I'm about to say something dismissive, when I see the look on Liz's face.

It's horror.

At the thought of sharing the stage with me.

She schools her expression, but I can still feel her

resistance to the idea like a cold front blowing from the stage. Her eyes meet mine, and I can feel her willing me to refuse.

I should refuse.

I should.

Smiling, I leave my seat, ignoring Kyle's surprise and Liz's palpable panic.

"I don't think..." she starts.

"What?" I'm still smiling. "It's just one scene."

Her brow furrows, and she turns away.

I know I shouldn't be doing this. She's the only reason I'm up on the stage. I'm still unable to resist the urge to push her buttons.

I start the scene with the first line. After a moment's hesitation, she responds. After that, my awareness of her merges into the desires, emotions and motivations of both characters. She transforms into her character. One moment she's behind me, her hand lightly stroking my arm, then she's standing in front of me, her fingers on my face, her eyes boring into mine. "Why not tell everyone how you feel," she pleads.

I have to tear my eyes away from her parted lips. "You're acting crazy. You've been acting crazy since this whole thing began."

She reaches for me again. Her eyes are beseeching yet desperate. She's innocent, tender, tempting, and all my resistance disappears. I don't care who knows.

I don't care what the consequences are. I'm tired of lying to myself, to her, and to everyone else. I close my eyes, reaching for her, cradling her body, trembling as I touch my forehead to hers. Then I lift my gaze to lock with hers. "You're so beautiful. So... innocent. I can't stop thinking about you."

"Then don't," she whispers, her voice quivering. "Don't."

I lower my head. My eyes on her lips.

"Door opens," I hear Cruz call the cue as if from far away.

There's a shocked female voice. "What's going on here?"

That's my cue to step back from Liz, to face the new arrival with an expression of guilt and shame, but my hand remains around Liz's waist. My eyes remain on hers. She's trembling, lips parted. A small breath escapes her, fanning my chin. I can feel her heart pounding as her body presses against mine.

I'm taut as a bowstring. I want to kiss her, so badly I can already taste her lips. The sweet ache of desire throbs in my groin.

Fuck.

Abruptly, I step back from her, and her face goes from pale in one moment, to bright red in the next.

"That's about what I have in mind..." I'm talking to Kyle, but I don't meet anyone's eyes. My voice feels thick.

"I'm..." Liz's voice is a squeak. "I need a few minutes," she blurts, half running, half walking off the stage, leaving me with an almost irresistible impulse to follow her.

"That was impressive," Kyle says. I hardly hear him. My blood is coursing hot, my body drawing me to Liz with an unfamiliar force...a force I know she's feeling too.

"Everybody, take five." I go back to my seat, unable to shake the knowledge that I'll need a hell of a lot more than five minutes to recover from what just happened.

CHAPTER NINE

LIZ

*H*ow do you get rid of an attraction that makes it almost impossible for you to function? I desperately need to know. It's wrecking my thoughts, how I can hate Aidan in one moment and in the next, I'm sneaking glances at him, my head full of fantasies, or getting goosebumps just from hearing his voice.

I can remember with a tortuous clarity how it felt both times he's touched me. I'm as hooked on him as if he's a drug and I'm an addict.

"It's hard to believe it's your first job," Kyle is saying. We spent most of the morning taking promotional shots for the play in full costume and makeup. Now, the others are posing, making jokes and shooting fun videos for their social media while I stew in my thoughts.

"Hmmm?"

"I said…it's hard to believe it's your first job. It's pretty sweet working with someone who's as talented as you." He flashes me a charming grin and I smile back.

"It's nice of you to say that."

He shrugs. "You have something special."

"Thank you," I reply, sincerely flattered to be getting compliments from someone who's been in the business for years.

"Too bad Aidan doesn't tell you that enough." Kyle continues. "Why is that anyway? What's with you two?"

"Nothing." I shrug and chuckle nervously. My denial is probably as convincing as that of a Disney villain. I'm not lying though. There is nothing between us. He's just my director. He gives me notes, and I perform. The fact that I can still remember what it felt like to stand mere inches from him and feel his skin under my fingertips, feel his face touching mine, his breath feathering my hair…The fact that the mere thought of that day fills me with intense longing…well, that's my business.

Kyle looks doubtful. "You sure?"

"Of course." I laugh. "I'd never met him before my audition."

"Must have been one hell of an audition then." He looks at his watch. "We have about an hour before we have to get back to rehearsals. Wanna go get lunch together? I know a place."

My stomach rumbles as if on cue. "That would be great."

Kyle's *place* is a vegetarian restaurant with a full menu of tasty items, which I enjoy, even though I'm unrepentantly carnivorous.

After lunch, we walk back to the theater. Kyle is telling me a funny story from one of his early auditions, making me double over in laughter as we walk in through the stage door.

I look up and see Aidan standing in the corridor, and the laughter dies in my throat.

Our eyes only hold for a few moments before he walks away, but I feel as if I've been hit by a sledgehammer.

Kyle pats my arm. "See you at rehearsal, kid."

"Yeah," I reply, my good humor gone. "Thanks for lunch."

After a short break in my dressing room, I go down to the stage and we spend the next few hours in rehearsals. We do the whole play from the first act, with Aidan stopping us now and then with his notes. By the time we finish, I'm almost too exhausted to move.

"Wardrobe," Cruz reminds me as I head out.

I groan my thanks and head toward the basement, passing by Aidan, who is talking with a bunch of lightning and sound technicians. They are all laughing and one of them, a pretty woman in her twenties, is standing much too close to him, her face upturned toward his.

Is she flirting with him?

Does he like it?

He says something to her, and she laughs softly. *He won't call you after,* I mutter under my breath, feeling resentful, and aching to experience a side of him that's not barking directions at me, or mocking me. The side of him with those perfect blue eyes sparkling in amusement or animation.

As if he can somehow feel my gaze or my thoughts, he turns around and sees me standing there. My cheeks flame and I hurry to wardrobe.

"Liz!" Clara greets me with a fond smile. She's a full-bodied woman with a huge laugh and warm eyes. She sweeps a large swath of fabric off a rack and holds it against my chest. "Hmm," she says, shaking her head and tossing it back on the rack.

"You have such a beautiful figure," Tammy, the other member of the wardrobe design duo says wistfully, tossing me a dress. "Put this on, okay?" She turns to Clara. "She has the longest legs. Going to be killing them on stage with more than her acting skills."

"Which are great from what we hear," Clara winks at me. "Go on. Get changed."

It continues like that for the next thirty minutes. They chatter non-stop and I can barely get a word in-between. Not that I want to, it's great to listen to them talk as they work.

By the time I'm ready to leave, the other cast members are mostly gone for the day. On my way to my dressing room, I head to the elevator, too tired to contemplate the stairs. The doors to the small elevator are already open and I rush forward, abruptly coming to a stop when I see Aidan standing inside.

He sees me and raises an eyebrow. His finger is hovering over one of the buttons on the panel, keeping the door open. Faced with no other sensible choice, I join him, keeping as much space between us as possible. It's only two floors, so at least I only have to spend a few seconds trapped in the small space with *him*.

The doors close.

I can feel him looking at me, but I concentrate on a spot above the closed doors.

"Isn't Kyle a little too old for you?"

I pause a moment before turning my gaze to meet his. He's watching me, one eyebrow raised. Why is he so cute, so infinitely beautiful to look at? Why is he such a dick, and why do I even care?

"Screw you," I mutter under my breath.

He chuckles. "Language, Liz."

The elevator stops and the doors slide open. He follows me into the empty corridor. I should walk away, but I hate that he's having fun taunting me.

I swing around to face him. "Let me translate," I snap. "It's not your business what I choose to do with Kyle or anyone else."

"Isn't it?" He takes a step toward me. "I'm very invested in the success of this play, and that success should be your major concern, not exploring your teenage fantasies of love and romance."

I flinch. If only he had a clue who really features in my fantasies. "You know," I start with a bitter smile. "Before I met you, I thought the world of you, but every day you've gone out of your way to show me what a dick you really are."

A shadow crosses his face. "Maybe you should stop building people up in your head before you get to know them."

"Maybe I will, that way I won't be disappointed again."

"While we're on the topic of disappointment, your main concern should be trying not to disappoint me, and the audience paying to see you perform."

Anger clouds my vision and I want to scream. "Oh, I won't disappoint them. I will give them the best performance they've ever seen. They will love me. You know that, Aidan. You've known it since the audition. So, stop pretending that my talent or dedication will ever be a problem."

My outburst carries me toward him until I'm looking up into his face. Once I stop talking, I realize how close we're standing. Blood rushes through my body, spreading warmth up my neck and into my face. But I don't back away, and neither does he. His gaze slides to my lips and his eyes darken with an expression that makes my stomach tighten.

"No." His voice is a soft whisper. "That has never been the problem."

I know what's going to happen next. I see it in his eyes, and in the way his body tenses, but still, when it finally happens, when he closes the tiny distance between us and covers my mouth with his, I'm not ready for it.

My heart explodes. The world lurches hard. Sensations hit me like a burst of cannon fire, touch and taste and smell. I'm enveloped by him, overtaken, captured, overwhelmed. Something bursts inside me like tension giving way to an explosion of freedom. I scream in silent exultation, straining closer to feel more of him, his lips, his chest, his hands.

His hands circle my arms, his fingers flexing on my skin. My body arches toward his. My breasts brush his chest, tingling with an urgent sensitivity. A soft sound escapes my lips.

It had never felt so good to kiss anyone.

It had never felt so terrible for a kiss to end.

He holds me steady as he backs away, hurriedly, as if I scorched him somehow. He's frowning as he releases my arms.

I don't need for him to say a word. I can see the regret painted on his perfect features, and in the face of that regret, the pleasure I experienced at his touch feels tainted, somehow. I recoil.

"Fuck." He runs a hand through his hair, tousling it even more.

"Language, Aidan," I say wryly.

He doesn't laugh. His eyes are still burning, but he holds himself away from me as if coming close to me would burn him up.

"Liz..."

I shake my head, stopping him from saying whatever it is he plans to say. "Goodnight," I mumble, then I turn around and walk away.

CHAPTER TEN

AIDAN

"We'll take five, then take it from the top."

There's a few exaggerated groans from the actors on the stage. "Last one today," I say with a smile. "I promise." I glance at my notes then turn to Liz, who's still standing in the middle of the stage. "Liz..."

There's a barely perceptible flinch when I say her name, but I notice. I notice everything about her. Especially after that kiss. She occupied my thoughts before the kiss, but now, after...I am helplessly obsessed with her.

I describe what I need for the scene, trying not to be too distracted while I talk. Everything about her is distracting...her eyes, the small pulse beating gently between her collarbones, the faint flush creeping up her cheeks.

My mind floods with the memory of her lips touching mine, the sounds she made, the sweet curves of her body, and arousal sears through me.

"...and when he says he wants to kiss you again—"

She frowns. "What?"

"What?" I look around and see the puzzled faces, then realize what I said.

"I mean...ah...when he says the line about wanting to see you again..." I clear my throat. "Pause a beat... include an action to convey your feelings, not just an immediate response."

She nods.

I reel off the rest of my notes to the other actors and watch as they get ready to do the scene again. My eyes keep going back to Liz, and it takes all my willpower to drag them away.

Why the fuck did I kiss her?

"Everything all right?" Cruz asks.

"Yes." I give him a tight smile, then my eyes go back to the stage, where Liz is saying something to Arthur. The older actor looks enchanted with her. They both laugh, and I desperately want to be the one she's laughing with.

As I watch, she pushes a stray hair back over her ear, lifts a water bottle to her lips and drinks.

God, she is beautiful.

"Fuck," I mutter.

"What?" Cruz asks.

"Nothing. Jesus!"

He gives me a quizzical look. "Maybe you need a break."

Maybe I do. A break. Or something to get my mind off Liz. Another woman, maybe. I grimace. Somehow, the thought of being with someone else is almost distasteful.

Liz has bewitched me with her dislike and her resentment.

It would serve me right to fall for someone who can't stand the sight of me. All the goddesses on Olympus would celebrate that one for all the ignored calls, blocked numbers, and unanswered messages their adherents have suffered here on earth.

I watch the rest of the rehearsal in silence, and when it's over, I'm glad to leave.

I spend the rest of the day in meetings with the production team and the set designers.

"We're planning to install a few additional tracks on the stage floor," Carter Hyong tells us. He's the chief set designer. "So we can rotate the sets for the final scenes..." He touches his laptop screen and the image on the screen shows what he plans. "Like so."

"How much does this go over budget?" Dennis McKay asks.

I try to hide my smile. Money and schedules, the producer's main worry. It's a valid worry too.

Creatives would go over budget every single time without firm refusals from the business side.

"What about the scenes that don't take place within these sets?" I ask.

"Yes, that." Carter nods. "We're still using the tracks that lead backstage, so we can move the rotating sets to the back and use a backdrop closer to the front of the stage."

Cruz frowns. "Did you test all the seats? What about people at the sides? Won't they see past the backdrop?"

"No." Carter shakes his head. "We projected all the angles, and the budget already covers most of this," he tells McKay.

After about half an hour of more questions and explanations, the meeting ends.

On the stage, a group of technicians are testing the lights. I hear McKay take a deep breath. "It never gets old, does it? Watching a production come to life."

"No, it doesn't," I agree, wondering what he would do or say if he got the slightest inkling that I kissed his daughter.

"Funny," he continues, oblivious to my thoughts. "I wasn't one of those kids obsessed with theatre, you know. One day, on a family vacation, my parents decided to see a play. It was unforgettable. It changed my life. I've lived and breathed Broadway since." He smiles at me. "Are we ready for tech?"

I nod. "The cast is ready."

"I don't want to be that parent..." He gives me a self-conscious grin that contrasts with his deep, booming voice, "but I am hearing good things about Liz."

"Well, yeah." I'm trying hard not to look as uncomfortable or guilty as I feel. "She's a natural. You should come watch her."

He laughs heartily. "She's banned me from doing so. Kids. One minute it's *daddy look at me*...and the next, they're twenty years old and starring in a play."

"Nineteen," I reply absently.

He nods. "Till tomorrow."

As he walks away, my thoughts go back to Liz. Why didn't I know about her birthday? I go to check the notice board, and sure enough it's there. I'm wondering why nobody asked me to sign her card, when Natalia finds me and thrusts the huge card in my face before handing me a pen.

"I've been waiting forever for you to finish your meeting. You're the only one who hasn't signed."

"I'm sure Liz would prefer the card without the taint of my signature," I say wryly, taking the pen from her outstretched hand.

"Oh, the director and the lead hate each other. How original." She rolls her eyes, making me chuckle as I scrawl my name at the bottom of the page full of messages and signatures and add the simplest message that comes to mind. *Cheers.*

A few minutes later, on my way to my office, I see Liz locking her dressing room door, the huge card under her arm.

I want to kiss her again.

I want to do more than kiss her.

"I'm just glad we have the day off and I don't have to see his face for one whole day," she says to the phone wedged between her ear and her shoulder. "Bliss."

She turns and sees me, and her eyes widen. My lips lift in a small self-mocking smile, and I give her a mocking salute. She scowls, then walks past me without a word.

ON MY FREE DAYS, I USUALLY TAKE THE TRAIN OR A town car to Windbreakers and spend the day with Wilson Hayes and Aunt Betsy, or hang around in my office and have long talks about old shows with Jimmy, the doorman who has worked at the theater since he was a kid, and knows everything that has ever happened on Broadway.

I still have no idea what I'm doing at Dennis McKay's home.

An older woman lets me in. Inside, the sounds of music contrasts with the silence outside.

Is Liz having a party?

Why the fuck am I here?

What happened to staying the hell away from her?

I walk into the living room, half listening as Fergie spells out the letters of the word *glamorous* in a soft, breathy voice.

There are a few people around Liz's age drinking from bedazzled paper cups. In an area of the room clear of furniture, a quartet of girls have formed a line and are dancing to the song.

One of them is Liz.

I stay near the door, watching the choreography, my eyes glued to Liz as she swings her hair, shakes her hips, in perfect step with the other three girls. Soon enough there's a chant of Liz! Liz! Liz! going around the room. I almost join in. She's good, a born performer.

The song ends, and the girls collapse into laughter. From where I stand, I can see the slight sheen of perspiration of Liz's skin. She's laughing, and even though I'm still unsure what I'm doing here, I'm glad I came, because I love seeing her like this.

She's mid laugh when she sees me. Her merriment disappears at once, and she straightens.

"Aidan!" It's a girl I recognize from Dennis

McKay's party the other night. Liz's friend. "I'm Fiona." She grins at me. "Liz didn't say you were coming."

"She didn't know."

Her grin widens. "Figures." She turns to where Liz is still glaring at me and her grin widens even more. "Looks like she's ecstatic to see you."

I chuckle. "I know, right?"

Fiona walks away, laughing, and I head over to Liz.

"Happy Birthday."

Her eyes flash as she studies me. Emerald-green and edged with a lovely shade of hazel. There's a whole universe of emotion in their depths, and I want nothing more than to decipher those emotions.

"I don't remember inviting you," she says, lips pursed.

"You didn't."

She's waiting for me to continue. "I didn't know there was a party," I explain over the music. Now it's hip hop, and T.I. is promising some lucky girl whatever she likes.

"It's mostly my friends from my drama program." She shrugs. "It's a goodbye party really, since I've dropped out."

I nod. "Can we go somewhere quiet?"

She crosses her arms. "Why? You want to talk about the play?"

"No."

She pauses a beat, then heads out of the living room, leaving me to follow her down a wide hallway and into a study with deep mahogany shelves lined with books and trophies.

She turns around to face me. "So...what is it you want to talk about?"

"I..." Why do I feel awkward? "Nothing, really...I just...I got you something."

She looks suspicious but accepts the small package. "What is it?"

"Why don't you open it?"

She fumbles with the wrapping, then goes silent as she pulls out a pair of sage cashmere socks. Someone has taken a lot of time to spell out the words Drama Queen on both cuffs with tiny rhinestones.

She chuckles.

"It's a joke," I explain.

"Yeah, I get it." Her eyes meet mine. "I'm keeping them."

"That's my intention." I smile. "Not so bad seeing my face, is it?"

She sighs. "I didn't mean for you to hear that...and really, if it had been anything else, anything tastelessly expensive, I'd have given it back and asked you to leave." She crosses her arms again. "I still want you to leave."

"Because I kissed you?"

"No." Color stains her cheeks. "Because you're a dick."

She's right. I am a dick. "I shouldn't have said you belonged on Disney junior. I assumed the fact that you got the part was apology enough, but it wasn't. You deserved the part, and an apology from me."

"I..." She searches for words, her eyes softening. "Is this an olive branch?"

"Yes. Kind of."

She breathes. "I accept it, and...I understand why you felt the way you did. I've tried to put myself in your shoes and I know how it must have looked. You'd never heard of me. I'd never done any work and as far as you knew, I was only being pushed on you because of who my father is."

I shrug. "I didn't have to sound like such a dick about it though."

She grins. It's the first time she has genuinely smiled at me and it blows me away. "No, you didn't," she agrees.

We stand facing each other for a long moment. I want to kiss her again, against my better judgement, against my every intention and instinct. Her face is turned up toward mine and I know she expects it too.

I stare at her lips, soft, inviting, beautiful as hell, and my dick hardens. I pull in a deep breath. "I should go."

Her throat works and her skin flushes again, deeper this time. There's a quick flash of disappointment in her eyes that makes me want to damn common sense and take her in my arms.

"I'm sure you can find your way out," she says, her voice low, then, without saying goodbye, she leaves the room and heads back to her party.

Oh, Liz.

CHAPTER ELEVEN

LIZ

"*L*ike...what do you actually want from him?" Fiona sounds curious from the other end of the phone line. "He apologized, now what? You want to be friends? Lovers? Professional colleagues and nothing more?"

"I don't know." I sigh. "I just know I can't stop thinking about him."

"I think you should seduce him," she offers. "For both our peace of mind."

I stare at my phone for a few baffled seconds before putting it back to my ear. "First, how? Second...fucking how? I can't just seduce him. It's not like I have a lot of experience in that field."

"No, you don't."

"Exactly."

"You still have weeks of rehearsals though. A lot could happen in that time."

A lot, like... what? What do I want?

I want Aidan. On my birthday, in my dad's study, I'd wanted him to kiss me again. I can't stop thinking about him, and I can't bear the thought that after the play opens, he'll walk away, out of my reach.

Even with my limited experience, I know he's attracted to me. But obviously, he doesn't want to be.

Frustrated, I mumble goodbye to Fiona and enter the theater through the stage door. Then, after a few minutes in my dressing room, I go down to the stage.

At first, I hear only singing and laughter. On getting closer, I see most of the cast watching Aidan and Kate. They're singing and dancing an old classic from one of Broadway's longest running shows ever.

Aidan is good, very good. He dances like a pro and his singing voice is a deep velvet baritone. If he chooses, he could be on the stage. Audiences would love him.

Like I love him.

Love doesn't work like that, Liz.

Love isn't supposed to be an uncontrollable emotion that takes over your senses and fills your thoughts with a certainty that you belong with this one person. It's supposed to be a slow-building emotion, born from familiarity and respect.

Or is it?

What I know is that I want him. I want him to belong to me. I want to share his smiles, his thoughts, everything. I want to ask him why he chooses not to be on the stage, if he believes in love, what his hopes are, his dreams. It makes no sense, but I wanted that even before I met him.

The song ends to loud applause and more laughter. Aidan is laughing too, teasing his fellow performer as he waves off the shouts for an encore.

"We've got to get to work," he says genially, just as he turns around and our eyes meet.

My belly twists. The laugh has frozen on his face, but he's still beautiful. A memory of his lips on mine bursts into my mind in vivid color and I'm flooded with a desire that almost paralyzes me.

He approaches me, smiling. "Hi Liz."

"Hi." My voice is soft. "I didn't know you could dance."

"There's a lot you don't know about me," he murmurs.

Our eyes are locked, and it takes a while for me to notice that everybody else has fallen into silence. They are all staring at me and Aidan.

Kyle breaks the silence by clearing his throat. "Liz. You must be in a good mood this morning."

Far from it. "Maybe I am." I'm still looking at Aidan, and as I drink him in, nothing escapes my notice. The way his thick, dark hair waves around his collar, the one lock that falls over his forehead, the way his lips seem to beg me to kiss them, the sexy smolder in his eyes. I notice the way his shirt stretches over his chest, his slim hips and thighs, his long legs.

I want him so much.

I'm familiar with curiosity, wanting to know what the fuss about sex is all about, but this...lust...it's more than I ever imagined I'd feel.

It's a long day of rehearsals and after, I join the other cast members in the dorm. Josie and the others have decorated the room with pink bean bags, and it has become the center for all gossip.

I half-listen to all the stories about who is dating whom, and what shows are closing soon. It's futile to try to stop obsessing about Aidan, and soon, I give up, retreating to my dressing room, too exhausted to contemplate the walk home or join the others for dinner.

I'm just going to nap for a few minutes I tell myself, but I wake up two hours later to knocking on my door.

"Liz," I hear Aidan's voice from the corridor and jump up from the couch, giving my face a quick once over in the mirror before opening the door.

He's right outside, one shoulder leaning on the door frame. His eyes linger on my body in a way that makes my skin heat and my heart race. I want to touch my skin to his. I want to weave my fingers through his hair. To fill my nose with his scent.

"You didn't join the others for dinner." His voice snaps me out of my dirty thoughts.

"Yeah...I was exhausted."

"Understandable," he says. "You're in almost every scene."

"Perks of being the star."

He laughs. "I got takeout." He shows me the brown paper bag. "Wanna share?"

My stomach chooses that moment to let out a loud rumble. I groan in embarrassment.

He laughs softly and follows me into the room. "I'll take that as a yes."

After settling in front of the dressing mirror, and turning the chair to face the sofa where I'm sitting, He hands me a pack of spicy Thai food, which I open and inhale, almost passing out from bliss.

"You like?" One side of his lips crooks upwards as he watches me, and I melt a little.

"I love," I reply, not sure I'm only talking about the food.

We eat in silence. After a while, he turns to look in my mirror and makes a pouty face like he's posing for a picture.

"Why don't you act?" I ask him, laughing.

He shrugs. "I'm not a performer. Being on stage does nothing for me. I prefer to direct."

"Being on stage does nothing for you?"

He nods, and I stare at him in disbelief. "What about the fact that you're good at it. What about fame? Recognition?"

"I'm good at a lot of things," he says dismissively. "I'm not planning to make careers out of all of them."

I don't doubt that he's good at a lot of things, but success as a performer has been a dream for me for so long, I can't imagine anyone not wanting it as desperately as I do. "I'm confused."

He chuckles. "What about you? Why do you want to perform?"

"Because I'm good at it and it's what I've always wanted to do. Also..." I shrug. "I want the world to know my name."

He looks genuinely curious. "Why?"

I look down at my almost empty bowl. "Because I don't want to be forgotten."

We are both silent.

"No one lucky enough to know you would ever forget you," he says quietly.

I can see that he means every word, and I want to explain why it's so important to me. It matters to me that he doesn't think I'm just a fame-hungry person. I want to show him my mother's picture on the wall and tell him about her. How she was making a name for herself. How she sang and danced even while pregnant with me. How she gave everything up after she had me, because she couldn't bear to miss a moment of being my mother. How, by the time of her death when I was seven, everyone had forgotten that she used to be a performer. She was only Dennis McKay's wife.

I don't want to be known only as a part of someone else's life. I want to tell him that, but it's hard to put the words together.

"I could say the same about you," I say instead. "No one could ever forget you."

"I don't care about acclaim or recognition." His voice is low. "I'm already lucky to do what I do. Lucky to be alive. Lucky to have people who support me, even when I don't deserve it."

I don't hide my puzzlement. "You're talented, driven and hardworking. You deserve all the chances you've had."

He looks like he's trying to believe me, and in his eyes, I see that haunted look again. "Where's this coming from," I whisper.

He shrugs, then chuckles. "Nothing...nowhere. Ignore me. I have a lot of dark places in my mind."

"Everyone has dark places in their minds."

"I guess."

When he remains silent, I return to my food, but after a few moments, I lift my gaze and find him looking at me.

"I'm made of a lot of dark places, Liz."

Is he warning me away? I pull in a soft breath. "I don't care."

"You should."

I shake my head. "I don't. You're talented, practically perfect..."

He scoffs. "You are young."

My face reddens. "Not that young."

"Liz..." There's a note of caution in his voice.

I ignore it. "I've been attracted to you for a very long time, Aidan. You'd have to start being an even worse asshole to me than before to prevent me from falling any deeper."

Abruptly, he rises to his feet, ignoring what I said. "Are you ready to leave? I'll walk with you."

No, I'm not. I want to stay here with him as long as possible. "Yeah, I..." I get up and meet his gaze. "I guess."

One moment we were looking at each other, and the next, he lunges toward me. Almost desperately, I reach for him and then his mouth is on mine, hot, demanding, sweet... I wrap my hands around his neck and cling to him as his tongue plunges into my mouth. There's nothing in the world I need more than his touch, with no inhibitions, no barriers.

His hands are around me, holding me pressed against his body as his tongue caresses mine. My skin is burning, my heart pounding. I'm wild with an insistent, undeniable desire. His lips trail down to my neck and I let out a soft moan.

He claims my lips again and as he kisses me, we both fall back on the sofa. His body covers mine, his hands setting fire to my skin.

"You're perfect," he whispers, holding my gaze before placing a soft kiss on my shoulder.

"You are perfect," I reply. My body is tingling all over from his touch and I want more. He kisses me again, his tongue teasing mine, then he lifts my top, one hand splaying over my belly.

His fingers create a tingling path on my skin. How have I lived for so long without his touch, without his kisses?

He slides his hand into the waistband of my tights, still kissing me as his fingers reach between my legs.

"I want to watch you come," he whispers. His hypnotic eyes are fixed on mine. His voice, his words, send hot tendrils of lust coursing between my thighs.

I wet my lips and part my legs, giving his fingers room to slide over the crotch of my panties. I let out a gasp at the first contact. When he starts to rub me in sweet, gentle motions, my eyes close and my legs go weak. His lips claim mine again, his tongue caressing mine as his fingers mimic the same movements between my legs. He works me gently, patiently, sending tingles of pleasure rocking through me.

Soon, I lose the ability to breathe. His lips, his fingers, *him*...it's too much all at once, and yet I want even more. My body arches into his touch, restless and eager. Something tightens inside me, hot and sweet and desperate, then I'm crying out, my body weakening as his fingers draw a gentle release out of me.

His eyes are on my face as I try to recover. I'm trembling all over, drunk on sensation.

"Are you all right?"

"Yes." I chuckle. "God, yes."

He slides his hand out of my tights. He's still watching me, his blue eyes dark with an emotion I can't identify.

"I should get you home," he says.

Disappointment cuts through me like a knife and the haze of pleasure recedes. "I don't want to go."

He rises and pulls me up to my feet. His eyes are like a dark cobalt flame, smoking and smoldering, and his lips are full and sexy. As if in a trance, I reach for his face.

"Liz." I hate the note of caution I hear in his voice. "It's late."

"Stop talking to me as if I'm a child," I snap. "I know it's late. I know what I want."

He combs his fingers through his hair in a gesture

that looks like irritation. "You do, do you?" He looks like he wants to say more, but instead, he gathers up the food packs, stashing them in the bag before tossing them in the bin. I stare at him, all the delicious feelings from earlier now shrunk into a tight ball of frustration.

"I don't understand," I mumble. "What did I do wrong?"

"Nothing!" He comes back toward me. "Nothing, you did nothing wrong." He pulls me into his arms. "You *are* perfect," he murmurs. "I don't want to ruin you, Liz, and if you let me, I will."

"You won't."

"That shows how much you know about me."

"I know that I love you."

His body stiffens. I close my eyes, regret and shame filling me in an instant. Of all the things I could have said.

"I mean..." I'm fumbling. I squeeze my eyes shut, embarrassed beyond words. "I mean...that I...love being with you like this."

He keeps holding me, but his body stays rigid, as if even though we are standing so close, he's trying to keep himself away from me. I want to cry. I wish I were more experienced. I wish I knew the right things to say instead of blurting out feelings I barely understand.

Silent, I push away from him and smooth my hair.

I don't look at him, but he waits until I'm ready and we go downstairs together.

"You don't have to walk home with me," I tell him once we're outside the theater. It's night, but the streets are brightly lit, and the evening crowds fill the sidewalks. I'm too embarrassed to bear another moment with him. I just want the day to be over.

He looks at me like I'm speaking in Greek. "Don't be silly."

We walk in silence.

I don't want to hurt you.

What does that even mean? How can he hurt me worse than this?

The walk seems longer than it usually is. When we're standing in front of the awning outside my building, I mutter a hurried goodnight and walk toward the doors.

"Liz..." His voice stops me.

I should ignore him and keep going, but I stop and wait, my eyes on the ground.

"For what it's worth," he says, his voice apologetic, "I loved being with you...like that."

Tears threaten to blind me, and I swallow a huge lump in my throat. "Goodnight, Aidan," I mutter without looking at him.

"Goodnight."

CHAPTER TWELVE

AIDAN

I know that I love you.

I keep hearing the words as if she's living inside my head.

It was tempting, so tempting, the possibility of letting go and allowing myself to enjoy what she was so willingly offering, but I couldn't, because she had no idea what she was asking.

"You don't even know me, Liz," I mutter to myself.

I've spent the last two days alone in my tiny cabin upstate, walking, running, and sometimes just doing nothing. I learned to clear my mind and detach from everything a long time ago, to deal with my memories, but now, it doesn't work.

I can't stop thinking about Liz.

She's young, talented and beautiful. She has a

world of possibilities ahead of her. The last thing she needs is me.

I know that I love you.

She's wrong, and her certainty is proof of how young she is.

You're barely four years older, Aidan.

But I've lived a different life. I wasn't sheltered by a doting father. I watched my mother die in a horrible accident and spent the next decade in therapy.

Hey, Liz. How would you feel about me if you knew I killed my father?

Would you still love me then?

Pain claws through me when I remember that winter almost ten years ago, when I finally lashed out at my father. My mother was leaving him when she had the accident, convinced he was having an affair. Landon and I survived, she didn't. My dad never recovered from her death, and he secluded himself in the house, barely acknowledging that Landon and I even existed.

I blamed him too, for everything, even as I longed for him to be the father I needed, the one I barely remembered, the man Landon sometimes described from his memories.

When I confronted him that winter night, I'm not sure what I expected. I said all the hateful things I'd thought about him for years, and then in the morning he was dead. I'd provided the final crack to a man who was already irreparably broken. When he walked out into the cold that night, he had no intention of coming back alive.

Because of me.

There's a whole ocean of blackness threatening to drown me if I let it. I've fallen into that darkness before, after my father's death. I drank. I left home and ended up in the basement of an abandoned church with a bunch of other teenage runaways, getting high, and hating myself when the highs didn't last long enough to make me forget.

And then one day, there was Landon, so out of place in that dark basement, he might as well have been a god. I thought he was my dad, come to take me to wherever he'd found his peace.

I spent the next year in rehab, with more therapy, and through it all, Landon was there. Working hard rebuilding the hotels and working just as hard rebuilding me. He even tried to save the other runaways by getting involved in the Shelter Project, a charity that helped the kids who didn't have a billionaire for a big brother.

I'm a fraud, Liz. A resentful little murderer who's only where I am because I have a brother who will always move the earth to fix me even though I killed our father.

I get to survive, to be admired for my looks and talent, because of luck, and family I don't deserve.

Just like I don't deserve Liz.

She's so beautiful, so young. What does she know about mistakes you can never take back? There's no way I can bear to let her see who I am under the persona of the *talented* Aidan Court.

I'm not anyone's fairytale prince.

I don't deserve to be.

Outside the cabin, the wind howls again.

On the table in front of me, three bottles of scotch are calling to me, promising the familiar comfort of deep, dark oblivion.

This is who you are, Aidan. Just like your father.

"What if I'm just like him?"

"If I end up even half the man he was before he lost the love of his life, I'll be proud, I guess. And I'll always be proud of you no matter what."

Landon's voice in my memories makes me smile. I drag my eyes away from the bottles. Outside the windows, the rain is a steady shower. The sound and the solitude are oddly soothing.

Go back to work, Aidan.

No. I need a few more days alone with my demons...just so I don't forget.

Just so I don't make the mistake of believing I deserve an angel.

I know that I love you.

The words are torture in my memories, because I so desperately want them to be true. I want her to know me inside out and still feel that way about me. I want to share everything with her. The temptation floors me and it scares me because I know once she sees who I really am, her feelings will quickly disappear.

I need to clear my head. Pulling on a jacket, then boots, I walk out of the cabin and into the rain.

When I return about an hour later, there's a gleaming black Cadillac parked at the end of the drive. The driver's window slides down and Landon's longtime driver Joe waves a greeting at me. I wave back.

Inside the cabin, Landon is standing by the stone fireplace, dressed in a suit with his fair hair slicked back, he looks like he just stepped out of a meeting.

I close the door behind me and pull off my jacket. "Hey man."

He studies me for a moment, one eyebrow raised. "You're running around in the rain now?"

"I needed some time." I join him by the fire and warm my hands over the grate. "I thought you were in San Francisco."

"I was, but...here I am." He gives me a look of faint disapproval. "You should change out of those clothes before you catch your death of cold."

My lips turn wryly. "How's that for poetic justice?"

"Don't be ridiculous," Landon says. I can tell from the way his body stiffens that he's also remembering that winter morning.

I killed him.

He exhales. "You skipped out on work, didn't tell anybody where you were, switched off your phone... Is there something you want to tell me, Aidan?"

I consider dumping everything on him. My fears... Liz. He'll know what to do. He always does. He'll move heaven and earth for me again and again and again.

He's always had to.

Now I need to do my own moving.

I shake my head. "Not really."

"Aidan—"

"Landon, I'm fine. I needed some time off to clear my head."

His eyes go to the bottles on the table. "So, it's the pressure from the play?"

"Something like that," I lie.

I'm not sure he believes me. "Aidan." His voice is even. "You've taken on a lot of responsibilities for someone your age. I know you have a commitment to the production, but if you want to pull out and start seeing a professional again, I'd understand."

I've seen professionals for most of my life. After the accident, I didn't speak for years. Professionals put me back on track to seeming like a normal human being, at least on the outside. They've helped me a lot, but I am sick of sitting on couches talking about problems nobody can solve.

"You always had a lot of responsibilities," I retort. "Even when you were much younger than I am now."

"That's different," Landon says. "I had to—"

"Take care of me? Be the responsible one?"

"Maybe."

"Maybe now it's time for me to be responsible for myself."

He studies me for a long moment, then smiles. "So, what are you doing hiding so far out here?"

I try to glare at him, but I end up smiling. "I painted myself into that corner, didn't I?"

He laughs. "You know I've always been smarter than you."

"Erm, who was it that mistook some girl trapped in an elevator for a hooker again?"

"Rachel isn't just some girl." I give him a curious glance, but he doesn't explain. "Are you ready to leave now, or do you need a few more days of staring into those bottles? I could give you a ride."

"I brought my bike," I say with a snicker, knowing how much he hates it.

He shudders. "Not in this rain. Stow the bike. I'm giving you a ride."

CHAPTER THIRTEEN

LIZ

I know that I love you.

What was I thinking? Of all the things I could have said to him.

I groan and bury my face in a pillow. Fiona, lying across the foot of my bed, looks up from her phone and raises her eyebrows.

"Stop beating yourself up. You slipped and told him how you felt, so what? He's the loser who's too blind to see how wonderful you are."

"He's not a loser, but thanks."

She sighs, "Just trying to make you feel better. Do you know when he's coming back?"

I shake my head. Aidan's been gone for three days. My dad is furious and worried, and Cruz is trying his best to manage the rehearsals.

Did he leave because I blurted out how I felt about him?

Good job, Liz.

Fiona hands me her phone. "You know how he said he's full of dark places," she says. "Maybe this has something to do with it."

Curious, I reach for the phone. I've already read every interview Aidan has ever done, so I'm not sure it will be something new. The article on Fiona's screen is old. An archived article from about twenty years ago. I start to make a comment about the date, then my eyes skim over the headline.

Wife of Swanson Court Owner Dead in Auto Crash.

A picture of two little boys wrapped in blankets causes an ache in my chest. The older one looks heartbreakingly sad, and the little one looks so tiny and confused.

Aidan.

Beside that is a picture of a beautiful couple, and another one of the burned-out husk of a car.

My eyes eat up the words, reading as fast as I can. "They watched their mother die."

Fiona nods. "Something like that has to leave scars, right?"

"I can't even imagine the pain." I see an image of Aidan in my head, smiling, teasing people on set, telling Clara in wardrobe how beautiful she looks, and it's hard to believe that somewhere in there is this sad, lost little boy.

"Maybe he hasn't gotten over it, and he's afraid to let people in?" Fiona is filling in the blanks with her overactive imagination. "He lost his father too, a few years after that. Maybe he's still aching inside and needs healing."

"If healing is code for sex, he gets a lot of that, believe me."

"What if he wants more, and he's afraid to reach for it because he's still hurting inside?" She gives me a dreamy look and I toss a pillow at her.

"This is real life Fiona, not one of your novels." As much as I want to believe the only reason Aidan rejected me is his childhood trauma, it's very unlikely.

It's more likely he's just not that attracted to me.

Not attracted enough to break his rules about dating actresses he works with. Not attracted enough to find out what my dad would think. Not attracted to take advantage of the fact that I'd thrown myself at him.

It rankles.

"Let's talk about something else," I say with a sigh, handing Fiona her phone.

THE NEXT DAY, AFTER ANOTHER SET OF REHEARSALS

without Aidan, the rest of the cast heads out to attend a photography exhibition headlined by one of Kyle's friends. I stay behind, even though he invited me. I'm too miserable about Aidan to want to do anything but be by myself.

After lingering in my dressing room for a while, I head home too, taking a last-minute detour toward the stage.

Most of the technicians are gone for the day and as I walk past all the boxes and material stacked offstage, I'm practically alone.

As always, the mere significance of my location overwhelms me. Especially with no one else around to detract from the beauty of the wide-open stage, the immense auditorium, and the ghosts of thousands of past performances hanging in the air like a fantastic daydream.

It's beautiful, and the beauty emphasizes my solitude. I feel almost as if I'm carrying the weight of all the thousands of heartbreaks that have been portrayed on the stage.

"It's amazing, isn't it?"

Aidan's voice jolts me out of my thoughts, overwhelming me with a mixture of shock, surprise and happiness.

"Aidan!"

My voice conveys everything I'm feeling...relief,

longing, happiness and a host of other emotions I can't even explain.

He's seated a few rows from the front, cloaked by the shadows. As I watch, he rises and walks toward me. He's wearing jeans and a sweater, and his hair waves over his collar, longer than usual, and devastatingly sexy.

My heart is racing, swelling. I want to run to him and tell him how happy I am to see him.

I know that I love you.

Taking a deep breath, I squelch my excitement and wait for him to come to me, focusing my thoughts on the memory of the humiliation I felt when he rejected me.

"I heard you were coming back tomorrow," I say evenly, even though my heart is aching.

"I got back into town last night." He climbs onto the stage with a lithe movement that makes me forget everything but how much I want him. There's something tender in his expression as he comes straight toward me, and something else, something that mirrors what I'm feeling. "I have to apologize, to you, and to the rest of the production."

With him so close, I can't think straight. I pull in a shaky breath. "My father has been livid."

"Understandable."

Just one step and I'll be in his arms. I can feel waves of intensity emanating from his body, and I'm aching, aching for him to touch me, aching for him to encourage me, to convince me the rejection of that night didn't happen.

He turns to face the seats. "I used to come to the theater with my brother when I was a child," he tells me. "Landon would get a backstage pass." He looks at me and chuckles. "I found it hard to communicate back then, but in theaters, I somehow came alive."

I can't take my eyes off him. I remember the image of him as a little boy, wrapped in a blanket, sad and confused. "It's hard to see you as someone who found it hard to communicate. It's easier to imagine you as a precocious, talkative child."

He meets my gaze, his eyes clouding with a heartbreaking melancholy. "You'd be surprised."

His expression makes me want to reach out and touch him. Instead, I turn my gaze to the seats in front of us.

"My mother was a performer when she met my dad. She'd been in a few shows and even received a few nominations, but she retired when she had me. I think she always planned to go back to work, but she never did. She died, and now it's almost as if she never existed."

I can feel his eyes on me. "Not to you."

"It's not like I'll ever forget her. She was my mom. But the audience..."

"I don't think the audience mattered as much to

her as you did." He searches my face. "Is that why you're afraid of being forgotten?"

He remembers our conversation. I swallow. "Yes, I think."

"I said it would be impossible for anyone who knows you to forget you." His voice is soft. "I meant that."

"Thank you."

We're both quiet, gazing at the seats. I steal a glance at him, admiring the way the work lights accentuate the planes and angles of his face.

He's so perfect.

"For someone who found it hard to communicate as a child, you seem to know all the right things to say these days."

He chuckles. "Just telling you the truth, Liz... And anyway, it wasn't like I wasn't always good with words. I just spent a lot of my childhood unable to say them out loud."

Because of the accident? I hold his gaze. "Tell me why."

He sighs. "After...after my mother died, I had this crazy belief that I'd caused the accident. That I'd distracted her with my crying..." he shakes his head. "I was a silly kid. I thought if I was silent for long enough, she'd come back and my dad would stop drinking himself to death." His eyes close, and a heartbreaking vulnerability creeps into his face. "I'm sorry. I don't know why I'm telling you all this. It's old history."

I place one hand on his. "It's fine. I'm glad you told me."

His eyes flare, and all I want to do is fall into his gaze and drown. I want him so much it hurts. It hurts to imagine all the reasons he's keeping his distance. Am I not good enough? Attractive enough?

Why doesn't he want me?

Do I even want to know?

"Liz." He's still gazing at me, almost as if he can't bear to look away from my face. "About the other night... There's a lot about me you don't know and..." He sighs and takes a step toward me. "You're incredible, Liz, and beautiful and you have this play and your whole life ahead of you. I shouldn't have let things get as far as they did that night. I just wanted..." He stops. "It was unfair to you, and I wish I could take it back."

I'm shaking, finding it hard to breathe. He's rejecting me all over again...letting me down easy.

It's not you Liz, it's me.

Of course.

I don't want to hurt you.

Yet, he's hurting me all over again.

I take a step back. "Stop."

"Liz..."

"No, seriously, stop." I close my eyes and imagine

myself on a stage, in front of an audience. "Forget what I said the other night. I was a little carried away." I give him a bright smile. "Understandable, really. You're very intense up close." I pause. "And as for letting things get as far as they did...come on, Aidan...It was only third base."

His eyes narrow. "Liz..."

"You're making a big deal out of nothing! It was nothing," I force a laugh. "I like you, but it has more to do with your work than with your personality." I shrug. "I got a little carried away that night. Now, I'm over it."

My insides are shriveling under the force of his gaze, but I stay in character. "I'm glad you're back Aidan. The play needs you." Then to show him how little I care, I go to him, and standing on the tips of my toes, place a kiss on his cheek. "Goodnight."

I almost lose my resolve when my lips touch his skin and my nose fills with his scent. Stepping back, I give him another easy smile. As I walk away, I can feel his eyes boring into my back.

CHAPTER FOURTEEN

AIDAN

*Y**ou're making a big deal out of nothing.*

I could tell that she was lying. She's a good actress, but I know a performance when I see one.

Still, I allowed it.

What was I supposed to do, insist she acknowledge that what happened between us meant something? Tell her how I can't help being insanely attracted to her, how I've dreamed about her every night, and then reject her all over again?

No. It's best to let her go.

Whatever she's feeling, she'll get over it.

Too bad I can't say the same for myself.

After a few moments, I make my way backstage. Liz is long gone, but Cruz is only just heading out.

"Hey." He stops when he sees me. "Just saw Liz."

I try not to glare at him. "And?"

He sighs. "Look. She's doing a great job. Everybody can see that."

"And you think I can't?"

"I'm just saying, man. She's your star. It doesn't serve the production if you're in a continuous conflict with her."

"I'm not."

"Good then." He looks me over. "It's great to have you back...and don't disappear on me again. I'm getting too old for that."

I nod. He doesn't ask me why I left. We've worked together and have been friends long enough for him to know that sometimes, I need to be alone.

He turns his concerned gaze away from me. "I was heading home, but if you want to hang out for a while, get a drink..."

I shake my head. "I know you'd rather go home to Cherise."

"Who wouldn't?" He laughs, his face brightening at the mention of his wife's name. "See you tomorrow, man."

We go outside, and after he rides off on his bike, I head toward my apartment. The sounds of traffic and pedestrians barely intrude on my thoughts as I walk.

You're making a big deal out of nothing.

I'm tempted to call Landon and unload everything on him, but after the events of the last two days, I'm hesitant to give him license to worry about me. Especially now that he's back in San Francisco with Rachel.

The mystery girl who appeared in his apartment.

He found her, and now they're together.

Well, if anybody deserves to have fun, it's Landon.

Once home, I'm about to order dinner when I decide I should think along those lines as well. Have some fun. Forget about Liz.

I scroll through the numbers on my phone. It would be so easy.

And yet...

Who am I kidding?

The only person who remotely interests me right now, is Liz.

SOMEHOW, I MAKE IT TO THE LAST DAY OF rehearsals before the preview without confessing to Liz that I can't stop thinking about her. It's a major triumph, especially since she's determined to prove how little she cares about me by flirting with me and every other guy on the production, while ignoring the fact that I'm constantly eating her up with my eyes.

She's acting like that night never happened while I'm becoming a wreck around her.

Very suave.

I'm counting the days till opening night, because God knows, I need to put some actual physical distance between us.

"Ready for tomorrow?" Cruz is heading toward the stage door.

I grin. "How many times have we done this, man?"

He laughs. "Not nearly enough times. I have butterflies in my belly."

"They'll pass." I watch him go, then head up to my office. Liz's dressing room door is open, and my steps slow, my heart kicking up a notch at the thought of being alone with her, even though I know she's just going to blow me a kiss and send me away with a few empty words and smiles.

Kyle is inside the small room with her. He has his hand on hers, and they're smiling in each other's faces. Liz turns toward the door and meets my eyes, but I don't wait to see or hear anything else. I keep walking, heading to my door and opening it just as she catches up to me.

"Aidan."

I step inside my office, not bothering to look at her. "What?"

"Can I come in?"

No.

No.

I hate that it's so obvious that I'm jealous. She

knows it. I know it. I want her. So much that I can barely think.

I step back to let her into the office, shutting the door then turning to watch as she walks to my desk.

"I wanted to talk about tomorrow," she says, her voice light. "Kyle was just telling me how he deals with stage jitters. I'm still a little nervous, and I wondered if you had any tips."

The easy casualness of her tone irritates me.

"Just show up." My voice is gruff and dismissive. "Is that all?"

She doesn't respond. When I look at her face, the careless mask is no longer there. Her eyes are imploring, wanting...... wanting what exactly?

"Is that all?" I repeat.

Her eyes don't leave mine. Slowly, she shakes her head. She wants much more. As I do. Desperately.

"What do you want, Liz?" I should ask her to leave, but the frustrations of the past few days, no weeks, have messed with my common sense. "You're bored with Kyle? Looking for someone else to play with?" I don't give her a chance to reply. I'm done acting like I'm not desperate to take everything she's offered me before.

With one step, I have her in my arms, then my mouth is on hers, tasting and taking. Instantly, she takes over my senses. All I feel is her. With my body, I press her against the desk as I cup the back of her slender neck with one hand while the other curves around her waist. She melts against me with a soft moan that drives me slightly insane. My head fills with her scent, taste, touch. All I want is to bury myself inside her and drown in exquisite pleasure.

I release her lips and my eyes drink in every feature on her perfect face, her wide eyes, flushed cheeks, her red swollen mouth. She makes a soft sound, then reaches her face up to mine, begging for another kiss.

I oblige, lifting her off her feet and setting her on the very edge of the desk. I'm standing between her thighs, with her slim legs wrapped around me. I grip her pert behind and pull her forward, letting her feel just how much I want her. She moans and moves against me, driving me crazy.

"Every time I saw you these past weeks, every damn time you laughed and flirted and acted as if what happened between us was nothing, this is what I wanted to do."

She arrests me with her deep green eyes. I don't miss the challenge in their depths. "Then why don't you?"

"Fuck, Liz." There's so much inexperience and trust in those eyes.

I know that I love you.

Guilt floods me. I can't. No matter how much I want to. If not for any other reason, for the fact that she deserves more than the wreck I am inside. I step away from the desk and run a hand through my hair. I'm aching with need and seeing her still perched on the edge of my desk isn't helping the situation in my pants. "I have a lot on my mind. You should go home."

"No."

I try for humor. "That's an order from your director."

"Right now, I don't give a fuck about my director. Stop treating me as if I don't know what I want, or like I'll break into pieces if you touch me. I want this just as much as you do."

Breathe, Aidan. "I know your daddy gave you every single thing you ever asked for, Liz, but you'll have to learn that you can't have everything you want. Go home," I add in a dismissive tone. "Get some sleep."

"First of all, I haven't always gotten everything I wanted. Second," She slides off the desk. "You haven't given me a good reason why this is a bad idea. You can't kiss me like that one moment and send me home the next."

"Can't I?" I laugh softly, watching as she comes to stand right in front of me. Temptation spikes and I take a deep breath to steady myself. "Liz, what do you want?" I lean my face close to hers. "You want me to strip off your tights and fuck you on my desk? You want me to bury myself inside you, make you come until you're too weak to stand?"

Her cheeks flush. "Why not?"

"For God's sake!" I lift her off her feet and head for the door, pulling it open and dumping her just outside. "Go get your beauty sleep, Liz. Tomorrow is a big day for you."

I close the door in her face.

"You're an asshole," I hear her mutter through the thin wood panel separating us.

"I know." I am an asshole, but hopefully, for the next few weeks, I'll try my best not to be the asshole that takes what she's offering, because I know more than anyone that I don't deserve it.

SHE'S SPECTACULAR.

From the moment Liz steps on the stage, she takes over, glowing with a luminous intensity that captivates me, as well as the preview audience. I can't take my eyes off her. It pains me to force my attention to the other parts of the play—the other actors, the scenery, the audience reactions, the lines I know by heart—when all I want to do is drown myself in her presence.

After the final applause, I don't dare go backstage. I'm buzzing with so much electricity from watching her, I know that one look from her eyes, and I will fall down to worship at her feet.

There's nothing she could ask of me tonight that I wouldn't give her. If she asked for my soul, I'd probably pull it out and hand it to her.

I meet Landon at the main reception. He's with Rachel, who's about my age, with a lovely, expressive face, unassuming expression, and eye-catching waves of red-gold hair.

No wonder Landon turned the city upside down to find her.

Her eyes widen when she sees my face up close. My resemblance to Landon usually has that effect. I like that she has none of the hard-edged sophistication of Landon's usual dates. It's refreshing.

"You must be Rachel," I offer before Landon can introduce us. "I'm Aidan."

Her smile is sweet and unpretentious. "It's great to meet you, and your play was very enjoyable."

Mostly thanks to Liz. For a moment, I wonder where she is and what she's doing. "I hope the critics thinks so," I tell Rachel, chasing off my obsessive thoughts with a laugh. "But let's forget about work. What's a nice girl like you doing with my brother?"

"None of your business." Landon's voice is gruff, but also amused, and relieved, I think. He likes that I like her.

Making a face, I watch as Rachel bursts into

laughter. Landon's eyes soften. "How're you coping with your ingénue?"

Liz. Again.

"Don't ask."

"I thought she was wonderful," Rachel says.

"Spellbinding, actually," I admit, though words are too bland to describe the combination of allure, torture and talent Liz represents to me. "But as I said, let's forget about the play. Landon promised to take me out for a drink. I hope you're coming?"

At the bar, I focus on entertaining Rachel with every hilarious anecdote I can remember from when Landon and I were kids. Landon pretends that he wants me to stop, but I can see how he drinks in Rachel's laughter, how he looks at her as if he would hand her the world if that would amuse her.

I've never seen him like that with anyone.

After a few more drinks, Landon escorts her to his car. He's staying behind, no doubt to make sure I'm all right, that after the success of the preview, I'm not about to crash like Icarus after flying too close to the sun.

He returns after a few minutes and settles opposite me, looking me over with his sharp gaze. "You look much better than you did last week."

"I'm much better, thank you."

"So, it was the play?"

No. It was a girl. A beautiful, innocent, talented,

maddening, infuriating, sexy girl I can't get out of my mind.

"Stop fretting," I reply with an exasperated groan. "Let's talk about Rachel. I like her."

Landon's smile is wryly amused. "Good, I like her too."

Like I couldn't see that from half a mile away. I remember our phone call from before the preview. *I wouldn't say it's as defined as that*, he'd said when I asked him if they were dating now.

"But...she's not your girlfriend, and it's not as defined as that?"

"Pretty much. We're good together. That's really all it is."

"It's hard to believe you're okay with that," I prod. "You seem really into her."

There's a faraway look in his eyes, and I just know he's thinking about her. "Liz was great tonight," he says after a moment, changing the subject.

I look down at my glass. "She's a talented actress."

I can feel his eyes on me, studying me, trying to decide if that's all there is to it.

"If today is any indication," he says, segueing away from the topic of Liz. "On opening night, we'll be talking about awards."

With Liz's performance tonight, it's almost a certainty. "Yeah...We'll see how it goes."

We spend about an hour together before he drops

me off at my place. Alone, in my empty apartment, my mind goes back to Liz.

Already, across the internet news-o-sphere, people are talking about the play, and about her, the new face who's going to blow audiences away.

The way she's already blown me away, professionally, and personally.

Disney Junior indeed.

One day, when she's a legend, she'll tell people what her first director said just before auditioning her, and they'll laugh and wonder how he could have been such a tool.

By then I'll be little more than a memory in her life.

By then, she would have forgotten all about me.

But I'll still be thinking about her.

Always.

CHAPTER FIFTEEN

LIZ

*S*tuff gets crazy in the weeks after the preview. In the countdown to opening night, things go wrong, installations malfunction in the middle of performances. Everyone goes a little crazy. It's exhilarating and terrifying at the same time.

The buzz for the play is crazy too. I'm still floating on the high from all the flattering feedback about my performance since the previews began.

...making her own name...

Sets the stage alight...

A pure new talent.

Aidan Court's new star.

I haven't talked much with Aidan since he left early on preview night. It's understandable. He has a lot to deal with as we barrel toward opening night, but even though our last conversation didn't end very well, at least, it was something.

Something more than watching him hurry away after rehearsals every day without a word to me.

I'm no longer pretending that what happened between us meant nothing, but it makes no difference when the only words we exchange have to do with the play.

On opening night, my dad makes sure to tell me how much it costs to replace each leg of the battens, and how, if I broke them, it would be worth it to replace them all.

Aidan sends a cookie basket filled with star shaped cookies.

Aidan Court's new star...

In my dressing room mirror, my reflection looks calm and composed. My makeup is done and I'm already in costume, waiting for the final call to go down to the stage.

I want tonight, so badly, and somehow, my desire for success has become so entwined with wanting Aidan that I don't know how to differentiate them anymore.

Something flutters in my stomach. All the butterflies in the state of New York have found their way there. I take a deep breath and close my eyes, saying a silent prayer to Ethel Barrymore, Vivien Leigh, and Katharine Hepburn.

There's a knock on my door.

"Come in," I call out.

The door opens and my heart skips when I see Aidan in the mirror.

We've been working together for weeks and even shared intimate moments, yet, whenever his amazing blue gaze focuses on me, I still feel like I'll melt.

"Hi." My voice sounds breathy. I don't care.

"Hi, Liz." He gives me a gentle smile, and I turn around to face him. I wish he wouldn't be so gentle. I wish he would back me against my dressing table and tell me again how much he wants me. I want to crash into him like a wave crashing onto a cliff and who cares if I break into pieces?

I don't.

I let my eyes roam over him. His hair is combed back, waving around the collar of his cocktail jacket. Even dressed semi-formally, he looks like danger and desire combined into one irresistible package.

"You look good."

He chuckles. "Me? You're the one who looks..." He stops and lets out a breath. "I came to say, break a leg."

I nod. "I got the cookies, thanks."

"You're welcome." He shrugs, and then he's holding my gaze again, and time seems to stop. Silence stretches between us like an ocean. A memory fills my head of his face hovering over mine, his lips capturing mine in a hot, searing kiss. I want him so much.

Too much.

I push the thoughts away. I can't afford to think them right now.

"I'll see you after?" My voice sounds like a plea.

He takes a few steps toward me, stopping just in front of me. I pull in a breath, filling my senses with his divine scent.

He lifts a finger to my cheek and strokes it gently. His eyes stay on mine, piercing and intense. "You were made to rule the stage, Liz. Out there, they'll have no choice but to love you."

I want him to kiss me, but his encouragement is almost as good. "Thanks," I breathe.

He takes a deep breath and steps away just as my call comes through the speakers, then he leaves without a word, and it feels as if he's taking my heart with him, tearing it out of my chest.

Which makes no sense, because he's had my heart for a long time now.

I've fallen hopelessly in love with Aidan Court.

"Five minutes, Liz." I hear Cruz announce from outside my door.

I take a deep breath. Later, I'll think about Aidan. I'll think about everything that's not the play.

For now, the only thing that matters is giving the

audience, and Aidan, the best performance they've ever seen.

THE APPLAUSE IS DEAFENING. CHEERS RING OUT inside the auditorium. A group in the audience is throwing loose petals at the stage. Tears fill my eyes.

I did it.

We did it.

Kyle is squeezing my hands, and Arthur can't stop smiling.

"Congratulations," he shouts over the applause.

"Congratulations," I shout back as my father, Aidan, and the rest of the production crew join us on stage. We bow, and the applause peaks again.

It's magical.

Backstage, my father has tears in his eyes as he draws me into a tight hug.

"You were spectacular, Liz."

"Thanks dad."

"I..." His eyes close. "Your mother would have been so proud."

My eyes sting. "I know."

He releases me. "See you at the party later."

He goes to schmooze with his business partners and sponsors and after a few more excited hugs, congratulations, and cheers backstage, I return to my dressing room to take off my final costume and makeup for the night.

I undress and put on a robe, then wipe my face free of the stage makeup. I'm so excited I could burst. My whole body is pulsing with a barely contained magic that feels like a potent drug in my system.

Where is Aidan?

I glimpsed him after the final curtain. I want to see him, desperately. I want to share the uncontainable excitement with him.

Only him.

Someone knocks and opens the door. It's one of the production assistants, Jules. Smiling at me she sets an armful of flowers on the floor by the mirror.

"They've been coming in since the intermission," she tells me.

"Wow!" I pick up a bouquet and inhale. "It feels so..." I search for a word. "Surreal."

"I can imagine," she tells me. "You were phenomenal."

My eyes mist. "Thanks."

The door opens again, and this time, my heart almost bursts at the sight of Aidan.

"Liz." He doesn't even see Jules by the door. He makes straight for me, a steely determination in his stride that makes me weak in the knees.

"Aidan."

He pulls me into his arms. "God, you are magic."

So close to him, everything else disappears, except for him, me, us.

"You think so?"

"Am I blind, and deaf? Of course I think so."

I can feel his heart beating in his chest, each thud is like a drumbeat directing me to surrender everything to him. "I was nervous."

"You had no reason to be." His eyes are shining. "There is no critic in the world who won't be singing your praises after tonight."

"And yours," I whisper. "I couldn't have done it without you."

"I think you could have."

"I imagined how it would feel," I close my eyes and breathe. "It's more than I thought it could be."

Aidan laughs. "Believe me, Liz. This is just the beginning." His arms tighten around me. "They loved you."

And I love you.

I don't say the words out loud. "And you?"

He chuckles. "You said you would blow me away. You did. More than you know."

He's so close I can barely breathe. His lips are curved in a small smile, his eyes roam my face. Desire roars like a tornado inside me.

"Kiss me."

At first, I'm not aware that I said the words out

loud, but then his eyes darken, and his hands slide down to clasp my waist. Through the silk of my robe, it feels as if he's touching my bare skin. My breath catches. One moment, I'm looking up at him, and the next, his mouth seizes mine with a hunger that verges on desperation.

Oh, Aidan.

My whole body ignites. His tongue delves deep into my mouth, tasting, each stroke like a new lick of flame, setting my body on exquisite, beautiful fire.

I don't hear Jules leave, or the door close behind her. All I know is Aidan's lips, his tongue, his hands. He tosses off his jacket then unties my robe, sighing as his hands encounter my underwear clad body beneath.

Still kissing me, he lifts me and places me on the edge of my dressing table. One warm hand cups the back of my neck and his finger massage my scalp. "Liz," he whispers.

"Hmm." My breasts are aching, and the throbbing need between my legs is driving me close to crazy.

He pulls my robe off my body, letting it fall to the ground in a whisper of silk, then with a flick of his wrist, he undoes my bra before pulling the straps off my shoulders.

"Jesus, Liz." His face is almost reverent as he cups my breasts in each hand. He draws his thumbs over each nipple, and I suck in a breath.

"I've thought about this." He looks at me and smiles crookedly. "I've obsessed, more like, and fantasized."

I swallow. "I've waited a long time. It feels like I've been waiting all my life."

He expels a breath, then lowers his head and draws one nipple into his mouth. His lips feel like heaven. His tongue feels like a sweet, sweet flame. My eyes close, and the throbbing between my legs intensifies. As if he can feel it, one hand finds the band of my panties and slips inside. He slides one finger between my folds and rubs the sensitive nerves of my clit, making my back arch as I cry out in pleasure.

"I want to make this good for you."

"Aidan," I sigh, already aroused beyond reason. "I only need you."

His chest rises, and he gets on his knees, sliding my panties down and tossing them away before pulling me to the very edge of the table and hooking my legs over his shoulders.

Spread out like that, I'm totally exposed to him, but I don't care. Anticipation renders me immobile as I wait for the first touch of his mouth, and when it comes, my body turns to liquid.

He tastes my clit, then licks me all the way down, pushing his tongue inside me before going back to suck my clit again. I cry out and grip his hair, my breath coming in sharp gasps as he devours me.

It feels so good.

So perfect.

Unlike anything I've ever experienced before.

"Oh God! Aidan."

When I moan his name, he responds by brushing the pad of one finger against my core, teasing the entrance, sliding in, then out until I'm shaking, dripping wet, moaning, crying and begging for more.

My climax takes me unawares. One moment, I'm rolling my hips against his onslaught. The next, I'm almost sliding off the table, moaning his name so loud, I'm sure everybody in the building can hear.

Aidan's hands grip my hips, holding me in place as he flicks his tongue over my throbbing clit again and again until I'm pushing him away, unable to take anymore. He rises to his feet, still between my legs, and I pull his face to mine, kissing him hungrily and tasting myself on his tongue.

"You're perfect," he growls. His lips travel along the curve of my throat, spreading soft kisses that leave me shuddering in pleasure. "So fucking perfect. You're making me crazy."

"Show me." I reach for his zipper, feeling the hard ridge of his erection pressing against the front of his pants. I stroke my hand down his hard, rigid length and he groans.

"Liz..."

I undo his zipper and lift my face up to his. The hunger in his eyes is scorching, and the force of it makes me whimper. "Don't even think about stopping."

With a sound like a growl, he flicks my hand away and frees his cock. My eyes widen at the sight of him, hard and stiff, and I reach for him, unable to stop myself from wanting to touch him.

He doesn't let me. He pushes my hand away and grabs hold of my thighs, spreading my legs even farther, then cursing under his breath, he reaches into his back pocket and retrieves his wallet, searching for a moment before finding what he's looking for. A single condom.

I don't think about why he has it in there, or about all the other women he's been with. I'm too eager, too hot, too aroused. He rolls the condom on, then meets my eyes.

"You ready?"

I nod, my tongue flicking over my lips in unrestrained anticipation. His fingers trail over my skin, the gentleness at odds with the hunger in his eyes, then gripping my thighs, he hooks my legs around his hips, presses the wide head of his cock against me, and slides slowly inside me.

My breath escapes as he fills me, stretching me so tight, I feel like I might burst. I hold on to his shoulders for balance, gripping him as he slides out and in again, slowly at first, flexing his hips, his eyes fixed on my face, dark, aroused, hungry...and so hot.

I'm moaning his name, almost in tears from the pleasure. His movements speed up, and sweet tendrils of exquisite delight snake up from my core and across my belly and thighs, until even my fingertips are suffused with the feeling. With each thrust, the pleasure builds until I can't take it anymore.

"Aidan," I cry out.

In response he fucks me harder and faster. Something explodes inside me and I cry out, my vision blurring as an orgasm rips through me.

His fingers dig into my hair. He groans and plunges so deep inside me, it feels like we're melded together. His body shudders as he comes. He lets out a shaky breath. One arm comes around me and he kisses my hair, then the side of my face.

I keep my arms around him, happy, languid, and too satisfied for words.

"You okay?" He tilts his head back to look at me.

"Better than okay."

He laughs, and he has never looked more beautiful to me.

"We have a party to attend," he says, making no move to pull away from me. "People to talk to."

I smile. "I know."

"My brother is around here somewhere, with his girlfriend. I should go say hello."

"I'll get ready for the party."

We're still holding on to each other, and he lowers his head and kisses me. "I'm crazy about you, Liz McKay. What have you done to me?"

"I bewitched you."

"I can believe that." He laughs and steps back, his hands lingering on my shoulders for just a moment before he bends to retrieve my robe from the floor, then starts to fix his clothes. "I'll see you at the party?"

I nod. "Yes."

"And after?"

I hold my breath. "After?"

He grips my face and kisses me again. "I'll tell the world that you're mine."

I kiss him back, loving him so much in that moment that I can hardly bear it... "Yours, Aidan. Always."

PRESENT

CHAPTER SIXTEEN

LIZ

I stand frozen as Aidan walks past me, willing myself not to turn around and watch him go. My heart is pounding in my chest, my blood rushing. Everything in me strains to follow him, to plead, to beg, to share the same space with him for a little while longer.

The temporary lull in conversation disappears after he leaves, followed by a buzz as people start to talk, probably about the fact that Aidan Court just snubbed me in front of the whole of New York's theatre crowd.

My face tightens in embarrassment, and I take a deep breath and try to smile. The bar is right in front of me and standing not far away is Celeste Granger, the hostess, gorgeous in a shimmering dress. Some guy is hovering close to her, trying to get her interested in whatever he is saying, but her eyes are on me, with a mocking half-smile dancing on her full red lips.

I return her smile and join her where she's standing, not because I want to, but because some survival instinct demands that I pretend that I'd been on my way over to speak to her and not the man who walked past me like I was invisible.

"Hello, Celeste. Great party."

She raises an eyebrow. "You're a good actress, Liz. I'll give you that. I can hardly tell that Aidan Court just walked out on you."

I shrug, ignoring the aching clump of emotions in my chest area. "Maybe he had somewhere more interesting to be."

The dig at her party makes her chuckle, and it makes me feel like an immature brat.

"Don't be mean," she purrs. "I was only complimenting your acting skills. You'll need them now that you're coming back to the stage, though..." A photographer approaches to take our picture, and she gives him a brilliant smile. "...if Aidan's reaction to finding out that you're in his play is any indication, you'll need more than acting skills."

With that, she abandons me. Deflated, I watch the back of her head as she walks away. A uniformed waiter passes with a tray of fluted glasses and I help myself to some champagne. Someone waves at me and I wave back. Someone I don't recognize approaches me and tells me how happy he is to see me again. Soon others join him, and I'm surrounded by people who know me, people hanging on to my every word.

And yet I can't stop thinking about Aidan.

I want to leave. Why had I agreed to come here in the first place?

Because you wanted a chance to run into Aidan. You wanted it to be oh so casual, like you haven't been yearning for him for seven years.

Except it hadn't turned out the way I'd expected.

What did I think would happen? That he'd talk to me? Act as if the past didn't matter for the sake of the people around? Of course, he wouldn't. Aidan has never cared about other people's opinions. He'd never pretend for the sake of spectators.

After draining my glass, I signal a waiter for another. At this rate, I'll be drunk before the evening ends. Well, if I'm going to stay here and try to save face after that snub from Aidan, I might as well enjoy it.

～

Did LKay just take a massive L?

What would you give for a chance to talk to sexy mega-star Liz McKay? Well, some people would give no fucks,

*apparently. Spotted last night: Liz McKay getting the cold
shoulder from award-winning director Aidan Court. Gossip
says they have a history. Darling Liz once dumped Aidan.
So, did she deserve to be snubbed? Tell us in the poll and in
the comments.*

"A poll! For heaven sakes." I sigh. "That's from
Celeb Observer. Have you seen it?"

"I have," Jenny replies coolly. My phone is on
speaker so I can scroll through the morning gossip
while venting to her. "I don't know why you bother.
It's just the stupid gossip rags. I only read them
because I have a web alert for your name. It's not a
big deal. You shouldn't care."

"I care because it's Aidan." My shoulders slump.
"If it becomes a thing, he'll hate the extra publicity."

"But...it will be good for the play, won't it?"

"If there's still a play after Aidan raises hell for
having to work with me. Judging by his reaction
yesterday, he can't even stand to be in the same
room."

"I'm sorry." There's a pause. "Would it help if I
said he's an ogre who has no idea how perfect you are
and how dare he presume to hate you for dumping his
ass when he should be overcome with gratitude that
you ever looked at him in the first place?"

I can't help chuckling. "He's not an ogre. Unless
ogres are hot, talented..." I sigh. "...and sexy."

"You still like him!"

I don't reply. How do I explain that I more than like him, even after spending seven years apart?

When I don't respond, Jenny sighs. "Well, if you do get to work with him again, the best it can be is awkward."

"And the worst?"

"Unbearable."

That's not helpful at all.

Moments later, the black SUV stops in front of a glass fronted building with a coffee shop and a jewelry store facing the street on the ground floor. I slip on my sunglasses and step out of the car, simply dressed in a burgundy jersey dress belted at the waist, paired with strappy heels. There are only a few people on the sidewalk, so I'm not very concerned about being recognized.

Still, a guy on the sidewalk does a double take when he sees my face. My friendly wave prompts a slack-jawed smile from him, and I hurry into the building before anyone else recognizes me.

The McKay Theater company is on the sixth floor. Inside, it's all glass partitions and blue-gray carpets. There has been a change in interior decoration since my father used to run the place—then, it was mahogany, leather and thick rugs. Natalia may have kept the name of the company, but she is making changes.

The receptionist gives me a dazzled smile "Liz McKay!" she squeaks. "I'm sorry...I mean...Good afternoon, Ms. McKay."

Her name is on her nameplate. "Hello, Daisy."

Her smile widens and just then, another girl in a colorful jumpsuit and spiked hair steps into the reception through a glass door. "Liz McKay. Welcome." She says my name like a solemn announcement, then leads me inside the main office. "Natalia is in an impromptu meeting right now. So, if you'd like to wait..." She gestures to a pair of armchairs, but I've already heard the raised voice coming from inside Natalia's office, familiar, achingly familiar, and obviously furious.

"Who is she meeting with?" I ask, even though I already know the answer.

The girl manages to grimace and look dreamy at the same time. "Aidan Court, the director."

I hear his voice again, carrying through the opaque glass wall of Natalia's office. I can't hear what he's saying, but I can feel the anger in his tone. It's grating that the thought of working with me is so distasteful to him, but I understand why he feels that way.

But maybe I can change his mind.

Taking a deep breath, I square my shoulders and smile at my escort. "I'll join them," I announce, ignoring the look of alarm that springs onto her face.

I walk past her and push open the door to Natalia's office.

"...I don't give a damn if her name sells millions of tickets. I will not work with her. It's disgusting that you're trying to arm-twist me into this. Frankly, I expected better of you."

"Aidan..." Natalia's sigh is a mixture of exasperation and patience. "Let's be reasonable..."

He stops pacing. "Fuck reasonable," he mutters, running a hand through his already tousled hair.

I linger at the door, frozen by the palpable waves of annoyance emanating from him. Natalia gives me an apologetic smile and I smile back. She's an attractive woman in her forties with copper hair in a short bob and creamy pale skin. She's also one of the toughest women I know. Whatever she has decided about the play, I know she won't back down. Not for Aidan, and not for anybody else.

Aidan follows Natalia's gaze, slowly turning to face me. I lift my chin as our eyes meet, and yet...the force of his gaze almost kicks me off balance. For a moment, we stare at each other, his deep blue eyes as cold as glaciers. My heart contracts and starts to ache all over again.

"Of course," he sneers, his voice dripping venom. "Of course, she's here."

I ignore his tone. "Hello, Aidan."

The flinch is barely perceptible, but it's there.

His body goes rigid and his jaw hardens. As if the sound of his name on my lips is something he can't stand.

"Aidan..." Natalia's tone is measured. "Think about the play...the potential, the publicity..."

"Oh, for fuck's sake," he explodes, leaving me weak as his gaze leaves me. His voice is full of anger, yet it remains deep and measured. "Fuck the potential and fuck the publicity. I couldn't care less. Get yourself a new lead, Natalia, or get yourself another director." He spares me another withering glance before he stalks out of the office.

The door shuts behind him and Natalia sighs, lifting two manicured fingers to her temples. "Bloody hell! Why do I always get these difficult projects?" she groans. "I have to deal with investors, with the unions, the theatre board trying to shaft us, and now an irate director." She narrows her eyes at me. "What are you doing here?"

"I had a few questions about the play, about Aidan." I approach her desk and lower myself into a chair across from her. "I guess I should have called ahead."

"You should have, then maybe, without your appearance here to set him off, I might have convinced him that your presence in the play wouldn't be a disaster, but you had to come here and start that...*je ne sais quoi* that happens whenever you

168

two are in a room together. Seven years and it's still the same. Who would have thought?"

I close my eyes, remembering the desire, uncertainty and desperation combined to create something I still can't explain, something that other people can sense whenever Aidan and I are together. "What happens if he pulls out?"

"A lot of paperwork. A long delay. He could sue us for whatever. Then we'd counter-sue. We could have a hard time getting a new director. Unhappy investors, loss of funding. It could become a disaster, and I don't need that. I haven't been in charge long enough to afford mistakes like that."

I know what she means. Theatre is art, but it's also a business, and nobody wants to spend their money and end up without the bragging rights of associating their name with a good play.

"What can I do?" I need to do this play. It's the only plausible answer to the questions people are asking about the reason for my extended stay in New York after pulling out of a big movie project. It's also the only opportunity I can see to get Aidan to listen to me, so we can confront what happened between us in the past.

But I don't want to cost Natalia her play. "I can pull out, if that will solve anything."

"Of course not." Natalia gives me an amused glance. "Don't undersell yourself, Liz. You aren't less valuable to me than Aidan is. The backers are already orgasmic about having you on the project. You know your name will sell tickets like nothing else will. And given your history with Aidan, the publicity will create itself." She gave me an apologetic smile. "I'm sorry if that sounded tasteless, or predatory. I'm just being candid."

"It's okay."

She taps a finger on her desk. "I just have to convince Aidan that this thing between you two is not as important or insurmountable as he thinks. That this is the perfect opportunity to give it a chance to fizzle out. He's usually not difficult, you know. Demanding, but not difficult." She looks at me. "When was the last time you two spoke?"

"Barring just now?" I shake my head. "Before I left for L.A. that first time."

Her eyes widen. "You're kidding."

"I'm not." I rise from my seat and walk to one of the walls, where framed pictures document Natalia's journey in theatre. "Why don't I reach out to him? Maybe I can convince him."

She gives me a look that states how little she thinks of my chances. "You can try," she says with a shrug. "What can it hurt?"

What can it hurt indeed?

CHAPTER SEVENTEEN

AIDAN

*H*ello Aidan.
 Hello Aidan!

The words mock me as I stride out of the building, desperate to get as far away from her as possible.

Hello Aidan.

As if mere words can breach the gulf between us. As if any rules of social interaction can ever form a bridge across which we can communicate and exchange meaningless pleasantries like the past never happened.

I can still see her standing there just inside Natalia's office. Hesitant, as if she needed my permission to advance. I can still hear the softness in her voice, the luminous imploration in her eyes. One look at her and I was a slave to my emotions again, with no idea what I wanted most, to wrap my hands around that tiny waist, crush her body beneath mine and fuck her till my ears filled with the familiar sound of her moans.

Or to beg her to explain, to make me understand why she walked away, why she had no qualms about moving on when I still felt like a crippled shadow of the man I'd been when we were together.

I still want her. That undeniable realization, that all the feelings I've suppressed and ignored for the past seven years have just been hiding beneath the surface, waiting for her to return...it enrages me.

How dare she?

How dare she waltz back into my life and act as if the past doesn't matter, as if we can just be friends? It leaves a taste like dust in my mouth. I'd rather live without directing another play for the rest of my life than pretend that she deserves anything but contempt from me.

Outside the building, I notice up to three people with cameras standing on the opposite sidewalk, and I mutter a curse under my breath. Of course, it was only a matter of time before the paps started following her around the city, hoping to capture images to satisfy her hungry public.

I wonder if she knows they're outside, if she knows to leave through one of the fire exits, to avoid them...

I stop my thoughts. Why do I care if the paparazzi mob her or not? Her problems are none of my business.

She is none of my business.

And I have no intention of working under her celebrity brand. For this play, there would always be another chance, another revival.

One without Liz McKay.

"Of all the gin joints in all the towns in all the world, she walks into mine."

I keep walking, tempted to go over to my brother's apartment at the Swanson Court and spill my frustrations to Landon, or Rachel. Seven years ago, they nursed me through the lowest period of my life. One day, I thought I'd found the love of my life, and the next, she was already on the other side of the country when I learned from an ecstatic press that she had left our play, was signed on to do a series of movies, and was already romantically linked with her future co-star.

Even the memories are painful. To avoid them, I spend the next hour punching a bag at the gym, not stopping until every muscle in my body is exhausted and I'm too tired to think.

After a quick shower, I head to my apartment, craving sleep. In the lobby, the doorman sees me and rises from behind the large reception desk, smiling like a man with a secret.

"Hey, Aidan." He rounds the desk, heading straight for me.

"What's up, Ted?" I return his smile. "Do I have a delivery?"

"No, but you have a visitor."

My exhaustion disappears and I tense. "Who is it?"

"I thought it wouldn't be discreet to keep her waiting down here. I didn't want people talking. We don't get movie stars here every day, so I let her into your apartment." He pauses, eyes shining, grinning as if he expects me to be as delighted as he is. "She said her name was Elizabeth Bennet. Must have been a joke, right? Because even a dead man would recognize Liz McKay."

"Right," I mutter, too angry to give him the lecture he deserves. "She's in my apartment?"

He nods happily, still drunk on her stardust.

I'm tempted to walk right out of the building and disappear for a few days. Let her have my apartment. Let her have the whole city. I'll leave and find my peace some place she'll never find me.

What the fuck does she want?

What does she want from me?

I head for the elevator, ignoring a wink from Ted. I'll deal with him later. On my floor, I let myself into the apartment. At first glance, it looks empty. There's nothing to show that anyone else has been inside, but

I know she's here. I can feel her presence like a crackle in the air, like a soft breath on my skin. She has disturbed the fabric of my home, just like she disturbed the fabric of my soul.

A few steps inside, and I see her curled up on the couch. There's a book in her lap, one of mine, but she's asleep. Her hair has fallen to one side, exposing her neck. Her lips are full and pink, parted as she breathes softly. I allow myself to study her in a way I haven't done in years, the perfect bones, the slender fingers, the outline of her body, slim yet curvy, lush and beautiful.

Everything is painfully familiar, yet so out of reach. My fingers ache to feel the silky waves of her hair. I want to bruise her lips with mine, to spread her legs and claim her body as harshly as I can, to demand to know why she came back into my life to haunt me like an unwanted, uninvited ghost.

As if she can feel the turbulence of my thoughts, she stirs. Even the way she wakes is beautiful. How many times in that long ago past did I worship that sleepy smile and that languid stretch?

She straightens and rises to a sitting position, her eyes on me.

"You're back."

I restrain myself from reaching for her. Instead, I glare, silently asking what the hell she's doing in my space.

"Aidan—"

"Don't." I raise my hand, as if to create a barrier between us. "What are you doing here?"

She rises and walks toward me, momentarily distracting me from the past seven years. She moves like a siren. She looks like a goddess. I want her. I want her with an ache that has only grown since we've been apart.

"We need to talk."

"No, we don't."

She sighs. "Don't be like this."

"Just stop, ok?" Her tone, and the implication that I'm being unreasonable... it infuriates me. "We don't need to talk. You shouldn't be in my home acting as if what happened between us was a little misunderstanding that you can smooth over by *talking*."

She doesn't back down. "If not talking, then what? What would it take to make you—"

"Nothing." I cut her off. "I want nothing from you. I don't want to talk. I don't want to see you. You've been dead to me for a long time, Liz, so get the hell out of my apartment."

She looks taken aback. Did she expect me to be glad to see her? Is she so drunk on her appeal that she thinks her appearance is all it'll take for me to forgive and forget?

"No." Even I am surprised by the stubbornness in her voice. "I'm not going anywhere."

I'm not sure if she's talking about my apartment or the play.

"Liz," I grind out her name. "Don't think I won't throw you out. And the next time you come here and get one of the impressionable young men downstairs to let you into my personal space, I will get him fired."

"You wouldn't." Her chin goes up, defiant. "The Aidan I knew wouldn't do that, anyway."

My laugh is bitter. "The Aidan you knew is dead. You killed him."

Her breath hitches and the elation I felt at landing the blow is suddenly colored with shame. I walk over to my bar and pour myself a drink. She remains beside the couch, watching me.

Expensive scotch burns my throat. "Go away, Liz. I don't want you here."

"I need to do the play."

I shrug. "Not with me directing it. Why do you want it so badly, anyway? Aren't you supposed to be on location shooting a big budget action movie?"

Her eyebrows arch, then one corner of her full lips lifts ever so slightly. "You know about that?"

I would rather be raked over hot coals, then whipped and flayed, than admit my unending obsession with her. "Sometimes I read movie industry news. Don't delude yourself into thinking I'm particularly interested in news about *you*."

Her face falls. "About the play..." She takes another step, coming closer to me. "I need to try something different from the movies I've been doing."

I don't take my eyes away from her face. She's one of the most bankable stars in Hollywood, but her movies haven't fully showcased her incredible talent. Is that why she's so desperate to do the play? Or is there something more?

"You're lying."

"There are other reasons," she says quickly, "but it's important to me, this play, and I trust you. I haven't been on a stage in years and people expect me to fail. I need you to work with me."

I put down my glass and go to her, not stopping until I'm standing right in front of her. A slow flush creeps up her cheeks, momentarily distracting me.

"Aidan—"

"You're pathetic," I say in a low voice. "It's all about you and your ego, as always. All the time you spent in la la land has made you even more selfish and egocentric."

Her eyes close. "I know you hate me..."

Hate? I laugh nastily. "You have no idea."

Tears spring into her eyes. "You don't have to be so cruel."

Curling one finger under her chin, I lift her face up mine. "*You* are cruel, Liz. You are selfish and cruel, and the only person who has ever mattered to you is yourself. You make me sick. Looking at you is an infuriating reminder that I ever allowed myself to fall in love with someone so vile. Go back to L.A. That's where you belong."

I release her, but she remains frozen, blinking furiously, as if to hold back tears, making me hate myself for hurting her.

But she deserves it.

"I'm not leaving," she whispers fiercely.

"Fine." I shrug. "Then I will."

We're standing barely inches apart, and her eyes are boring into mine, challenging, defying. My nose fills with the flowery scent of her shampoo, and the soft fragrance that reminds me of white satin sheets and soft skin.

White satin sheets and her soft, naked skin.

Arousal clouds my thoughts and I swallow hard.

"Do you hate me so much you're willing to derail the play?" Her voice is a heated whisper. She places a hand on my chest, and I freeze. "Think of all the hard work that's already gone into it. All the people who dedicated the last few months to trying to get it off the ground."

I take a step back. She's trembling, and less noticeably, so am I. I'm also hard as a rock, only a few moments away from succumbing to the temptation to push her against the wall and find out if being inside her still feels as good as I remember.

If her moans still sound as intoxicating as I remember.

I take a deep breath. "You're being dramatic, and manipulative. And guess what? That doesn't surprise me. Natalia can get another director, or you can leave."

"Why should I leave? Just because you're afraid to work with me."

My laugh sounds hollow even to my ears. "I'm not afraid, Liz. I'm unwilling. I have no respect for you, either as a person or as an actress."

She flinches at the lash of my words, but she doesn't retreat. "I don't believe you." She gives me a pitying half-smile. "You're a coward, and you're afraid of what would happen if we work together. You know why? Because I'm not the only one who has spent the last seven years thinking about what we had."

Her words are like a thunderclap in my head. How dare she? "You were thinking about what we had? When, Liz? Between the high-profile relationships and the helluva short engagement? When did you have the time?"

"You'd be surprised."

I chuckle. "You think you can insinuate that you still care and that would somehow change my mind?

Get out, Liz, and keep going until you get back to where you've been for the past seven years."

"I'm not going anywhere. I won't run away, but I bet you will." She smiles, looking pained and disappointed at the same time. "It's amazing how much you've changed, Aidan. The man I knew would never have run away from a challenge."

With that comment, she strides to the door and out of the apartment. I hear the door slam behind her, bristling as I go back to the bar and start to pour myself another drink before I think better of it.

You're afraid to think of what would happen if we work together.

"No, Liz," I mutter. "I'm not."

I watch the clear amber liquid swirling in the bottle for a long minute before pushing it away. If this continues, I'll be a relapsed alcoholic before the play opens. Working with her would likely drive me crazy, but I'm going to do it, because she challenged me, and she knew when she did it that I wouldn't back down.

CHAPTER EIGHTEEN

LIZ

*D*ad is sitting up in bed while his nurse hovers over him. She watches him swallow his medication, then satisfied, she gives me a smile and leaves the room.

"Being sick is boring," he complains.

"I can imagine." I pat his hand. "Would you like to go out?"

His eyes go to the window and he grimaces, shaking his head. The soft classical music playing from the speakers lends a melancholy air to the room. I wish he'd let me change it to something livelier.

I walk over to the windows and open the blinds. "We could go for a drive."

"Maybe another time." He closes his eyes as a haunting interlude from Chopin fills the air. "Your mother could listen to this for hours."

He rarely talked about my Mom when I was growing up, but now, he mentions her every day, and even though I want to hear his reminisces, I'm also scared that it means he has resigned himself to an imminent reunion.

I return to the side of the bed and take his hand. "She wouldn't want you to give up, not when I still need you."

"I'm so proud of you, Sweet Pea." In his lined face, his eyes are sharp. "You know you don't have to come here every day. Especially since you'll soon be busy with the play."

"Never too busy to see you."

He smiles. "I hear Aidan is not quitting the play after all."

Remembering my last encounter with Aidan, I sigh. "Natalia confirmed he's staying."

"She says you persuaded him."

I snort out a laugh. "Persuaded is not the word I'd choose. I mean...I tried, but the only person who can make Aidan Court do anything is Aidan Court."

"Maybe," my dad concedes. "At least you've got what you wanted."

Have I? I only have to think about Aidan for my mind to be flooded with images of all the things I want from him... with him. I pull in a sharp breath and smile brightly.

"Did I mention there's a presser later this

afternoon? Part of the publicity for the play. I have a few hours before I leave. Would you like me to read to you?"

He nods, and I read until he falls asleep, glad for the moment not to have to answer any more questions about Aidan.

A FEW HOURS LATER, I ARRIVE AT THE PRESSER. AN intern from the publicity company leads me to a back room, where the other members of the production are waiting for the cue to join the press in the conference room.

I recognize my co-star Todd Feldman and wave. A wiry man with black-framed glasses and a shock of frizzy white hair introduces himself as Gary, the publicist for the production. Natalia is across the room with the sound, lighting and production designers. Busy interns buzz from one corner of the room to another like bees, offering coffee and water.

Aidan is absent.

Since that afternoon at his apartment, public interest in the play had grown to a crescendo. There have been numerous articles speculating about my acting skills, my history with Aidan, why I'm choosing to do theatre instead of a guaranteed box office hit at this point in my career. There are always paparazzi waiting outside my apartment and even my father's place.

It's madness.

The presser is a chance for the production to offer an official story to the world, and they are making a huge production of it, offering the press access to the whole production team instead of doing something easy like releasing a statement.

Where is Aidan? I glance at my watch, nervous at the thought of seeing him and at the possibility that he won't show.

"Hi," I look up to see Todd smiling at me. He's handsome, with short brown hair, gray eyes with nice crinkles at the corners, and the tight athletic body of a dancer. "I don't believe we've met. I'm Todd Feldman."

"I know," I return his smile and take his offered hand. "I saw your last musical a few times."

His grin widens. "That's great to hear. I'm...I'm honored."

"Why?" I look around again for Aidan, but he still hasn't arrived. "You were the one lighting up the stage."

Todd laughs and I smile, still nervous. I grab a bottle of water from a table stacked with refreshments and take a few sips. Someone comes in from the conference room and I hear the racket from the crowd of reporters on the other side of the door.

Lord! Seven years in the public eye and I haven't gotten used to it. It still boggles my mind that people are so interested in me. Interested enough that thousands of questions pour into my social media daily.

"Five minutes," an assistant from the production company announces. "Keep answers to the point, and short. Only about the play." Her eyes skip to me. "They'll want to ask about personal stuff, relationships...direct them back to the play and if they get insistent, we'll shut them down."

I nod. My publicist said the same thing earlier on a call from L.A.

Natalia comes up beside me. "How're you doing?"

"So so." I shrug and take one last sip of my water. Just as I drop the bottle in the trash, Aidan walks into the room. He's dressed in an ashy gray shirt, black jeans, and a dark jacket. His hair is wavy and messy, as if he's just rolled out of bed, or some lucky girl has just run her greedy hands through it.

I swallow a sigh.

His eyes are alert, and when they land on me, his lips quirk in a dismissive smirk.

At least you're here. A triumphant smile creeps onto my lips. *You're doing the play. You're going to work with me, and you won't be able to avoid me.*

He ignores me after that one glance, speaking to Natalia and a few others until it's time to enter the conference room. Then he strides past me and through the doors.

The buzz of voices intensifies as all the others go out. I'm the last to enter the conference room and as soon as I do, the noise intensifies and the flash of cameras nearly blind me.

There's promotional art for the play everywhere, with a huge banner that reads, The Break of Day across the back of the stage. An intern leads me to my seat as someone addresses the press. After a few words, Natalia takes over, and her firm voice details the aims of the production and introduces the production team. I give a small wave when she says my name, stealing a glance at Aidan, who looks uninterested, bored even.

Natalia keeps talking and I can feel the hundreds of eyes on me. I'm the reason most of them are here —the entertainment network reporters and the tabloid magazines with their half-page *art and theatre* sections. They want to see what the Liz McKay brand is up to. They want to see the body language between me and Aidan and decide if there's a story they can magnify.

The questions start with one for me. "Why did you pull out of your last project? Many of your fans were eager to see you in that role."

"I'm sure my fans understand that I'm making the right decision for my career by choosing to work in an acclaimed play such as the Break of Day. It's a powerful story that needs to be told and I'm honored to be given a chance to tell it."

"But wouldn't—"

"We would appreciate it if you kept your questions to issues relating to this play." The interruption comes from Gary and I gave him a grateful smile.

For the next few minutes, the questions revolve around the play. Natalia answers a few about production schedules, previews and such. I focus on the timbre of Aidan's voice while he talks about ensuring that this run of the Break of Day preserves the artistic integrity of the story.

"You choose your projects carefully. Why did The Break of Day appeal to you?" The question comes from a reporter from a lifestyle magazine.

"This play is a seminal work with its exploration of grief, repressed emotions and catharsis. It demands that the audience question long-held beliefs about the expression of human emotion. It's an important story, one that I feel honored to bring to the stage."

His gaze swings in my direction, and I realize I've been staring at him. I turn away, wondering if everyone in the room saw the stark admiration on my face.

"Ms. McKay. Is your father involved in this play in any way?"

I exchanged a short glance with Natalia. "My father is retired," I answer. "This production is entirely due to the hard work of Natalia Barrow."

"There are rumors that you pulled out of your last movie project because your ex-fiancé Devlin Coates signed on to co-star."

I feel the burn of Aidan's gaze on my skin, and I let out a small laugh to buy time. "You have a fascinating imagination," I tell the reporter, earning a few laughs. "Devlin and I are very good friends. In fact, we've been friends longer than we were engaged. I would have been glad to work with him, but doing this project is more important to me at this time."

Despite my better judgement, I steal a glance at Aidan. His eyes hold mine for a fraction of a second, his withering contempt for me all too clear in their depths.

"Well, forgive my imagination," the same reporter continues. "I'm curious. This is the second time you're doing a play on Broadway. The first was the critically acclaimed Edge of Madness seven years ago, which Aidan Court also directed. Did the fact that you're *intimately familiar* with the director factor into your deciding to work with him again?"

I don't miss his emphasis, but I smile brightly. "Aidan is a very talented director. This play is lucky to have him and I'm glad to be in such good hands."

Another reporter chimes in. "You pulled out of

the Edge of Madness in the first month of the initial one-year run, leaving your stand-in to take over. Can you assure your audience that you won't leave this play as abruptly as you left the last one?"

"As I said, this production is very important to me and I've learned the lessons about not fulfilling contracts." There are a few laughs. "So...no, I won't be leaving this play abruptly."

The next question is directed at Aidan. "Where do you see this play fitting into your impressive body of work?"

He answers the question, not bothering to mask the boredom in his voice.

"Do you have any concerns about working with Liz McKay?"

There's a pause. "Is that a complete question?" Aidan's voice is stinging and I can hear his irritation. "What exactly are you asking?"

"I mean it's common knowledge that you have a romantic history. Is that a concern for either of you seeing as you will work closely together, and can we assume there is substance to the rumors of a reconciliation?"

Aidan's jaw hardens. I fully expect him to announce his distaste for me in front of the world. Desperation churns my belly.

Leaning toward my mic, I start to talk almost without thinking. "You know, I was very young when

I left New York and Broadway. I loved Aidan then, and I loved his work. I still admire him...I admire his work and I still love him. Seven years ago, I didn't deal with the situation I found myself as well as I should have, but now I'm determined to give us another chance and to do better."

The questions explode.

"What does that mean?"

"Does that mean the rumors are true?"

"Are you two together?"

Aidan is glaring at me. If eyes could kill, I'd be a shriveled husk six feet underground. I jerk back from the mic, as if it was somehow to blame for my impulsive word vomit. Regret drowns out the certainty I felt only moments before.

Why had I thought he'd see my words as a public apology, a public declaration that I wasn't unaware of how badly I'd acted seven years ago, of how inconsiderate I'd been of what we had, of how desperate I am now to make him understand?

At that moment, it doesn't seem like he's interested in anything I have to say. He looks royally pissed. When he speaks, his voice is tight with suppressed anger.

"Gentlemen, and ladies... We have a play to produce and I promise that like professionals..." He gives me a withering glance, as if to say that I don't belong in that group. "...We won't let personal feelings and histories get in the way of doing the best job we can."

He rises, as if, as far as he's concerned, the briefing is over. Then he turns his back on the rest of us and walks out of the room.

CHAPTER NINETEEN

AIDAN

I take the subway, as if hurtling through underground tunnels surrounded by an eclectic mix of people would somehow clear the thought of Liz from my head.

It doesn't.

When I emerge from the train, I watch a man wearing a coat at least two sizes too large playing passable music on an old violin. I place a few dollar bills in the hat in front of his boots and keep walking.

I still love him.

Fuck her!

"You don't get to come back into my life and say things like that," I mutter under my breath.

Why couldn't she just stay away?

I still love him.

My soul is stirring with uncontrollable emotions

and I hate it. I hate that beneath my anger, there's still hope, hope that we can make it work.

There's also fear, and the certainty that she will wreck me again, just like she did before.

As soon as I emerge into daylight, the first thing I see is Liz looking down at me from a jewelry ad covering the two-story windows of a large department store. Her shoulders are bare, a half-smile plays on her full lips, and her hair is expertly disheveled. I stare, hating her almost as much as I want her.

It's always a game with her. She drops her little cues and watches as everyone scrambles, and yes, I'm scrambling. She has ensured that I'll spend the next few months unable to think of anything but what she said.

I still love him.

God! I hate her.

I really do. As much as it's possible to hate her and yet know deep down that there'll never be anyone else like her for me. Never.

It's a sad thing to know for sure at my age.

I reach the Swanson Court hotel and nod a greeting at the doormen before walking into the familiar lobby. It has changed little since I was a child, but it still looks impeccable. Landon is a perfectionist with his properties, especially this one, the flagship hotel.

In the penthouse, the elevator deposits me in the foyer. Rachel redecorated a few years ago, and the spacious entrance is warm and welcoming. From the foyer, a carved metal door leads to the rest of the apartment. It's one of the extra security measures Landon added after the horrible attack that almost took their lives seven years ago.

It takes a few moments before Esmeralda, the housekeeper, unlocks the door.

"Mister Aidan!" She sounds delighted. "Is so good to see you."

"You too, Esme." I grin and hand her a box of sweets I got from the gift shop downstairs. She loves them. "You look beautiful today. Is it the hair? Did you do something to your hair?"

She laughs, her eyes sparkling. "No! It's the same!"

"Impossible!"

"Uncle Aidaaaaaaan!" I hear the scream from the top of the stairs a moment before two small bodies fling themselves at me with the speed and strength of high-velocity projectiles.

"Uncle Aidan!" Preston repeats, hanging unto my neck with his tiny arms. He's the oldest of the two boys, a little over six years old and the exact image of his father.

I puff under their weight. "How are my boys?"

"We're bored," Preston proclaims.

"Will you take us to see the zebras in the park?"

Damien lisps imploringly. He's a sweet-faced boy who looks more like his mother than Landon.

"Of course," I reply, placing them on their feet and tousling their hair. "That's why I'm here. Where's Miss. P?"

Damien giggles at the nickname for his baby sister. "She's not Miss. P," he corrects me. "She's Penelope, and she's sleeping. She's always sleeping."

"And crying," Preston adds matter-of-factly.

"And eating," Damien says, not to be outdone.

"And trying to talk like this," Preston mimics baby noises and both boys double over.

"I remember when you only knew how to talk like that. You weren't so smug then."

"What's smug?"

"It means when you think you're perfect."

"I think you're perfect, Uncle Aidan," Damien tells me, coming closer for another hug.

"Awww." I kiss the top of his head. "But I'm not. Not really. Where's your mother?"

"I'm here." Rachel is coming down the stairs. There's a small white Labrador under one arm who starts barking enthusiastically and squirming once he sees the boys. "Look who it is," she says with a smile, setting the dog down once she reaches the bottom of the stairs. "We've missed you around here."

"Work." I explain, going to hug her while the boys roll around on the carpet with Scribbles, the dog.

"I know." She studies my face, concern etched on her features. Apparently, Landon's penchant for worrying about me is contagious. "I've seen some of the press about your new play."

My mouth twists. "You can say her name."

She sighs. "I read that Liz signed on to star. Are you okay with that?"

I know she is thinking about the day I discovered that Liz was gone. I'd come here, looking for my brother, and I'd found Rachel. She'd been pregnant, tired, and still recovering from the attempt on her life, but she held me while I cried my eyes out, unable to pretend that I wasn't devastated.

I shrug the painful memory away. "At this point, there's nothing I can do about it."

"Nothing you can do about what?"

I turn at the sound of Landon's voice as he enters the living room, casual in a t-shirt and lounge pants. The children run to him and he picks them up, carefully avoiding the dog running circles around his feet.

"Hey, bro," I grin. "Good to see you slumming it in sweats like the rest of us mortals."

He laughs. "I am working, though. Just doing it from home." He sets the boys on their feet before pulling me in for a hug. "What's going on? Are there problems with the play?"

I almost start complaining about Liz, but I stop

197

myself. Landon has spent most of his life taking care of me and making my problems his. I've worked for years to change that dynamic, especially now that he has a young family of his own.

"There's no problem, really."

"Only that Liz is starring in the new play." Rachel gives him a pointed look.

"Liz?" Landon frowns. "Liz McKay?"

Rachel nods. Landon turns to me and I shrug like it's not a big deal.

"That's..." Landon looks from me to Rachel. "... potentially awkward. I thought she was doing movies."

"Who's Lis Macray?" Damien pipes up.

"Is she your girlfriend?" Preston asks, tugging at my sleeve.

The innocent question causes an unexpected tugging in my chest. "No," I reply firmly. "No, she's not."

"Uncle Aidan is working with her on a new play," Rachel explains to the boys, before shooing them upstairs to join their nanny and the baby in the nursery.

After they finally leave, very reluctantly, I collapse into an armchair.

"So," Rachel prompts. "What will you do?"

"Nothing." I meet Landon's concerned gaze. "I get that you guys are worried, but this is not seven years ago. I'm not going to descend into a spiral of misery and depression just because of a girl."

"Not just any girl," Rachel amends. "It's Liz. Have you seen her? Spoken to her?"

"Yes."

"And?"

I still love him. "And...Nothing. It's not a big deal."

"It's only a few months at the most." Landon shrugs. "Seven years is a long time. You've both grown a lot since then... and moved on."

Except I haven't moved on. I still want Liz. I'm still mourning the loss of what we had...what we could have had, and sometimes the pain is enough to make me want to scream at the sky in frustration.

Rachel is looking at me, almost as if she can read my thoughts. "Maybe at least there'll be some closure."

The idea is tempting, too tempting. I shake my head. "Closure is just another name for letting someone back into your life to reopen old wounds because you can't bear to let go."

"I disagree." Landon hands me a drink. "But closure isn't necessary when you've both moved on."

"They haven't..." Rachel sighs. "Men," she mutters under her breath. "Aidan—"

I rise from the armchair, shaking my head. "I'm done talking about her for today. Now, I'm going to see my niece, and then I'm taking my nephews out for sunshine and ice-cream."

"Please." Rachel accepts at once. "They're driving me crazy with their energy."

I reach the top of the stairs before I hear Landon's voice. He's talking to Rachel. "You don't think he can handle it? It's been years. He got over her a long time ago."

Rachel's reply is low but heated. "Except he didn't." She snorts. "You men are so blind it's a miracle that you can find your way around."

Landon chuckles. "I have you to show me the way."

She giggles. "Aren't you lucky?"

Done eavesdropping, I make my way to the nursery, cooing at little Penelope in her crib before taking the boys out. I need all my energy to keep up with them, even with their nanny helping. And yet, through it all, somewhere in the back of my mind, there's Liz, whispering over and over again.

I still love him.

CHAPTER TWENTY

LIZ

"What were you thinking?" Fiona exclaims, handing me a margarita. We're in the kitchen of the lovely Brooklyn townhouse she shares with her husband Lionel and her four-year-old daughter, Lily.

"I wasn't...I wasn't thinking at all."

"Not even a tiny little let-me-shake-things-up bit?" She raises an eyebrow in my direction.

"No!" I place my hands over my face, remembering Aidan's fury at the presser.

"That was some stunt," Natalia had said afterward. "That'll generate even more buzz, but Aidan is livid. Did you think about that? His reaction?"

I hadn't expected him to be so mad, that was for sure.

Fiona is still looking at me, one eyebrow raised. "Maybe...a little," I concede. "I thought...I wanted to stop him from telling everyone how little he thinks of me, but yeah, a small part of me also hoped that hearing me say I still cared..."

"That it would soften him a little? Make him more amenable to give audience to the woman who tore out his heart and left him bleeding?"

I sigh. No matter how everyone else in the world treats me, I can always count on Fiona to tell me what she really thinks. "If you don't think he can forgive me, then maybe there's no point."

Fiona refills my drink. "Maybe his anger is just a mask and he hasn't gotten over you, but you should think carefully before making any public statements about you two." She seems determined not to coddle me and even though it hurts, I appreciate it. "It's not all about you and what you want. If he's so important to you, then you should also think of what he wants and what he deserves."

I swallow. "Something or someone better than me?"

"Of course not." Her face softens. "You, but... more considerate of his feelings."

I take a sip of my drink then place the glass on the counter and stare at my fingers. She's right. I've been so focused on the fact that I want Aidan to forgive me. I assumed that if he loved me before, he can and will love me again.

Is that too arrogant? The assumption that because the whole world loves me, he'll love me too.

It probably is. It's also selfish.

You are cruel, Liz. You are selfish and cruel, and the only person who has ever mattered to you is yourself.

Aidan's sneering words are like a whiplash in my memories. "How's your new book coming along?" I ask Fiona, changing the subject.

She grins. "The plot is still secret, and I'm not sharing, but my hero is such a delicious hunk of alpha goodness..."

I spend the rest of the evening badgering her for details about her latest novel, then Lionel returns with Lily from her ballet class and we have dinner together.

Later, in my apartment, I consider Fiona's advice.

It's not all about me and what I want.

So, what does Aidan want?

And how can I do my best to give it to him?

"LADIES AND GENTLEMEN, WELCOME TO THE TABLE read for The Break of Day."

The stage manager, Reed Dyker makes the

announcement with a flourish then stands grinning as we all clap.

"Okay," he continues after the applause. "First, introductions, and then we get on to familiarizing ourselves with our roles and characters. As most of you already know..." He gestures toward where Aidan is seated with a brooding smile on his face. "This is our director, Aidan Court."

There's more clapping. Aidan smiles tightly and lifts one hand in something that barely passes for a wave.

"He's so cute," I hear someone whisper from a few seats to my right.

As if a word like *cute* can ever describe just how amazing he is. He is talented, dynamic, extraordinary, unbelievably beautiful... And even without the aid of my memories, my body still reacts to him with barely contained lust.

He keeps his eyes on whatever he's reading, not looking up even when I introduce myself and earn a few laughs from the rest of the cast.

The whole world already knows who you are, Liz.

After the introductions, we discuss for a while, then read our parts. The atmosphere is relaxed, and it would be fun if I were not so acutely aware of Aidan, and if he wasn't so intent on ignoring me.

I didn't lie, Aidan. I still love you.

As the reading progresses, I keep my gaze on him.

Surely, he can't really be so immune to the memories of the past?

Look at me, I urge silently, but his eyes stay on the pages in front of him.

Almost as if I don't exist.

Suddenly he looks up and our eyes meet. He looked bored, his face impassive, but my body jolts, thrilling like an excited puppy.

"Liz." He says my name drily, without inflection.

"Yes?"

He frowns, and then I notice that everybody else seems to be waiting for me. Aidan's expression curls with unconcealed contempt.

"Your line, Liz."

Someone giggles, and I swallow, feeling stupid and unprofessional. I say the line from my head, holding his disdainful gaze with a steady one of my own.

With a curl of his lips, he turns away.

Pushing aside my embarrassment, I continue with the rest of the reading. Fine. Let him go out of his way to show me he still hates me for what I did to him.

If only he knew.

He can't possibly hate me more than I hate myself.

He can't possibly punish me more than I punished myself these last seven years, knowing that I threw away the best thing that ever happen to me.

AFTER THE SESSION, AIDAN DOESN'T WAIT TO CHAT. He picks up his notes and strides out of the rehearsal space. Gathering my things, I hurry after him.

At the door to his office, he turns around and sees me trying to catch up. His face hardens.

"Wait..." I reach him before he can close the door. Thankfully, he doesn't slam it in my face and break my nose.

"What do you want now?"

"To apologize?"

"For what? Your behavior at the presser? Your presence here? Your actions seven years ago?" His laugh is bitter and mocking. "I don't have the kind of time it would take for you to attempt a decent apology."

"You can at least let me try."

"Why?" He takes a step toward me, then stops and his eyes rake me from head to toe. "You know what, Liz? There's no point. Just leave me alone."

"I'm sorry about the press thing," I say quickly, before he turns away. "I don't know what I was thinking. I was afraid that you'd say something cruel about me before I even had a chance to convince you I'm not the same person I was seven years ago."

"You're still the same person." His voice is almost pitying. "You were afraid I'd say something that wouldn't be flattering to your image? That's your explanation?"

When I don't reply, he continues. "Fuck it, Liz. You're so out of touch with reality. Don't you care about anything but how you look to your adoring fans? Are you even real anymore?" His voice drops to a whisper. "Were you ever real?"

I am. I was, and he's wrong about me. "I care what you think," I tell him. "I told the whole world how I feel, how I still feel about you. Doesn't that mean anything to you?"

He looks tired. "No, it doesn't. You already told me how you feel about me, remember? You told me loud and clear seven years ago."

"Aidan..."

"Aidan!"

We both turn toward the female voice at the same time. The newcomer is an attractive woman with a lithe model's body in a sheath dress and black pumps.

She's almost as tall as Aidan, and when she walks past me and takes his arm, she plants a slow kiss on his lips.

The granite in his expression relaxes into a smile. He doesn't bother to introduce me, and she walks through the doorway into his office without a glance in my direction, all the while looking at Aidan with a smile that reeks of familiarity and intimacy.

Jealousy twists my insides. I hadn't even

considered that there would be someone else. How stupid of me. I know he hasn't been celibate all these years, but seeing him now with another woman, tears at me in a way I never imagined possible.

I want to confront her and tell her Aidan belongs to me.

Except, he doesn't, and I have no right in the world to feel this crippling jealousy and possessiveness.

"Are we done here?" Aidan's voice jerks me out of my thoughts.

"For now," I smile and lift my chin, hiding my pain. "I guess I'll see you later."

CHAPTER TWENTY ONE

AIDAN

"*I*t's been forever since you returned my calls," Claire says. Her eyes hold mine and I compare them with Liz's luminous green gaze. "I was almost too proud to say yes to lunch." She gives me a coquettish smile. "What would you have done if I'd refused to see you?"

I shrug. "Nothing."

"You wouldn't bother to change my mind?"

I don't reply. Our food arrives, and I watch Claire push her steamed broccoli around on her plate. Randomly, I think about how she hardly eats. Randomly, I compare that to my memories of Liz's healthy appetite.

Somewhere inside, I'd known that calling Claire to distract myself from Liz would turn out to be a mistake. Claire is beautiful, smart, entertaining, and sexually uninhibited.

But she's not Liz.

Nobody is.

She drops her fork and reaches out to cover my hand with hers. Her eyes mist, and I know something big is coming.

"I was glad when you called, and I couldn't wait to see you. I just...I wish you'd try to make me feel like I mean something to you, something more than sex."

Halfway through her speech I'm already thinking about Liz again. I pull my hand back with a sigh. Lunch was a mistake, and I don't want to lie to her.

"Listen—"

"How about we go over to your place right now, and I'll show you just how much I've missed you?"

"Claire..."

Something about my tone makes her stop. I feel like an asshole.

I am an asshole.

"I just...I'm busy with the play. I don't think I have the time for any distractions right now."

She scowls. "That's ridiculous. It never stopped you before."

Because none of the other plays had Liz in them.

"Is that why you asked me to lunch? To dump me?"

"I'm not dumping you." You can't dump someone if you were never dating.

"It's because of her, isn't it?"

"Who?" My voice is blank, though I know exactly who she means.

"Liz McKay." She curls her lips when she says the name, and my back stiffens in instinctive defense. "You two used to go out, and she practically admitted to the whole world that she's still in love with you. Maybe you're the one who's still in love with her."

"Don't be ridiculous."

"Fuck you!" Her voice rises, then she sniffs. "Why did you even ask me to have lunch? You could have ignored my messages and ghosted me forever. That would have been kinder than letting me think there was a chance..." She throws her napkin on the table. "You know what? Goodbye, Aidan. I guess I was foolish for thinking I could live up to *the* Liz McKay."

She pushes away from the table and heads for the exit. I watch her go, but I don't stop her. As she nears the doors, they open and Liz walks into the restaurant.

She's dressed the same as she was back at the theater. The same oversized sweater and black tights with boots in the same color. Her hair is different. It was in a topknot earlier, now it's flowing free around her shoulders, and her full lips are glistening with a fresh coat of lip gloss.

Desire, acute and uncontrolled, pools in my groin. My fingers curl and ache with the sheer need to feel the softness of her skin.

It makes sense that she would come here, to this restaurant. It's popular among the theatre crowd. Still, seeing her fills me with a raw frustration. I don't need the constant reminder of her presence and proximity. I don't need the constant reminder that I'm still helplessly under her spell.

Claire stops walking, and as I watch, she spits a few words at Liz, who only smiles in response. Next to Claire, she looks like a goddess, dripping with almost unbelievable beauty and equanimity from her hair to her toes. Claire sweeps past her and out of the doors.

Liz lingers at the entrance for a few moments, then, meeting my gaze, she walks over to my table. The neckline of her sweater slips over one shoulder, exposing smooth, delicate skin and calling attention to the soft swell of her breasts.

I want to stroke my tongue over that exposed skin, and everywhere else.

Fuck me.

"I'm not stalking you," she says with a soft smile.

I tear my eyes away from her. "I don't care."

She expels a small, amused breath. What does she think is there to be amused about?

"I've just been told that you're an asshole and I'm welcome to keep you."

"The first part is true. I am an asshole. The second part, not so much. I'd rather sip lava than spend more time with you than I absolutely need to."

"Aidan..." She draws out my name in a soft plea. Then she sighs. "Can I join you?"

I rise from my seat. "I was just leaving, Liz. The table is all yours."

I can feel her eyes on me as I walk away, and it gives me an immense, though immature sense of satisfaction to feel her frustration as she watches me go.

THAT NIGHT I BURY MYSELF IN MY NOTES FOR THE play. There's a note for every performer, for every scene. I make additions and changes, my mind absorbed in my vision for the play.

Until I get to Liz's part.

Thinking about her, her performance, her lines, her words and gestures, the extra something she brings to every role...and my mind goes from work mode to an unproductive, daydreaming, longing mode.

I want her...so much.

I put the notes aside and massage my temples, as

if that would somehow get Liz out of my head. I switch on my rarely used TV and navigate to one of the streaming apps, then to the list of saved movies in my library.

They all have one thing in common.

Liz.

Watching her movies has been my one indulgence these past years, and I've seen them all at least half a million times.

This time, I choose a romantic comedy. It's one of her early movies, a box-office success that reinforced her reputation as a bankable movie star. The movie starts, and she takes over the screen, and I can't take my eyes off her long enough to focus on the story which I already know by heart.

Liz.

My Liz.

Beautiful, effortlessly sexy, and incredibly talented.

My phone buzzes, pulling me out of the spell of Liz's face and voice. Reluctantly, I reach for it and flick my finger across the screen.

Aidan...I'm terribly sorry about the presser and for all the awkwardness. Let's talk. Liz.

Staring at her words on my screen, with her voice coming from the speakers, it feels almost as though she's in the room with me.

Let's talk.

Why does she keep pushing this insane demand for a conversation as if mere words can change anything for us?

I ignore the text, but even as my eyes go back to the screen, I find it impossible to focus.

My phone buzzes again.

Dinner. At Sardi's. Nine o' clock. Just like we used to. I'll buy.

Just like we used to. I almost smile at the memories, before nostalgia is replaced by the familiar sense of betrayal. Does she know she is assaulting my peace of mind? She probably does. That's her style, after all.

I should go to the restaurant and drag her back here. There are a lot of things I'd gladly do with her. *Just like we used to*.

The image of her in my arms, in my bed, sends a powerful thrill of arousal through me, and my cock hardens.

I resist the temptation to take matters in my hands. With her face on the screen and her voice coming from the speakers, it would be easy to close my eyes and imagine her hands touching me, her voice in my ear, her mouth around my cock...

Fuck her.

From nowhere a memory creeps into my head. Liz, years ago, laughing as she snuggles in my arms. "I never knew it was possible to be this happy."

Then why did you throw it away?

I switch off the TV and toss my phone to the far edge of the sofa before going to pour myself a drink.

No, Liz. I won't have dinner with you.

We're not going to talk.

I won't let you push me over the edge.

She had my heart once, and she destroyed it. Now, I have no intention of giving her anything else, especially my time.

CHAPTER TWENTY TWO

LIZ

"There is no close up." Aidan's voice is like a whiplash. "You've got to show more emotion for the audience to understand what you're going on about. There's no sound mixing. It's just you and them. Can you at least act as if you understand?"

I bite back a sharp retort. "I'm trying to give you what you want."

"Try harder." He paces a few steps then turns around to glare at me.

When I don't move, he leans forward, raising his hand questioningly. "Is there something you want to say?" His voice takes on a mocking tone. "Or is there something you require before you can give us a passable performance? Is your trailer not luxurious enough? Would you prefer a different brand of bottled water?"

I grit my teeth. "Stop it."

"Do your job and give me a scene."

What a bastard!

Pressing my lips together, I prepare for another attempt to do the godforsaken scene. Since he ignored my invitation to dinner, I've made no headway with him. Sitting in a restaurant for two hours waiting for him had been humiliating enough to make me think maybe I should give it up. Having my picture taken by a fellow diner and leaked to the press with headlines talking about how I'd been stood up only added to the humiliation.

As if that's not enough, his attitude at rehearsals is close to unbearable. Every day is the same. He snaps and snarls at me during rehearsals, and after, he acts as if I don't exist.

I spend most of my evenings with my father, and long after he dozes off, I wrack my brains for ideas on what to do about Aidan.

I can seduce him. The force of my attraction to him has not diminished over time, and I have no doubt it's the same for him.

But Aidan will not react well to any attempts to manipulate him, especially with my body.

No, I have to convince him some other way that if he shelves his hatred of me for long enough, he'll see reason to give me a chance.

"So, from the top?" Todd, my co-star, looks from

Aidan to me. He gives me a small wink as if in solidarity.

I give him a grateful smile.

"For fuck's sake," Aidan growls. "I know you two are having a moment, but can we please get back to the scene?"

"Aidan seems to have it in for you," Todd observes later. We're both exhausted from trying to give Aidan his perfect scene.

I hate that I feel compelled to defend Aidan, even though he's treating me like I'm dog poop stuck in his shoe. "He's a perfectionist."

Todd raises an eyebrow as if he can't quite believe I'm defending my tormentor like some sort of masochist.

"Forget Aidan," he says. "Would you like to get lunch?"

I shake my head. "I'm exhausted and aching for some quality shut eye."

After he leaves, I briefly consider heading over to Fiona's when my phone rings. It's a number I don't recognize.

"Hello." My voice is wary.

"Hello, Liz." The voice on the other end is light, friendly, and vaguely familiar. "This is Rachel Court."

Rachel...Oh! Rachel. I met Aidan's brother and his charming sister-in-law, a long time ago, in what now seems like another life. Different, unlikely reasons for her call run through my mind. "I...Hi!"

"Hi!" She laughs, probably at my confusion. "It's been a while. How are you?"

"I'm fine." I'm not. Not really. I have a sudden and unbidden memory of the night Landon proposed to her. It was a party, and I'd been there as Aidan's date. We'd been so happy and in love, and I was just days away from breaking his heart into pieces.

A wave of longing washes over me and I stifle a sigh.

"I've just spoken to your publicist," Rachel is saying in her sweet, lilting voice. "We want to do a feature on you for Gilt Review. I imagine she'll call to let you know, but I wanted to find out from you if you'd be interested."

"Of course," I reply, remembering now that she is an editor at one of the prestigious Gilt magazines. "I'd love to."

"Okay. I'm sure our people can arrange the scheduling and logistics." There's a pause. "I'm having a party later in the week," she tells me. "I wondered if you'd like to come."

Will Aidan be there? The question hovers on the tip of my tongue. Does she know? Does she know how much I hurt him and how much I'd give to get him back? Does she know how much he hates me?

He'll probably hate me more if he sees me socializing with his family.

Or maybe it'll give me a chance to talk to him outside work.

"I'd love to come," I tell Rachel.

"Great! I'll send you the date and time, Okay?"

"Okay."

Back in rehearsals, Aidan is as impatient and caustic as ever and I wonder if he knows his sister-in-law has just reached out to me, and what he would do when he finds out.

Probably find new ways to torture me.

After rehearsals are finally over, everybody leaves, and I head over to Aidan's temporary office.

It's just a few doors down from the rehearsal space. In a few days, we'll move rehearsals to the theater, and I'll be standing on a real stage again.

I've missed being on the stage. I've missed the audience and the applause. As much as I appreciate what I'd achieved in cinema, I know being onstage will feel like being back home.

If only Aidan would stop torturing me.

I reach his door and knock. It's slightly ajar, and the force of my knock pushes it open about an inch.

"Yes?"

He sounds distracted. I step into the office and close the door behind me. The space is bare, with only a simple desk and a chair. Aidan is leaning on the wall beside a small window with open shutters, scrolling through his tablet. He doesn't look up when I enter but I sense the stiffening of his body.

Like I'm a poisonous reptile he'd rather avoid.

"Nice place."

He doesn't reply. He lifts his gaze to my face, his blue eyes conveying both irritation and dismissal without diminishing his beauty one bit.

"Oh look, it's Cruella de Ville," he says with faux excitement. "What do you want?"

I walk over to his desk and settle on the edge, facing him. "Can you be honest with me?"

He scowls. "Are you being serious?"

"Answer the question."

"It seems a bit redundant for me to have to point this out, but I'm not the one who has a problem with honesty."

I ignore his statement. "Do you sincerely think my performance is horrible?"

He watches me for a moment, his eyes measuring. "Will you pack up and leave if I say yes?"

"Maybe," I shrug. "But you agreed to be honest."

He runs a hand through his hair, tousling the waves. My fingers itch to smooth them back, but he'll likely bite my hand off if I so much as touch him.

"Liz." He sounds bored. "You either do the play or you don't. If you want to leave, go. Don't look to me to give you an excuse."

"So, you can't answer my question. You can't tell me the truth, can you? Because then you wouldn't have an excuse to bully and humiliate me all day."

"Humiliate?" He laughs. "You want me to coddle you? Is that what you want? You want me to tell you how great you are? To flatter you and feed your ego?"

"That's not what I want!"

"Good. Because you may get that in Hollywood, but not here."

I take a step toward him. "You don't want me to leave, do you?" He raises an eyebrow, but I continue. "If you did, all you had to do just now was lie and tell me how poor an actress I've become. I'd have left. But no, you want me to stay so you can lash out at me and call it direction."

Silently, he pushes off from the wall and set the tablet down on his desk. He glares at me, then rubs a finger at his temple, like he's tired of my presence.

Well, I'm not leaving.

I go to stand right in front of him. "Why, Aidan?" I whisper. "Does it turn you on to torture me?"

His eyes are burning. With less than an inch between us, I can feel the heat of his body. His scent fills my nose, a heady combination of mild cologne, body wash, and *him*. His chest rises and falls, and I'm fully aware that if I make even the smallest move, my body would brush against his.

Not that I'd mind.

"You know nothing about torture." He bites out every syllable, and each one hits me like a lash.

"Aidan..." I pull in a breath. "I shouldn't have said what I did at the presser, but I meant every word. When I left here—"

"Me."

I blink at the interruption.

"When you left me," he clarifies, his eyes burning.

I close my eyes. "When I left you, Aidan, I thought I was doing the right thing. I know you're angry and you have every right to be, but I can't keep apologizing forever."

Abruptly, he puts some distance between us, walking over to the other side of his desk. "The thing is, Liz, nobody is asking you to."

I follow him. "So that's it? You're going to keep pretending I mean nothing to you?"

"I don't have to pretend." His eyes are expressionless, his voice brutal. "You mean nothing to me."

"Liar."

He shrugs. "Close the door behind you, Liz."

I stare at him, frustrated beyond words. "I asked you to have dinner with me and I waited for you. I waited for hours. Did it make you happy to think of me, alone, enduring the whispers, wondering if you would bother to come? When did you become so heartless?"

He lowers his head, bringing his face so close to mine, we're almost touching. "If anybody here has the right to talk about heartlessness, it's not you." He places his hands on my shoulders and gently moves me backward, creating some space between us, then he walks over to the door and pulls it open. "Since you refuse to leave, have fun staying where you're not wanted." Then he walks out, leaving me alone in the tiny office.

CHAPTER TWENTY THREE

AIDAN

*S*he has some nerve, really, accusing me of cruelty. Cruelty!

Look in the fucking mirror, Liz.

I stride through the theater, making for the stage door. Outside, a few people are waiting, hoping to catch Liz on her way out. Many are the wide-eyed young girls who make up the majority of her fan base. I scowl as a few of them raise phones and take my picture.

"You don't deserve her!" someone yells.

Jesus!

My scowl deepens and I hurry away from the entrance, leaving them to their vigil. Liz will probably disappoint them by leaving through one of the more discreet exits.

Not that I care.

I walk past a few shops, then stop when I spy the headline on the front page of a tabloid stacked on the display rack of a tiny grocery store.

Another big L for Lkay!

There's a grainy picture of her waiting alone at a restaurant table. The picture was taken with a smartphone but from a bad angle, like the photographer was trying to be discreet. Liz's face is turned away from the camera, but there was enough detail for me to make out the dejection on her face.

My fingers clench.

When did you become so heartless?

I push my hands into my pockets and keep walking, squashing the guilt that makes me want to go back and apologize to her.

What do I have to apologize for?

I didn't ask her to come back and try to upend my life. I didn't encourage her, and my lack of response to her text should have told her I would not come running to meet her for dinner just because she asked.

I'm not one of her loyal fans.

I'm just the man who loved her enough that I fell to pieces when she left.

Screw her anyway.

Is it really my absence at the restaurant she cares about, or is it the headlines? Gossip rags spreading the news that she'd been stood up can't be good for her ego, or for the McKay brand, and those are the only things she cares about.

I ignore the doubt nagging in my mind.

I meant every word.

I still love him.

I can hear her voice in my head, like the last notes of a siren's song.

What if she really cares?

What if there's a chance that something has changed?

What if there's hope for us?

I'm not immune to her, and God knows, I have enough fantasies stored from years of vacillating between hate and desire, enough images of the life we could have had together...the life we could still have, together.

I shake my head. I'm being a fool, but then, haven't I always been a hopeful fool with Liz?

The saddest part is, I'd gone to the damn restaurant. I'd gone as far as the hostess booth, separated from the tables by a glass panel. I'd watched her as she waited alone at the table, almost ethereally beautiful, with her hair falling down her bare shoulders like a gleaming dark waterfall. I'd imagined us talking, digging up the past. I'd imagined laying my pain at her feet, opening myself to her and drowning in the pleasure only her body could deliver.

I knew then that if I gave her even an inch, I'd be lost, so I left the restaurant and went back home.

It wasn't cruelty or heartlessness. It was self-preservation.

I keep walking until I reach my apartment. I work out for a bit, take a shower, then order takeout while warring with my desire to put on another one of Liz's movies. As I wait for the food to arrive, my phone buzzes with a message from Debra.

I delivered your notes for the cast. Liz was lovely. I can't believe you guys used to date.

Even my assistant is under her spell.

There's another message, this one from Rachel.

I'm having a dinner party on Friday and you're required to attend. It's semi-formal, just a few people. Heads up. Liz will be there, but that's no excuse for you not to show. Love you loads.

I close my eyes, ignoring the ringing in my head. I select a movie from the list and soon, Liz's face fills my screen. Why do I even bother to resist her? No matter how hard I try, there's just no escaping her.

CHAPTER TWENTY FOUR

LIZ

"*O*h, look at you," Rachel exclaims as soon as I walk into the spacious penthouse. She's a beautiful woman, a few years older than me, with burnished red-gold hair and an aura of friendly intimacy that instantly puts me at ease. She pulls me into a quick, warm hug. "You look spectacular."

"Thank you. You look great too." My eyes skip behind her, surreptitiously searching for Aidan.

"He's not here yet," Rachel says with a knowing smile.

"Oh! I..." *God!* Am I so obvious? I smile weakly. "It looks like a great party."

She laughs and takes my hand, leading me further into the intimately lit room. There's a smattering of guests, about twenty people. Soft music fills the air from hidden speakers. A table on one side of the room is loaded with an assortment of cocktail dishes, and beside it, Landon Court is pouring drinks.

"You remember my husband?" Rachel leads me toward him. He looks up at us and even though I've met him before and I'm expecting the resemblance, it still knocks me off balance.

He's an older version of Aidan, with wavy dark-gold hair. His eyes are a lighter shade of blue, but with none of the animosity that I've come to expect from Aidan.

He also seems more relaxed, more at peace with the world, but why wouldn't he be? He and Rachel are obviously crazy about each other.

It makes me long for what I could have had with Aidan.

"Liz!" Landon grins at me, then hands me a champagne flute. "This is exciting. I can't remember the last time we had a genuine movie star in our home. I hope Aidan isn't working you too hard."

I shake my head. "He tries, but I'm used to working like a packhorse."

"Really?" Rachel looks concerned. "Well, here now, relax and forget about work."

"Aidan here yet?" Landon asks, looking around the room.

They exchange a glance I can't quite decipher. "He's on his way," Rachel replies, then with a smile at her husband, she leads me away.

Most of the guests are people from the publishing world and a few faces I recognize from trending business news. There's a wickedly funny woman who Rachel introduces as her cousin, Laurie. I spend the next few minutes confirming or denying some of the more scandalous stories from the Hollywood rumor mills.

"I hope Aidan isn't being difficult to work with," Rachel is saying. "I know he can be...intense."

I shake my head, that need to defend him again trumping my desire for a confidant. "He's a great director."

She laughs. "Now there's one way to avoid answering a question." She beckons at a tall, youngish guy who has just arrived, and he walks over.

"Have you met Liz," she says. "Liz, this is Finn McDonald. Finn, Liz McKay."

He stares at me, almost slack-jawed. "I've seen all your movies," he stutters. "Some more than once."

"Me too." I manage a laugh, watching him double over like I've just said the cleverest thing. I have a vague idea of who he is, something to do with investment and finance tech. He is one of the latest additions to the Forbes billionaires list.

Many women would be glad for the opportunity to meet him. He seems nice, and is good-looking in a wide-eyed, nerdy way.

Too bad I'm obsessed with Aidan.

"Why don't you two get to know each other while I go get another drink?" Rachel gives me an encouraging smile, and I wonder what she's doing. I'm sure she knows I came here for Aidan. Doubtless, she knows why I keep looking at the door.

She pats my arm and walks away.

"I heard you were in New York, but I never dreamed I'd get the chance to meet you," Finn is saying.

"I'm sure you can meet anyone you want."

He thinks for a moment, then nods. "You're right. Sometimes I forget."

I smile up at him. "So, which of my movies did you see twice?"

He lists them. He's obviously a big fan. We're talking about my experiences filming in the Moroccan desert when I feel the air thicken around me.

Don't look.

I know I should keep talking with Finn, even flirt a little, maybe encourage him to ask me to dinner. Maybe Aidan needs to see that some men would give the world for a minute of my time.

But knowing he's in the room, and I can't hear what Finn is saying anymore.

I turn toward the door.

Aidan is right by the entrance, leaning on the wall, his arms crossed as he looks straight at me.

My breath catches. Finn's voice fades into background noise. My eyes follow Aidan as he peels himself from the wall and walks over to his brother for a quick hug, before kissing Rachel on both cheeks. When he turns to look at me again, his eyes are cold.

"...I always thought there'd be a sequel. It's been years, and we've been waiting for an announcement."

I have no idea what Finn is talking about. I watch Aidan pour himself a drink.

I should go talk to him.

What would I say that I haven't said hundreds of times already?

It's getting exhausting, and it hurts to consider that at some point, I'll have to give up the dream that there will be a future for us.

Aidan throws back the rest of his drink, then without saying a word to anyone else, he walks out of the room.

"Liz?" Finn is giving me a quizzical look. He laughs self-consciously. "I'm probably boring you with my fan-boying."

"I'm sorry. I'm just a little distracted." I look in the direction Aidan went. "I gotta go."

Without waiting for a reply, I hurry after Aidan. I reach the door just in time to see him disappear inside one of the many doorways leading off the hallway.

I follow him, pausing only for a moment before pushing the door open. It's dark inside the room, but I can see Aidan silhouetted against the window, the brightly lit city a brilliant backdrop to his tall, masculine figure.

I close the door behind me just as he turns around.

"Are you still *not stalking me?*" he mocks, his voice as dry as dead grass.

I shrug. "You knew I'd be here."

"Did I?" I hear him chuckle. He moves in the darkness, coming toward me. My heart thuds against my ribs. I feel him brush close to me, but he only moves past me to flick a switch close to the door.

The room fills with warm light, and I blink, turning around to face Aidan.

He places one hand on the door knob.

"Don't go," I whisper.

He looks pained. "Whatever it is you want, Liz, give it up. I closed the chapter on you a long time ago."

There's a finality in his words I can't bear. I can't let him go. "You don't want me to leave."

"Really?" There's mockery in his eyes. "How would you know what I want?"

"Because I know you." I take a step toward him. "I know under all your anger, you still have feelings for me."

"Feelings?" His laugh is harsh, but he doesn't deny it. He reaches out a hand, almost languidly, and cups my chin, then with his other hand, he pulls me to him. His back is to the door and I'm flush against him. I can feel the tenseness in his body, the heat washing off him in waves. I feel his chest rise against my breasts and I pull in an aching breath.

"What feelings?" he whispers, his lips close to my ear, so close, I can feel his warm breath on my skin. "I want to kiss you until your lips are bruised." He fingers the fabric of my top and beneath it, my nipples harden and start to ache.

"I want to tear this off you and taste your skin. I want to feel your breasts in my palm, your nipples pebbling in my mouth. I'm aching to taste you, to feel your hips jerk and your thighs convulse when you come on my tongue. I'm aching to fuck you all night, till you're sore and exhausted and neither of us can walk." He draws one hand down my back and cups my butt, pressing me to his body so I can feel the hard evidence of his arousal.

I close my eyes, weak with desire. My lips part with my breaths. I want him to do everything to me he's just said. I'm wet, aching and going crazy with want.

"Are those the kind of feelings you mean?" he continues, "because I have them, plenty."

Me too, but this thing between us isn't only about sex. I know it, and I know he knows it too.

"I love you." The words leave me in a rush. "I've never stopped loving you."

He flinches, and where we are touching, his body seems to turn to stone. Abruptly, he jerks away from me, his expression almost livid.

"Why do you play these games, Liz? Does it make you feel good to torture me?"

I move forward, trying to regain the distance he has put between us. "You know that's the last thing I want to do."

"Yet, here you are." His eyes close and he draws in a deep breath, making his chest shudder. "Why did you do it? Why did you leave? Was I too damaged for you? Too wounded, too insecure? Did I lose you because I let you see the person I was inside?"

"No!" Tears fill my eyes. Everything he'd shared with me—his guilt over his father, his depression, addictions—all of it had made me love him even more. The idea that I left him because of that is something I can't bear. "Of course not."

"So, was it the fame? Did you think I'd stand in your way?" His eyes are bright. "I would have given everything up. I would have uprooted my life over and over, just to be with you."

"And you would have hated me for it. Just as I would have hated you if I'd given up the opportunity to go...because I wanted to, Aidan. I wanted to stay with you so badly I was willing to tell one of the most powerful directors in Hollywood to go to hell. What we had was so perfect I was willing to throw the recognition I'd always wanted down the drain just to be by your side. It scared me...It scared me to think we would ruin it somehow, that it wouldn't last, and then we'd hate each other. It scared me because it was too much, too intense, too good to last...and at the time, it felt like the best thing I could do for the both of us was to make a clean break."

I close my eyes and a tear rolls down my cheeks. "I was young and stupid and afraid. I thought I knew what love...what life was about. I was afraid that if we tried too hard to keep what we had, we'd ruin it."

"So, you left without a word, and I had to read about your new movie role in the news. I had to read about your whirlwind romance with your co-star. I saw you move on like I never existed."

"None of it was real." I reach out to touch him and he flinches. "Aidan, it was all publicity for the movie. All the fans wanted me and Devlin to be dating, like a wish fulfillment couple. The studio liked it and told us not to deny the rumors. We didn't start to date until more than a year later."

His face tightens at the mention of my ex.

"I thought it was time to move on. I thought you had too, but now... I know that..." I swallow. "I shouldn't have left like that. I should have given us a chance, even the slightest chance, instead of thinking I knew all the answers."

He reaches for me, cupping my face with one hand and wiping a tear from my cheek with his thumb. He holds my gaze for a long moment, and it's almost as if he can see into my soul.

Can you see that I always loved you? Always.

Pain flashes across his eyes, and with a sigh he places his forehead against mine. I hold on to him, feeling his muscles beneath my hands. "Liz," he whispers.

My heart swells and bursts into a million aching pieces. I want to bury myself in him. I want to open my heart and my soul and beg him to give me even a fraction of what I once had.

"Liz." This time, his voice even more tender than before.

I pull in a breath. "Aidan."

He lifts his head from mine, and for a moment I think he's going to kiss me, but instead, he releases me and takes a step back.

"I don't want your love," he says, his gaze steady on my face. "I have to work with you now, but when my work is done with the play, I hope to God I never have to see you again."

Something breaks inside me. If he wants to crush me, he has succeeded. He starts to open the door, and without thinking, I place one hand over his on the door knob and curl the other around his neck, lifting my face to press my lips to his.

It's a desperate move, but I am desperate. I kiss him, sliding my lips against his firm, yet tender lips, feeling his implacable stiffness and hoping to melt the ice beneath.

After a few moments, I give up and place my hands on his chest. His muscles stiffen under my touch. "You have to stop hating me," I whisper helplessly. "I can't bear it anymore."

Gently, he takes hold of my arms and thrusts me away from him. "You should have thought of that before crushing my heart, Liz," he mutters. "Now it's far too late."

CHAPTER TWENTY FIVE

*W*alking away from her is the hardest thing I've ever done in my life. I step out of Landon's study, unable to think or function clearly. I don't wait to see if she'll follow me. I run up the stairs, taking them three at a time, trying to put as much distance between us as I can.

I never stopped loving you.

In the boys' room, my nephews are already asleep, and after a few moments spent watching their peaceful faces, I go to the nursery to see little Penny sleeping with her thumb in her mouth.

"Hey."

I turn toward the voice and see Rachel in the doorway. "Are you all right?" she asks.

"Yup," I lie, keeping my voice low so as not to wake Penny. "Why wouldn't I be?" I leave the room, closing the door behind me. "You know parties aren't really my scene, so I came up to see the kids."

Rachel cocks her head to one side and gives me a look that says she knows I'm full of shit. "Liz just left. What did you say to her? She was...She looked miserable."

I breathe through the ache in my chest.

I never stopped loving you.

She's inside my head, holding my heart, unwilling to let go, and I'm a willing slave, unable to push her away.

"I have no idea why that would be," I say lightly, trying to smile, but failing spectacularly. "I think I need another drink."

Rachel puts a hand on my arm. "Aidan, I know you think you're punishing her, but she's not the only one who's suffering."

I don't reply. I give her a thin smile and return downstairs. The party is almost over, and after one more drink, I leave for home, battling the ghosts of Liz's words as they repeat in my head over and over.

I never stopped loving you.

THE REST OF THE WEEKEND PASSES IN A BLUR OF obsessing about Liz and torturing myself with images of us together, like we used to be. I tell myself I'm an asshole for pushing her away, then convince myself she deserves it. By the time I got to rehearsals on Monday, I'm a wreck.

I walk into the auditorium from the back of the stage. There are people everywhere, cast members and crew, but my eyes are only for Liz. She's standing in the middle of the stage, listening to Todd read lines he's trying to memorize. She draws me to her somehow. I'm not even aware I'm going to her until I'm standing right beside her.

She stiffens and angles her body away from me, focusing on Todd and keeping her attention on him even when he stops reading and waves at me.

"Hey, Aidan."

"Todd." I nod at him. Beside me, Liz stays quiet.

Why do I want to grab hold of her, right here, in front of all these people, and make her tell me again that she loves me?

Because I want her with a desperation I have no words to articulate.

And I want to punish her for making me hope.

Our chapter closed a long time ago, Liz. Why won't you let it go?

Why can't I?

Reluctantly, I pull my attention from her and find a seat. Rehearsals start, and I watch the performers intently, trying to block out everything but the form the story is taking.

Liz is doing an emotional scene, and in that moment, she stops being Liz. She becomes a young mother, battling depression, trying not to blame the people she loves even as cracks appear in all her relationships.

She's incredible to watch. She looks like she would shatter into pieces right there on stage, give the audience exactly what the story says, send them home with an experience they won't forget.

The scene ends and her eyes find mine, holding my gaze only for a moment before sliding away.

Has she given up on me?

The possibility fills me with an acute sense of loss.

Is this the end for us, Liz? The question is a silent echo in my head. *Is this the end?*

We finish early, and as the cast members leave the stage, I get a message from Debra.

You have a visitor. Your office.

Who?

Claire. You want me to tell her to leave?

I think about it, then reply in the negative.

I'm already feeling like an asshole over my last conversation with Liz. The least I can do is not be an asshole to Claire.

Claire is waiting outside my office. She greets me with a friendly smile, almost as if our last conversation never happened. "Hey."

"Hey," I reply, unlocking my door and letting her

in. Just before I close the door, I see Liz on her way to her dressing room. Our eyes meet, only for a second, then she looks away, but not before I see a flash of something in her eyes. Jealousy? Hurt?

Why do I feel so guilty?

I should want to hurt her for what she did to me.

Instead, I want to apologize for causing her pain.

Fuck me.

"I'M SORRY FOR THE OTHER DAY," CLAIRE IS SAYING. "I don't know what came over me. I was jealous, I guess."

"You don't have to apologize." We are at a lounge close to the theater. The music is good. Not too loud, just lively enough to allow a conversation.

"No, I do." She sighs. "You're not a bad guy, Aidan. It's not like you ever promised me anything more than casual fun. It's not fair for me to blame you because I started wanting more."

In that moment, I wish more than anything that I can push Liz out of my mind and give myself a chance with Claire, or anyone else.

But I can't. Not as long as even the memory of Liz exists.

I've known that for years. Yet, I keep fighting her. Why?

I never stopped loving you.

Liz.

She will burn me to ashes.

And I want to let her.

Because I'm still in love with her.

"You don't have to apologize," I repeat. Claire looks at me with wet eyes, and I know she wants me to say more, to say I want to try again, that I'm open to more casual fun.

But there's no room for that, or for her.

Only Liz.

I place some money on the table for the drinks then rise to my feet. "I need to get back to the theater. I have some...business to take care of."

A look of disappointment crosses her face. "I guess."

Outside, I shove my hands in my pockets and start to walk. What am I doing? I don't know. I just know I want to see Liz. I want to talk to her. Even if we fight or argue, the hope that we'll come to some sort of resolution, that I won't lose her again this time...it's too much for me to ignore.

It's silent inside the theater with most people gone for the day. I head for Liz's dressing room, hoping she's still around.

Tell me again that you never stopped loving me.

Her door is ajar, but she's not inside the room.

Where is she?

In the mirror, my reflection looks, desperate, sad, and purposeful all at once. I breathe in the lingering scent of her perfume, mixed with the musty smell of the old building.

My Liz.

In the corridor, two of the younger cast members walk past me, talking and giggling. They wave at me and I wave back, distracted.

I walk to my office, trying to decide whether to go to her father's place or to hers. I'd wait until she shows up. I just know I need to see her tonight. I enter my office and the first thing I see is Liz, asleep on my couch.

She looks so small lying there. I close the door behind me, resisting the urge to pick her up and cradle her in my arms, to kiss her neck and breathe in the soft fragrance of her skin, claim her as mine and make sure she never leaves again.

Except she will. She always will.

I lean back on the door. Frustrated. The wood creaks behind me, waking her. She starts, then relaxes when she sees that it's me. Her eyes water, filling me with a tenderness I don't want to feel.

"You're back," she murmurs.

I'm suddenly angry again. She's twisting me around, leading me on with hints and words and tears and I'm helpless to it.

"Obviously," I snap. "What are you doing here?

Did you find my couch comfortable? You want to take it with you when you leave again?"

She sighs. "Is your date over already?"

"That's none of your business."

"It is my business..."

I laugh bitterly. "Screw you."

"...because I care about you," She continues, ignoring my outburst. "and because I'm jealous."

I hold her gaze as the words flow through me, stirring a fire of possessiveness, longing and hope. "You have no right to be."

"Well, I am jealous," she admits with a rueful smile. "Devastated even. Wasn't that your intention, to hurt me again the way you did at the party the other night?"

The pain in her voice dampens my anger. "If you know that then why are you here?"

"Because that's how I know you still care about me." She rises and approaches me slowly, every deliberate step she takes calling to something inside me, something wild that wants to lift her up and put her over my shoulder. To take her to a remote cave and mark her as mine so she'll never doubt it again.

"I stopped lying to myself a long time ago Aidan. I stopped telling myself that I could get over you. I can't. I know you feel the same way. Something like what we had...it doesn't just end."

She's right, of course. "It might...if one person

ruined it and the other person wanted to forget badly enough."

"You don't want to forget. You'd rather hold on to the pain."

I snort. "Try this, Liz, I have already forgotten."

"You're lying."

I advance toward her, closing the distance between us. Her bottom lip starts to tremble, and I resist the urge to taste it, to feel the sweet trembling against my tongue. "Life is not a script where you write in a second chance romance when things get boring. I'm not your entertainment to spice up your life."

"No, you're not." Her voice is steady. "You're the man I love. You're the man I'll always love."

I stare at her for a long time. Her eyes are wide, imploring, her lips are begging to be kissed. When my hands finally move, it's almost of their own accord. I cup her shoulders, feeling her tremble.

I don't know if I want to push her away or claim her as mine.

"Aidan..." Her voice is a soft plea, like a whisper of silk.

I don't let her say whatever it was she means to say, because I'm done with listening...and I'm done fighting. With a low groan, I pull her into my arms and crush her mouth with mine.

CHAPTER TWENTY SIX

LIZ

*H*is lips are firm and hard, uncompromising and brutal, yet my heart swells and almost bursts with delight. I open myself for him, letting him inside to plunder my mouth with his tongue. I want him so desperately, and I'll take this, this pleasurable punishment, if it's all I can get.

A moan escapes me. I'm eager for him to devour me, to touch me everywhere. His fingers round my nape, tangling in the hair at the back of my head, bringing my face closer as he kisses me, his tongue lashing firm strokes across my soul.

Desire pools between my legs. Hot and insistent.

Finally.

I thread my fingers in his hair, curling my fingers into his scalp, bringing him closer. He groans and moves his hips against mine, the ridge of his arousal hard and insistent between us. Another moan escapes me.

Finally.

He releases my lips long enough to pull my top over my head. His eyes are wild and clouded with naked, hungry lust. He tosses the top and unhooks my bra with one flick of his fingers. My breasts spill out, heavy, my nipples swollen and sensitive.

"God, Liz." The words come out in a whisper, and there's a note of wonder in his voice. He cups both my breasts, and I sigh, closing my eyes as his thumbs brush my nipples, once, then again, filling me with almost unbearable sensation. Then he lowers his head to take one nipple in his mouth and I cry out.

He responds by lifting me, not gently. His mouth is still on my breast when he grabs my waist and pulls me up along his body. I spread my legs, wrapping them around him. He turns, and now my back is to the door. His tongue laps at my breast, swirling around an engorged nipple. Once some of my weight is on the door, he moves one hand between my spread legs.

My hips roll eagerly, awaiting his touch. I've waited so long for this. I've waited for what seems like forever to feel this way again, because it had never been like this, not with anyone else. I cradle his head in my hands and gasp when his fingers slide into the waistband of my tights, stroking me through the thin silk of my panties only for a moment before he flicks the silk to the side with his thumb and slides his fingers deep inside me.

My hips jerk and my body tightens around him.

"Fuck!" The word is both a groan and a prayer. His eyes lock with mine, then he plunges his fingers deeper, stroking them in and out of me until I can hardly bear the pleasure.

My eyes flutter closed. "Aidan," I moan.

"Look at me." His voice is thick and harsh.

I meet his gaze, drinking in the dark storm in his eyes. He claims my lips, but only for a short kiss. His fingers slide out of me, and my body clenches greedily, missing him. Still holding me against the door with his body, he unwraps my legs from his waist and drops to his knees.

Anticipation tears a moan from my lips. My throat bobs, and my fingers dig into his hair. He tugs my tights down, pulling them clean off and tossing them aside. My panties soon follow. Then he grabs one of my legs and lifts it over his shoulder. His lips find me, pressing into my mound in a soft kiss before, his tongue slides between my folds.

I scream out loud, caught in the pleasure of his touch. His tongue rounds my clit, flicking and tasting until my legs are shaking uncontrollably. Then he is plunging deeper, lashing at me with deep strokes of his tongue, tasting every part of me, licking my trembling slit and sliding his tongue inside me. I'm moaning incoherently, my fingers tight in his hair, gripping on for dear life.

"Easy." His face is still between my legs, and the rumble of his deep voice along with the soft warmth of his breath adds to the pleasure of his tongue. My hips jerk forward, and he places a hand on the lower part of my belly, steadying me. Then he's tasting me again, fucking me with his tongue, taking ownership of me until I explode with indescribable pleasure, knowing for sure that my body will never be mine again.

I'm still shaking when he rises to his feet. There's a satisfied smirk on his perfect face as he lifts my pliant limbs around his waist again.

"You still have the most beautiful pussy I've ever seen," he tells me, kissing my neck. "The best tasting too." His lips find mine and I kiss him back, tasting the musk of my pleasure on his lips.

"I'm all yours," I whisper earnestly. "For as long as you want me."

Silent, he undoes his pants. I hear the zipper slide down, then I feel him, hard and rigid, the smooth head of his cock sliding between my legs and teasing my slit. I reach for him, eager to stroke his length, but he moves too quickly, spearing me with one smooth thrust that jerks my back against the door.

My body screams with the sensation of fullness, the delicious pleasure. My legs tighten around him, pulling him closer to me. My head falls back. "Oh God!"

"No, just me." There's some humor in his voice, but I have no time to appreciate it. He starts to move, his eyes closed as he pulls back then slides inside me in a deep thrust.

"Liz." His voice is somewhere between a whisper and a plea. "Fuck, Liz!"

My response is a soft cry. I've been waiting for this feeling for seven years, this heat, this unbearable pleasure.

"Don't stop," I moan as he thrusts deep into me again and again. "Aidan!"

In reply, he picks up his pace, fucking me so deeply I can no longer tell where he ends and I begin. He lowers his head to place soft kisses on my breasts. His fingers dig into my waist and my thighs and I know there'll be bruises, but I don't care. I just want more of him, more of the pleasure only he can give me.

"Did you think of this?" His voice is a low growl. "Did you think of how good we were together?"

"Every day," I moan. "Every damn day."

"Fuck you, Liz." He punctuates every word with a hard thrust of his hips. "Fuck you for coming back here."

Pleasure builds inside me like an uncontrollable wave. "I couldn't stay away," I pant.

"Fuck. You. For. Leaving." He bites out the words, his chest heaving, his eyes darkening almost to black. My head falls back as pleasure spreads through me in a warm tsunami. I cry out and my body tightens, bowing off the door. I slide against him as my body contracts over and over, my climax rocking me almost to oblivion.

I hear him grunt, feel him stiffen, feel his hands tighten around my thighs as he enters me so deep his balls press against me. Warmth explodes deep inside me as he comes.

We are both silent. Both breathing deeply, chests rising and falling, our hoarse breaths the only sounds in the room.

Then I hear my name escape his lips in a soft sigh. "Liz."

We stay motionless for a while, his body pressed against mine. I wrap my arms around his neck and bury my face in the crook of his neck. He smells of skin, sweat, sex, and faint cologne. I breathe deeply, taking him in. My nipples rub on the soft cotton of his shirt. My belly is pressed against the hard board of his, and his muscled thighs remain between my legs.

It's perfect.

I kiss his neck and feel his chest rise. He turns his

face to mine and slowly slides out of me. I smile languidly, pleasure still coursing through me.

"Hey," I say softly.

"Hey." He releases me, letting me slide to my feet. He holds me steady, which helps because my legs are still too shaky to stand on their own. I'm naked, but in no particular hurry to get dressed.

I watch him fix his pants, then his eyes return to my face. I wish he would say something, anything to make me feel like we are going somewhere from here, that we've moved past the animosity and into a place where we can work on us.

The silence continues.

What now, Aidan? my heart screams.

"You should get dressed," he says without emotion. His eyes are on my breasts, and he makes no move to step out of the way so I can find the items of clothing he peeled off me earlier.

I pull in a breath. "I should, probably."

He nods and lifts one finger to trace a line around my nipple. My eyes close.

What now?

"If I let you go, I am lost," he murmurs, then cocks his head to one side. "Not quite accurate in our case, is it? If I let you in, I am lost."

I shake my head, almost pleading. "I was lost when I let you go."

He swallows visibly, then turns abruptly, picking

up my top and my bra and handing them to me. "Here."

I reach for them. *What now?*

"I wanted to leave," I admit in a low voice. "Hollywood promised everything I wanted. Bigger, brighter, the kind of stardom I thought I deserved. I wanted it so badly, at least I thought I did, at the time."

He doesn't look at me, doesn't say anything, so I continue. "But I didn't want to leave you. It was confusing, how willing I was to give up dreams I'd had my whole life just to be with you. I knew if you tried to convince me to stay, or if we tried to make it work and the distance got between us, I'd choose you, and it scared me."

"I couldn't tell you the truth, Aidan. You'd have convinced me we could make it work. You'd have offered to uproot your whole life and move to L.A. with me, so I left. I broke your heart intentionally, because I thought if I hurt you enough and you had no choice but to move on, then maybe I'd move on too."

Silence follows my words. Aidan is standing as still as a statue. That's the only indication that he heard me.

"Aidan..."

He shakes his head, stopping me. "One day you were the love of my life, and the next you were gone."

His eyes search my face and I can see the pain in their depths. "I couldn't reach you, and the next time I saw you your pictures were splashed all over the news with your new co-star who was suddenly the love of your life..."

"You are the love of my life." I place my hands on his chest. "I already told you, that relationship was all for the studios...and to say the truth, I agreed because...I thought maybe it would help you move on..."

His voice is still accusing. "You almost married him."

I almost did. I try to remember the craziness of my Hollywood engagement, the eager fans who wanted to believe the relationship I had with my co-star on screen was real, the ache for Aidan that never went away. "That was almost three years later. I was unhappy. So unhappy. I missed you like crazy. Work was crazy. I knew you wanted nothing to do with me. I was lonely, and Devlin was lonely too. We were prisoners in the same fishbowl... and I found out..." I stop.

Aidan gives me a sharp glance. "You found out what?"

"I found out you were dating again. I cared more than I should have. I was miserable, and Devlin was there, but I never moved on. He's just a friend. A good one."

"So that too was my fault." Aidan chuckles bitterly and pushes my hands away from his chest. "You know what? This is who you've always been. I just didn't see it before. You do something unforgivable and you think just because you want forgiveness, you should get it. It's still all about you. You're still the same selfish Liz."

"It's not about what I want. I wouldn't be here if I didn't care about what you want."

"And you think I want you?" His laugh is cruel. "I want to hate you. I want to hate you so much that hurting you would give me pleasure."

"But you can't."

He sighs. "Get dressed," he says again. "You should go."

I reach for him. "No."

He gives me a warning look. "Nothing has changed. We fucked, and that's it. It was just sex. This wasn't a reconciliation. It was just two people making use of each other's bodies."

I almost stamp my foot. "Stop lying to yourself."

He abandons me by the door and goes to his desk, lowering himself into the seat behind it. "Go home, Liz."

"Come with me," I offer, desperate again. "Let's go to my place. Let's talk about this."

He ignores me.

I approach his desk. "I hate what I did to you. I'm

so sorry I can't find the words to explain how sorry I am. I regret that we are not together, but what I regret the most is turning you into someone willing to punish himself, just so he can make me suffer."

"You're right," he replies, spearing me with his eyes. "I'd give anything to make you suffer just as I did, and it still wouldn't be enough."

"You'd give anything...even the chance to be together?"

He is silent.

"I already suffered, Aidan. Just like you did."

He makes a frustrated sound. "This was a mistake," he mutters. "Working with you was a mistake. This..." He gestures at me. "Us... It was a mistake." His chest rises. "You need to accept that there won't be a happy ending to our story. We will never work. The sooner you accept that and go back to your life, the better for both of us."

I hold his gaze. "Can you look me in my eyes and tell me you don't love me anymore?"

He rises suddenly and rounds the desk, coming to take my face in his hands. He gazes down into my eyes. His chest rises, and he starts to speak, then stops.

"Aidan..."

"Liz," he says slowly and firmly. "I don't give a fuck what you want. Just leave me alone."

He walks out of the office, leaving me to nurse my

pain alone. I fix my clothes and returned to my dressing room. I've tried. I've done everything I can think of. Maybe it's finally time to give up on Aidan.

The thought fills me with agony and an image of a lifetime of loneliness stretches before me. No, I don't want to forget about him. I don't want to resign myself to a life without him.

In my dressing room, the first thing I hear is my phone ringing in my drawer.

Panic sets in when I see that the call is from Gertie.

My dad is fine.

My dad is fine.

My dad is fine.

"What's happened?" I ask as soon as I connect the call. A weight of foreboding settles on my shoulders. "Is it Dad?"

"Liz." I've never heard Gertie cry, but she's crying now, and suddenly, I don't need her to tell me what's happened. Grief seizes me like a demon. "Oh Liz," Gertie sobs. "It's your father."

CHAPTER TWENTY SEVEN

AIDAN

*S*ince she wouldn't leave, I left her in there. That's what I should have done from the start. I should have left the production, stayed as far away from her as possible.

Now I have the taste of her mouth on my lips. The weight of her breasts is a vivid memory in my hands. I can still feel myself buried inside her silken heat. I can still hear her moans, her abandoned cries as she exploded from my touch.

All mine.

In my head, I'm already a slave to her. My body aches for her. She conquered my heart a long time ago. She owns me totally...but I can't give in.

Giving in would be setting myself up for the kind of pain I know I won't survive.

Outside the theater, I see a black tinted SUV pull

up near the stage door and idle for a few minutes. After a while, Liz emerges from the building wearing a huge jacket, with massive black shades covering her eyes. She doesn't see me on the sidewalk, and I keep walking, lengthening my strides to put as much space between us as I can.

I head to the gym and train for about two hours. I run, do weights, then do an impromptu session with one of the martial arts trainers. I end up with a few bruises, but I don't care. Nothing on the outside compares with the pain I'm feeling on the inside.

Don't think of what could be if you let her into your heart again.

Empty your mind.

Feel nothing.

If only.

Even in my exhaustion, I can't stop thinking of what would have been if I'd taken her up on her offer to go to her place, to talk. Except we wouldn't talk, not at first. I'd be making love to her again right now...making up for seven years of wanting with seven years of taking...and giving.

Liz.

She knows me, inside out.

She knew how much she meant to me.

And she left.

So why can't I stop thinking of what could have

been? Why can't I stop imagining love, happiness, a future with her...

At my apartment, I pour myself a drink and go out to the balcony. It's cold and windy, and I let the chill seep into my bones. The physical suffering can only help to distract me from the turmoil of my chaotic emotions.

Only, it doesn't work. My head is filled with Liz's smile, her scent, her taste, her moans.

"Fuck me," I mutter. "And fuck you Liz."

Once, she'd knocked my legs out from under me, and now I'm supposed to believe that she'd done it for me, because in her own way, she cared too much about me? Loved me so much she wanted me to forget about her and move on?

Fuck her lies.

Back inside, I switch on the TV, then settle on the couch and flick through the channels, not really interested in the images on the screen.

Then I see something that makes me pause.

A news anchor is talking about international politics, but the Chyron visible across the bottom of the screen leaves me reeling in shock.

Dennis McKay dead of a heart attack.

Fuck.

The news switches to two entertainment correspondents.

"Sad news from here in New York, Dennis

Mckay, the renowned Broadway producer, best known for many successful productions has died earlier tonight of a heart attack. He has been battling cancer for a year and according to sources, seemed to be on the road to recovery. His daughter is actress Liz McKay who is in the city and was with him when he passed. We understand she will release a statement soon.

"Sad news," the co-anchor intones. "Dennis McKay fought a valiant battle with cancer, and the sickness took a toll on him, leaving him vulnerable to this attack."

There's a sober silence. "Sad as Broadway loses a legend. We will bring you the statement from McKay's family as soon as it's available."

I put my head in my hands.

When was the last time I saw Dennis? More than a year ago at a charity function.

After Liz. After that play, I'd never worked with him again, not because I didn't respect him, but because he was a reminder of what I'd lost.

I hadn't known that he was sick.

Even when Natalia took over his company.

Poor Natalia...

And Liz.

Jesus! Liz.

I recall her face as she walked past me, hurrying into the SUV. Had she known then? Probably. She'd been hurrying to be with her father in his final moments.

To deal with losing him after having to deal with my cruelty.

I'm already walking out of the apartment. I have to go to her, and I don't care if she doesn't want to see me. After the things I said to her, I deserve for the door to be shut in my face, but I'll try. I'll be there for her.

If she'll still have me.

CHAPTER TWENTY EIGHT

LIZ

*O*nly two days, and now I have to say goodbye forever.

My hands are shaking. It's quiet in my dad's room, and his bed stares back at me, mocking me with its emptiness. I'm desperate to close my eyes, open them again and see him lying there, or walking around, healthy, the way he used to be.

Guilt racks me. I'd spent so little time with him since I left to pursue my career. I'd missed so much, but I assumed there'd be time, after the next movie, after the next...whatever...and now he's gone forever.

"Dad."

The only answer is silence.

I grip his blanket, and when I blink, tears splash down my cheeks. "Dad, how am I supposed to survive with you gone?"

There's no reassuring voice to tell me everything will be all right.

Concerning arrangements, I don't have much to do. Dad took care of everything.

The funeral service is taking place in a few hours. After that he'll be laid to rest in the cemetery right next to my mother. The memorial service is tomorrow. That one I'll find harder to face, because all the people who knew and admired him will be there and I'll have to listen to them remind me of my grief.

There's a knock on the door and Gertie opens it and steps inside the room. "We should leave in about thirty minutes," she says softly.

I nod. "I'm ready." Though I'm not. I'll never be ready.

She sighs. "He's here again."

I pull in a painful breath.

Aidan.

"You have to see him sometime," Gertie urges. "He's been here every day since your father passed. You can't keep sending him away."

Why not? I don't have the strength to face him, to remember that while I'd been reeling from his rejection. I'd lost my father.

I wipe my eyes. "I'm coming," I tell Gertie. "He can wait in the study."

After she leaves, I rise from the chair and smooth

my clothes. My plain black dress is a metaphor for my mood, dour, dark and bereft.

In the study, Aidan is standing in front of the shelf of plaques and pictures, wearing a dark suit to fit the occasion, and looking down at the picture of us with my father at the opening night of the Edge of Madness. As I watch, he reaches up a hand to the frame, only the glass stopping him from touching my face from seven years ago.

I step into the room and he turns to face me. As our gazes lock, I pull in an aching breath. His hair is neatly combed and laying almost smooth on his head, and on his face, there's so much compassion I almost start crying again.

It takes all my strength to resist the urge to run into his arms, bury myself in him and let him take away my pain, because I know he would. I can see it in his eyes.

"Come here." He holds out his arms to me, his voice so gentle I could cry.

I walk into his outstretched arms, and he wraps them around me. He smells like comfort and peace. Like love.

"I'm so sorry, Liz."

I step back from his embrace, breathing deeply. Being so close to him puts me in danger of losing myself, of forgetting how much he despises me, and how his presence here is nothing more than pity.

SERENA GREY

"He'd been sick for a while." I smile wanly. "I was trying to spend as much time with him as possible without letting the world know how bad he was."

"The play." There is a sudden realization in the blue depths of his eyes. "That why you wanted…"

"Yes…to an extent."

He exhales. "How are you Liz?"

Miserable, despondent. Desperate to come back into your arms and cry if you'd let me.

I shrug. "I'm holding on, I guess. I'm sorry I couldn't see you earlier."

"I understand." His eyes bore into mine, vivid and searching. "After the things I said. I wouldn't blame you if you never wanted to see me again."

I blink back tears. "The funeral is today."

"I know." He gestures at his suit. "I was hoping to come with you, if you'd let me."

Why? I want to ask. Why are you offering your support now? When will you take it away again? When will you remember how much you hate me for breaking your heart?

"Are you sure?" I say instead.

He nods.

Holding out one hand to him, I try to smile. "Okay."

∽

Outside the funeral home, there's a crowd of photographers waiting for me. I ignore them, cringing at some of the questions they shout over each other.

Is it true you were only in New York to be with your father?

Will you be returning to L.A. now?

Without a sick father keeping you here, when are you going back to do your movie?

Didn't you think your fans deserved to know why you were really in New York?

Aidan is holding my hand, and he squeezes it as we both hurry to the door.

"Are you two dating now?" Someone screams just before we enter the funeral home and the door closes behind us.

Natalia and Fiona are waiting inside. Natalia's eyes are red-rimmed. She's grieving too. She puts her arms around me and hugs me for a long minute. "How are you holding up?"

"I'm okay. You?"

She shrugs.

"Sweetheart." Fiona wraps her arms around me, and I sniff. "It's going to be all right."

I nod and try to smile. Aidan is talking to Natalia and Fiona smiles in his direction before turning back to me. "It's going to be all right," she says again.

There are about thirty people at the service.

Some are there for me, but the majority are there for my father, the people he was close to, people who worked with him. A woman I vaguely recognize from pictures as my father's cousin is crying into a handkerchief. They hadn't seen each other in decades, she tells me later, ever since they were children. They'd made plans to have a family reunion but kept on postponing.

"That'll never happen now," she sniffs.

"At least you're here," I tell her.

The service is short and beautiful and after, we go to the cemetery. I watch the pallbearers lower the coffin into the ground and I have to fight the feeling that the earth is going to swallow me up too.

The chaplain is talking but I can't hear a word he says. Past the graves, outside the wrought-iron fence, I can hear the commotion of waiting photographers in the distance.

Panic seizes me. I want to go somewhere quiet and cry. I look around, searching for a way to escape, but Aidan takes my hand, and the feel of his warm palm enveloping mine promises me safety. The solid mass of his body invites me to lean on him, to draw on his strength.

But I can't, not now. Not after he has rejected me for so long.

I swallow hard and start to pull my hand from his.

"Please," he whispers. "Let me."

I feel his words like a warm blanket on a cold day. I close my eyes, letting him hold me, knowing somehow that he will be here, as long as I need his comfort.

After the funeral, we return to my dad's apartment. Gertie has worked her miracles and there are light refreshments awaiting the guests. People come to talk to me, to offer me their condolences. I accept them.

Tomorrow, we'll do this all over again. There'll be more people, stories, speeches about my dad.

It will be goodbye.

After a while, people start leaving, first stopping to wish me all the best. When I can't bear their compassion anymore, I escape to the guest room.

Natalia is in there, wiping her eyes. Her relationship with my dad was a complicated one, but I have no doubt they loved each other deeply.

"He was one of a kind, you know." She shakes her head. "I always knew I'd never find another man like him."

"I always wondered why you both never—" I stop talking, not sure if the funeral is the right time to ask.

"Why we never went public with our relationship, or made a commitment to each other?"

I nod and she sighs.

"He was always going to be in love with your mother, Liz. He was my once in a lifetime love, but she was his. There are just some kinds of love that when people lose, they never recover. Like your parents.'"

She pats my hand and leaves me alone.

A once in a lifetime love.

Like mine, for Aidan.

By the time I return to the living room, Gertie is clearing the dishes with Aidan's help.

"Why don't you get some rest," I tell her. "You must be tired. We can take care of this."

She hesitates but does as I say. She's grieving as much as I am.

Aidan and I work in silence, clearing and cleaning. When we finish, he follows me to the study, coming to sit beside me on the sofa. Still silent, he takes my hand in his own.

I close my eyes, drawing comfort even from that small touch.

"Everything fell apart when I left," I mutter. "I hurt you, disappointed my dad..." I shake my head. "Did you hear the questions today? That's what people care about. When I'll make them a movie. Sometimes I feel like going to L.A. was the worst decision I ever made."

"You can't think that," Aidan's fingers tighten around mine. "You've done some excellent movies and brought a lot of joy to your audience."

"But not to myself. Everyone I love has been hurt

by that decision. Seven years ago, I had him, I had you. Now..." I stop and give him a helpless look. "He was sick for a while before he told me, Aidan, because I'd become such a stranger to him, he had to consider what his sickness would mean for my *brand*."

Aidan's arms circle my shoulders. "He cared about you. He was proud of you. You made him happy. He was prouder of you than anything he ever accomplished in his life, which is saying a lot."

"I keep thinking I didn't deserve that pride."

"You followed your dreams and succeeded where many others failed. That's what he wanted for you."

I close my eyes, wondering what it cost Aidan to say that. Pursuing those dreams broke us apart. I hold back a sob, but he notices and draws me into his warmth. "You were here for him at the end."

"Yes, whatever that's worth."

Aidan smooths my hair. "Liz, I'm certain it was worth a lot."

I rise to my feet and walk over to the shelf, because it's torture to remain in his arms, so close to him. "He was still here when I got to the hospital. He talked about my mother. He never stopped loving her, I think in the end he was certain he would see her again."

"Maybe he will," Aidan smiles ruefully. "I always hoped there was a place where my parents could be happy again."

"Oh Aidan." The reminder of his parents' tragedy makes everything seem so much more painful. I go back to the sofa and take his hand, burrowing into his arms. We remain there, quiet companions in our shared grief but somehow, feeling better because we're together.

Later, in the living room, I open a bottle of wine and put on one of my father's favorite classical records. On the couch, I rest my head on Aidan's shoulder.

"What do you think would have happened if I hadn't left?" I ask softly.

He thinks for a few moments. "Who knows," he says finally, his voice oddly unemotional.

I already know the pain of dwelling on opportunities lost, but somehow, I need to experience it again, with him.

"We'd be married," I murmur, "With a child, maybe two."

I feel his chest move. "I'd work less," he says. "I'd take care of the kids when you go on location."

Tears threaten my eyes. "My dad would have had grandchildren."

He squeezes my shoulder. "We're just dreaming Liz. Don't torture yourself over dreams."

"I thought we'd try to make it work, and the trying would destroy us, but it wouldn't have."

"No. I would have done everything possible to make us work."

"I believe you."

He doesn't reply.

"You're the best man I've ever known, Aidan Court. The best."

He kisses the top of my head. We don't say much after that, and soon I fall asleep in his arms.

CHAPTER TWENTY NINE

AIDAN

I let myself drift off, but after about an hour, I carry Liz to one of the bedrooms in the apartment. She doesn't wake up when I take off her shoes and lay her on the bed. When I place the covers over her and arrange her head on the pillows, I hear her murmur something. My name.

I place a kiss on her cheek, the urge to take her in my arms and spend the rest of my life making sure she has no reason to cry causes a tightening in my chest.

I never stopped loving you either.

She stirs, and murmurs my name again, so I get up and leave her in the room, letting myself out of the apartment.

What now?

I have no idea, but I know I'm ready to stop lying

to myself. I'm ready to admit that I don't want to let her go, not again.

The next day at the memorial, the tiny church is packed, and everybody has a story to share about Dennis McKay.

Liz is seated in front, and she's quiet throughout the ceremony, through the clapping and the muted laughter that follows the funny anecdotes from people who knew her father.

I should have gone to sit with her. This is not a time for her to be alone. She still needs...

Needs what Aidan... You?

I close my eyes. Why not? I've fought it for weeks, but I know I can't fight my feelings forever. I know I've been lying to myself, telling her I want her to leave, because if things don't change between us and she leaves again, I won't be able to bear it.

After the ceremony, Liz thanks everyone and people walk to the front to pay their respects. I join them.

She smiles when she sees me. "Hello, Aidan."

I take her hands. "You okay?"

She nods and squeezes my hands. "Thank you for yesterday."

"You don't need to thank me."

Her eyes hold mine, luminous with unshed tears. "Aidan..." she starts. There's a pain in her voice that I suspect has more to do with us than with her father.

My heart freezes. "What?"

She looks behind me at the person waiting to talk to her. "We'll talk later."

I feel dismissed. I consider waiting to talk to her but decide to go home instead. We'll have many opportunities to talk whenever she returns to work.

If she returns to work.

I've seen the headlines, already speculating about unknown reports that she's returning to her movie. I'd dismissed them because...she wouldn't.

Would she?

She wouldn't return to L.A. so soon after losing her dad.

She wouldn't leave the play.

She wouldn't rip my heart open like that again.

Let's talk later.

About what?

At home, I try to stop focusing on the chaotic thoughts and suspicions.

She's torn the earth from beneath my feet before. Why would she hesitate to do it again?

I fall asleep and wake up to the sound of knocking.

When I open the door, I'm not surprised to find Liz on the other side. She's changed from earlier and is now wearing a light sheath dress and walking shoes. Her face is hidden by a big pair of dark glasses.

"Can I come in?"

I step back to let her inside. She pulls off the glasses and watches silently as I close the door.

I want to ask her about my suspicions, but now they're the farthest thing from my mind.

I take a step toward her and she falls into my arms, naturally, as if she belongs there.

Because she does belongs there.

She is mine. She has always been mine. The same way I'm hers, body and soul.

"Aidan," she moans, burrowing into my chest.

My arms tighten around her. I kiss her forehead, then smooth her hair.

"I need you," she whispers. Her voice is shaky, heavy with a mixture of sadness and surrender.

"You have me," I murmur in her ear.

She releases a choking breath, then lifts her face toward mine. Our lips meet and I forget everything else.

Just her.

And me.

As it should be.

Her lips are sweet and soft. Her mouth tastes like peaches. Her skin is soft and smells like fresh flowers. She takes over all my senses, and I don't care. It's exactly what I want.

She moans against my lips and I lift her up, carrying her the short distance to my bedroom, laying her on the bed and covering her body with mine. She puts her arms around me and clings to me like she will never let go.

I kiss her again, trailing my lips from her mouth to her neck. Her body arches and her fingers twine in my hair.

"Take off your clothes." Her voice is soft. "I want to look at you."

I chuckle. "Anything you want, ma'am."

Her eyes follow my movements as I rise to my knees and pull my shirt over my head. I slide off the bed and remove my pants, and she gets on her knees, running one hand over my chest, her fingers sliding over my stomach before coming to rest on the ridge in my briefs. Her touch is like a catalyst to my cock, and it hardens even more, pushing against her hand.

"I want you so much," she whispers.

I take her face in my hands. "I will never stop wanting you." My hunger for her is an insistent, never-ending flame, the undying inferno at the center of the earth. Reaching behind her, I unzip her dress and pull it over her head, exposing her slender body in a lacy bra and panties.

Her eyes meet mine, waiting and expectant.

I curl my fingers in one cup of her bra and nudge it down until her nipple peeks out, then I lower my head and draw the hard, pink nub into my mouth.

She says my name on a shaky breath, and the sound is intoxicating.

Grabbing my free hand, she guides it between her legs. Her panties are soaked. Unable to wait, I push the flimsy material aside and my fingers find her. Hot and wet. Silky and eager for my touch.

She moves her hips in a rolling motion, inviting my fingers to explore deep inside her. I join her on the bed, on my knees facing her, still teasing her nipple with my lips and tongue, still stroking her most intimate places with my fingers, drunk on the sound of my name from her lips.

With one hand on her back, I keep her upright as her body reacts to my touch. She's already trembling when I roll the pad of my thumb around her clit, spreading my fingers inside her at the same time. Her body jerks and stiffens, and she falls apart, clutching my shoulders as tremors shake through her.

When her body finally stills, she meets my eyes and smiles softly. "Magic fingers."

"And tongue." I return her smile and push her gently, so she falls back on the bed. "Want to test that one out?"

She shakes her head, pulling me down on top of her then rolling, so she's straddling me.

"I have something else in mind," she tells me, holding my gaze as she trails her hands down my body.

I lock my fingers behind my head. "Why don't you show me, Ms. McKay?"

She chuckles and lowers her lips to my chest, licking one nipple then the other, then she trails a long kiss down to the edge of my briefs.

My cock strains inside the restriction of the fabric as she strokes me, her hands firm. With a quick flick of her wrists, she frees me, making a soft sound in the back of her throat before wrapping one hand around me, and stroking up and down along my length with a glaze in her eyes that's almost dreamlike.

Her hands are heaven. My body strains and my eyes close. Just when I think I can't possibly bear any more, she takes the tip of my cock inside her mouth.

A curse rips from my lips. She tightens her mouth around me and sucks me deep until I'm touching the back of her throat, then she releases me, trailing her lips and tongue back to the head of my cock and flicking her tongue around me like she has never tasted anything better.

I release a string of curses. My hips flex as she moves her head up and down, each sucking motion of her mouth driving me crazier than the one before.

"Liz..." I warn.

Holding my gaze, she licks the head of my cock in several quick flicks. I let out a groan, unable to bear anymore. Reaching for her, I pull her up to my chest and roll so I'm on top of her.

She laughs softly, placing a quick, playful kiss on

the corner of my lips. "You can't stand not being in control?"

"Oh, I can, but right now I just want to be inside you."

She licks her lips, silent as I reach behind her and unhook her bra, freeing her breasts. I tug her panties down and toss them away. A moan escapes her when I spread her legs and position myself between them, meeting her eyes and holding her gaze as I enter her.

She surrounds me like bliss, hot bliss. She feels so good. So good, I know I'm going to lose my mind.

"Fuck, Liz!"

Her response is a soft groan. Her body strains, her chest rising and her breasts rolling as she moves in time with me, meeting me thrust for thrust.

She's perfect.

I lower my head to her breast, catching one nipple between my teeth. Her fingers twine in my hair.

"Don't stop," she pleads.

As if I ever would.

As if I ever could.

Her body tightens around me, straining, pulsing and throbbing, drawing me in. I lose the capacity to think as pleasure takes over and my hips are thrusting of their own accord. My groans mingle with the sounds of her moans in a perfect carnal symphony.

She clutches my shoulders and screams my name,

her body seizing as her climax rips through her. As soon as the tremors subside, I pull out of her, then turn her to her side before entering her from behind. She whimpers softly, still trembling with pleasure. I lock one arm around her leg and lift it high, holding it there while I thrust into her.

So hot.

She moans my name over and over, urging me on, shuddering as she nears another climax. Her muscles tighten around me and she cries out. This time, I go with her, my climax powering through me like a crazed beast as my pleasure explodes inside her.

We're both panting. My arms snake around her and I pull her close to my chest.

"Don't even fucking think of leaving ever again," I growl in her ear.

She doesn't reply, but she snuggles closer to me, her perfect ass curved against my groin. My heart is thudding, and I can feel hers too.

"I love you," she whispers.

The declaration washes over me and my arms tighten around her.

I love you too. My response is silent, inside my head. I never fucking stopped.

SHE SLIPS OUT OF THE APARTMENT IN THE EARLY

hours of the morning after we spend the whole night making love, untiringly rediscovering each other's bodies until we are both totally spent.

"I'll see you at work," she tells me at the door, placing a kiss on my lips.

I reach for her hand, stroking her satiny skin. "You don't have to come in. Take a few days off."

"No." She shakes her head. "I need to be around other people. I need to work."

There are multiple questions raging in my head, but I say nothing as she kisses me, steps outside the door, then turns around to kiss me again.

"See you later, Aidan."

I watch her walk to the elevator and wait until the doors slide shut before going back to my bedroom. There, the rumpled sheets on the bed, the mild scent of sex in the air mixed with her perfume...it all reminds me of her.

Before, she was like a wound in my soul that could never heal, now, she's fused to me, body and soul, and I know I have no hope of ever separating myself from her.

"SHE'S REALLY SOMETHING, ISN'T SHE?"

Reed is standing beside me at the edge of the stage, watching Liz. She's exceptional, bringing such a radiant, shimmering quality to her performance that I'm finding it hard to choose the right words to describe it.

"Yes, she is."

Between scenes, she smiles graciously as people offer their condolences, but she doesn't dwell on her grief.

"Dennis McKay was a great guy," Reed continues. "He'd be proud of how strong she is."

I nod my agreement. She is strong. Stronger than I could have been in the circumstances.

She leaves the stage after rehearsals and it takes me a while to extricate myself from a tense discussion with the lighting technicians, but when I do, I go to find her, drawn by a longing I can't control.

The excited conversation from the few people I pass on the way to Liz's dressing room should have given me a clue, but I'm not paying enough attention. I enter her dressing room before I realize she's not alone.

She's standing beside the chair in front of her mirror, wearing only a silk robe. Beside her, with one arm around her shoulders, is a man whose famous face I'd come to hate almost as much as I told myself I hated Liz all those years.

Devlin Coates.

Her first big co-star.

Her tabloid love interest.

Her ex-fiancé.

"I'm so sorry I couldn't come earlier," he whispers to her. "I came as soon as I could get away."

Jealousy sears me like a hot knife. I should walk away, but I can't. Devlin notices me first and with excruciating slowness, he releases Liz and turns his megawatt smile and capped dentition in my direction.

Liz turns at the same time. "Aidan..." Something like guilt crosses her face. "Devlin, this is Aidan Court, my... director. Aidan, Devlin Coates."

Devlin stretches out his hand to me with a good-natured smile. "A pleasure to meet you. I've heard of you and seen your work."

I bare my teeth in a semblance of a smile. I'd much rather throw his plastic ken-doll face and body out of the room, the theater, the city. "Same."

"I came to offer Liz my condolences." He smiles fondly in her direction. "I'll leave you two..." He stops and touches her cheek and I want to punch him. "I'll call you later."

She nods. He gives me another pearly smile as he walks past me. The door closes behind him and I find Liz watching me, her face uncertain.

"I didn't know you had a guest." My voice is tight.

"He just stopped by. I had no idea he was coming."

I take in her state of almost casual undress. In her

robe, she looks young and delicate and excruciatingly beautiful.

A view I hate to share with anyone, especially her ex.

"You seem very comfortable around him."

She takes a step toward me. "Aidan, he's just a friend."

Is my jealousy so obvious? She's grieving. I should be more considerate, but I just want to remind her, again and again, that she only belongs to me.

Except she doesn't.

Not really.

"You don't have to explain." I force a smile. "It doesn't matter what I think about your relationship with Mr. Synthetic-smile Hollywood heartthrob."

She sighs. "It matters to me."

Why? I want to ask. Why do you need me to believe we have a chance? How soon until you crush my heart again?

"I just came to check how you were doing." I continue. "Obviously, you're fine."

I turn to the door, but her voice stops me.

"Aidan, don't be like this. Don't leave."

I take a deep breath, waiting as she takes the few steps to where I'm standing.

"Don't leave like you don't know how much I need you."

I breathe in her scent, intoxicated by her.

For how long, Liz? How long will you need me?

"Don't leave," she says again, then holding my gaze, she shrugs off her robe. Underneath, her skin is smooth, and I recall how it feels to my touch, like the softest silk. Wordlessly, I let my fingers trail over her shoulders, feeling her tremble at my touch.

My Liz.

I cover her lips with mine and her breath escapes in a low moan.

I will never get enough of her. I know that now, more than I know my own name.

"I need you," she whispers.

"And I need you." I let her see the truth in my eyes. "I need you more than I need to breathe."

She wraps her arms around my neck and lifts her face up to mine.

And I'm lost.

CHAPTER THIRTY

LIZ

*a*idan carries me over to the small couch that sits along a wall in my dressing room and lowers me onto the soft cushions. When I reach for him, he pats my hands away and covers my body with his, his weight supported by his strong arms.

I look up at him in wonder, almost unable to believe that he's here with me. He looks down at me, incredible in his beauty. Arousal surges through me. He's like an aphrodisiac, and he owns my body, every inch of it.

He slides his lips over mine, probing gently with his tongue and then surging inside my mouth. I give myself to him, hungry for the taste of his lips, the feel of his tongue against mine.

He trails a kiss down from my lips and along my body until his head is between my legs. Hungrily, as if he can't wait to taste me, he spreads my thighs and covers me with his lips and tongue.

I moan, helpless with pleasure. His tongue flicks around my clit, then starts to explore, soon he's teasing my trembling slit, pushing his tongue inside me, while using one masterful finger to play with my clit.

I'm weak, unable to do anything except surrender my body to him. He's skillful and attentive, and he knows exactly how to reduce me to a screaming, shivering mass of pleasure.

I come with a soft cry, my core throbbing as pleasure explodes behind my eyes, and then he's ripping off his shirt and undoing his pants, teasing me with the hard, rounded head of his cock and the promise of more pleasure.

I thrust my hips forward as he slides inside, taking him so deep inside me, my eyes roll back with the unbelievable sensations.

He starts to move, and I hold on to him, clutching at his shoulders and meeting every thrust as I urge him on. I want all of him, everything he has to offer.

"Don't stop," I moan in his ear. "Don't ever stop."

"Never." His chest heaves and my breath hitches. I'm panting, breathless, but I want more, more of him.

He rises to his knees and lifts my legs around his

waist. My eyes fix on the bunched muscles of his chest and belly as he makes love to me.

So perfect.

He rolls his hips and plunges deep into me, again and again, until I'm incoherent with pleasure, repeating a garbled version of his name.

In response he thrusts faster, deeper. My body twists as I let go. My vision explodes and I hear his cry as he loses control, spilling himself inside me. He's still for a moment, holding my legs, breathing hard, then he lets out a deep shudder and lays over me, careful to put his weight on his elbow.

Cupping his face in my hands, I kiss him full on the lips. The last thing I want to think about is Devlin's brief appearance and the other aspect of my life calling for my attention. "I've wished for this moment for so long."

"Good thing you have me to make your wishes come true." His lips quirk in a small smile, but it soon disappears, replaced by a worried frown.

"Tell me," I whisper.

He shakes his head. "It's you who has something to tell me, but I'm guessing you will when you're ready."

To leave or to stay.

He has guessed that I'm thinking about leaving, and with Devlin's appearance, how can he not be concerned?

"Devlin was here as a friend," I tell him. "Not as an emissary to lure me to back to L.A."

Aidan shrugs. "Something will lure you back though, won't it?" His tone is bitter. "Sooner rather than later."

I don't reply. Pain is churning in my chest. I turn my face away from his, finding something on the wall to capture my attention.

A week ago, I'd have said no, without hesitation.

But now?

He's waiting for me to say something. I close my eyes and take a deep breath, then turn back to face him. "Why are you here with me, Aidan? Why are you supporting me?" I hate the words even though I have to say them. "Is it because my father died?"

He pushes off the couch and takes a step away from me, then turns back to glare in my direction. "You've got to be kidding me."

I rise from the couch and pick my robe up from where it's lying on the floor, putting it back on before facing Aidan again.

"I can't forget the things you said to me just days ago. What changed your mind about me?" I jerk the sides of my robe together and secure the tie. "My loss? I want your love, Aidan, not your compassion or pity."

He makes a sound that's not quite a laugh. "I can't believe you're making this about me. If you don't plan to stay, Liz. Own it. Don't try to tell me you're leaving the play because I didn't let you seduce me as soon as you arrived."

I pull in a breath. "A week ago, you couldn't stand to be in the same room with me."

"Right now, I'm returning to that particular state of mind." He laughs bitterly. "So, you're leaving?"

I exhale. "I am."

I watch him freeze. I watch the air around him still and turn icy. He doesn't say a word, but the coldness in his eyes makes me flinch.

"You never intended to stay." His voice is hard and condemnatory, like frostbite on my skin. "You want me to believe you came back for your dad and also because of me, but you're lying, aren't you?" His eyes rake me. "I was a coincidence, an attractive little entertainment to amuse you while you spent time with your father. All this..." He makes a wide gesture. "It's all been another one of your selfish games."

My eyes are tearing. "You know that's not true."

He takes a step toward me. "No, Liz. What I know is that you don't care about anyone but yourself."

"Don't act like I didn't try everything. You kept pushing me away. I gave up. You made me give up on you."

"So, it's my fault?" His voice is laced with anger. "You can tell me you never meant to stay. You can tell me I never meant as much to you as you tried to make me believe." His voice cracks. "Tell me that truth at least."

"I can't."

"Why not?" His chest rises. "Damn you, Liz. Why couldn't you just leave me alone?"

My eyes fill with tears, and soon they're running down my cheeks. "Because I love you."

"Fuck love. It can burn in hell." He laughs. "Nothing is enough for you. Not me, not the play. The only thing that matters is you and your ego, and now, after playing the hero daughter to your dad, you can go back to feeding on the adulation that's everything to you." He glares at me, his eyes dark and stormy.

Tell me you love me.

Ask me to stay.

His eyes burn into mine, and when my eyes fill with tears, he makes a move toward me, his expression almost tender, then changing his mind, he turns on his heel and heads for the door, and out of the room.

CHAPTER THIRTY ONE

AIDAN

I had to resist the urge to take her in my arms and comfort her.

Ridiculous.

Comfort her for breaking my heart, again.

I'm angry. Angry, sad, humiliated and fucking desperate. I slam out of her dressing room, eager to get as far away from her as possible.

After a quick train ride home, I get my car keys and head out of the city, wishing I still had my bike. To Landon's relief, I gave that machine up after Liz crushed my heart the first time.

I can measure my adult life by the heartbreaks by Liz. The realization is darkly funny, but I'm in no mood to laugh.

A few hours later, I pull into the driveway at Windbreakers. The beautiful mansion stands on a bluff, overlooking the ocean on one side. It's the house where I mostly grew up. It's the place where my father died when I took his already broken heart and shattered it even more.

Maybe Liz is my punishment.

The house looks empty from the outside. Wilson and Betty, the Hayes, have a built-in apartment and rarely use the multitude of rooms in the main house. I let myself in, and as I close the door behind me, the light comes on and I see a bleary-eyed Wilson in a dressing gown.

"Aidan." He looks surprised to see me.

"We didn't know you were coming." Betsy follows close behind him, concern etched on her face. She hurries up to the door as fast as her cane will let her, and studies my face, looking for signs of stress, or residue from Liz's destruction.

I offer a smile to put her at ease, feeling bad for giving them reasons to be concerned. "It was a spur-of-the-moment thing."

"Is everything all right? With work? With the play? Have you spoken to Landon?"

I shake my head. "I'm just tired," I tell her. "Go back to bed. I'm going straight to sleep."

"After I make you something to eat," she insists. "A sandwich?"

I accept and we all go to the kitchen. Wilson makes conversation about the play while Betsy watches as I dutifully consume the sandwich.

They linger for a while before going back to bed. I head to my old bedroom and stay only a moment before heading out to the back porch.

It's dark, but the moon is full, and I can see the waves as they crash on the beach. I try not to think of my dad, and that last night.

I killed him.

Now, it's my turn, to lose what I love. To watch my life return to the emptiness of lacking Liz.

Is this what I deserve, dad?

There's no answer.

I walk along the beach until the cold drives me back inside. Then I go up to my room and fall asleep.

"UNCLE AIDAN!"

"Is he awake?"

"No, he's asleep."

"How do you know?"

A small hand pulls my eyelid open. I groan and turn over.

"He's awake!" a childish voice announces jubilantly.

"No, I'm not," I grumble.

"How can you talk if you're sleeping?"

I crack open my eyes and see Preston looking at

me, waiting for an answer. Damien sidles up to the bed. "You have hair on your face," he lisps.

"That's because..." I grab them both and pull them onto the bed. "I'm a monster... grr grr grr."

They're laughing hysterically when I notice their mother at the door.

"Breakfast," Rachel announces. The boys whoop and run out of the room, abandoning me. "You too." She peers at me. "You look like hell."

"That's how I feel." I shrug, then frown. "You weren't here last night."

"Nope. We decided on an impromptu visit this morning."

"Or last night when Wilson called and told you I was here, in a state."

"Actually, it was Betsy." Rachel shrugs. "She said you looked like you were going through a lot."

I groan and roll off the bed.

"Why don't you take a shower and join us for breakfast?" she suggests. "We'll talk later, okay?"

She leaves me alone to do as she asked. Downstairs, the kids are joyous at the unplanned family reunion and they laugh and scream and race around the house despite all attempts to calm them.

Landon hovers between amusement and disapproval at their antics. He's feeding Penelope, and the little angel is kicking in her highchair like she'd love to be running around with her brothers.

"Where's the nanny," I ask, settling at the kitchen table.

"Day off," Rachel says. "It's just us."

After breakfast, the children go to play on the beach, and we watch them from the back porch while Penelope snoozes in her rocker.

"So, you want to tell me what happened?" Landon asks.

"Nothing that required you to bring the whole family down here," I reply with a shrug.

He laughs. "We needed a vacation, anyway."

I snort to let him know what I think about that lie.

Rachel calls out to the children then turns to look at me. "If it's Liz, you shouldn't be giving her a hard time. Not now, after she lost her father."

Oh, I'm the villain giving saint Liz a hard time? "She's leaving the play," I mumble.

"Oh!" Rachel looks from me to Landon. "Oh Aidan, I'm so sorry."

I'm quiet. She knows what that means to me. I'm probably the only one who has spent all this time denying what Liz leaving again would do to me.

Rachel exchanges a look with Landon, and he rises to his feet. "I'm going to watch the kids and make sure they don't get too close to the water."

We both watch him walk toward the children and

they race to him, screaming with joy as they launch their small bodies at him.

I'm silent for a while, just watching my brother and his kids. "It's not just what she's doing to me," I say, my voice sober. "Look at what she's doing to the play. People want to see her, not an unknown stand-in." I sigh. "She's selfish, just like she's always been."

Selfish.

Self-centered.

What do you think would have happened if I hadn't left?

We'd be married. With a child, maybe two.

I'd resisted for as long as I could, but finally I'd bought into the fantasy that we could recover what we lost.

Had she been stringing me along, looking to see how long before I broke?

I wish I knew for sure.

Rachel sighs beside me. "I'm betting she's not in a good place. She just lost her father. Grief does things to people's minds and they make bad decisions."

I snort. "She always knew she would do this. All that talk about wanting me to forgive her, wanting to give us another chance and make it right between us, it was just her manipulating me for her own amusement."

"You can't believe that." Rachel shakes her head. "Not Liz. I don't believe that one bit."

I laugh bitterly. "Days ago, she was sure I still loved her, that I was angry because I'd never gotten over her, but now, according to her, I'm only with her because of *pity and compassion*." I mutter a curse under my breath. "I'd feel far better about my chances for the rest of my life if she just tells me it was all a game to her."

"And what if it wasn't?" Rachel pats my hand. "You rejected her for so long, what was she supposed to think? How many times did you ask her to leave? How often did you tell her that there was no way to undo what she'd done? I'm guessing you kept telling her you didn't love her anymore."

"Well, I was lying."

"Then you'll have to convince her."

You made me give up on you, Aidan.

My eyes go to the beach. The boys are pulling Landon by the hand and he's laughing. It's so familiar, it could be a scene from my childhood.

Beauty from ashes.

Here, close to the bliss of my brother's marriage, it's tempting to buy into the fantasy that all Liz needs is for me to step up, to do or say something.

But I know better.

I know she'll wreck me. No matter what I say or do.

I turn back to Rachel. "There's no point."

She gives me a pitying smile. "I'm sure if you look inside your heart, you'll find that there is."

I PLAN TO LEAVE LATER IN THE EVENING. AFTER lunch, I head to the garden and after a while Landon finds me there. We sit in silence for a long time.

A cool breeze ruffles my hair and sweeps a few dead leaves around my feet. Here, the sound of the ocean is almost too far off to hear.

"Rachel thinks you're letting your anger cloud your judgement," Landon starts.

"My judgement was clouded when I allowed myself to think there was a chance for me and Liz."

Landon chuckles. "You are angry."

Of course I am. I pull in a cool breath. "There's a part of me that hopes I never see her again."

Landon nods. "Yet, there's another part of you that wants a chance to make her happy, to make you happy. A part of you that knows things will never be the same without her."

I glare at my shoes. "Yes."

"You know better than anyone that grief can make people irrational. She's grieving. Maybe with time..."

I shake my head. "With time, she'll be long gone, back into the circus that's her life."

"I'm sure you can brave the circus to be with the woman you love, to be happy."

Yes. If I thought she loved me, but Liz...Liz exists to punish and torture me. To take me high and drop me so low, I'm nothing but wreckage on the ground.

"Maybe I don't deserve to be happy," I mutter. "Maybe I exhausted my store of goodwill the day I pushed Dad to kill himself."

"Don't be ridiculous." There's an edge to Landon's voice. "To think that, you have to ignore every other wonderful thing that's happened in your life." He gives me a stern look. "I used to focus so much on everything that went wrong, I forgot to be grateful for all the things we had...the Hayes, grandpa and nana, the summers in France, the hotel, the financial safety nets... It was easier to think about what we lost and use it as a reason to be unhappy."

He pauses. "I had to decide I deserved to be happy, to stop blaming myself for things I couldn't change, to focus on the present and make the future I and Rachel deserved."

"You need to stop blaming yourself for that night. You had a fight with your dad. Lots of teenagers do. What happened after the fight was not your fault, Aidan. I used to think I was a bad person for thinking this, but dad died the day we lost our mom. Every other moment he spent here... he was just waiting for a chance to go to her. Was he a bad father for that? I won't judge anymore, but the man he was, before the accident...he'd have been proud of the man you are, the success you've become. They both would. Stop thinking you deserve pain or punishment. You don't."

I stare at him for a moment, then I smile a little. "Years of therapy and I just needed my big brother to set me straight."

He laughs. "That's why I'm here."

"You really think he'd have been proud of me?"

"Yes. I am proud of you."

I smile. "Best thing I ever did for myself was hoodwinking you onto my team."

"You were always devilishly charming, even as a baby."

We both laugh and he pats my back. "Don't give up on Liz. You deserve a happy relationship with a woman who loves you, and if she's the one, then you'll both find a way to work through this."

If she's the one.

She's always been the one for me.

But I've never been enough for her.

And if I open myself up to her, she's just going to destroy me, all over again.

There's no point telling Landon that, so I just smile.

"In any case," he continues. "What matters right now is that she's going through a lot, and she needs you. So, are you going to be there for her, or are you going to let your resentment steal this time you have together?"

"After seven years, I have an almost symbiotic attachment to my resentment."

"I can tell." Landon laughs. "I can also tell that it's keeping you miserable."

Later, on the drive back to the city, I think about our conversation. Seven years, and the only moments of life, of brightness, were the moments I spent with Liz.

My life has been a desolate winter without her, and I can't deny that these few weeks with her here, have meant far more than all the time we spent apart.

I want her to stay, but I won't beg. I won't open my heart for her to scorch it all over again.

But as long as she's here, then I'll give her what she needs. My time, my support...and when she breaks my heart all over again, maybe it will have been worth it.

CHAPTER THIRTY TWO

LIZ

*S*omehow, I get through the next day of rehearsals. Aidan's absence is conspicuous, but we manage.

"Don't forget," Reed announces jovially. "Dress rehearsal tomorrow, then after that, previews. Prepare to charm the public."

There are a few tired cheers as people leave. "Any news from Aidan?" I ask Reed.

"Just that he needed a day off. Did you want to talk to him?"

"No, not really." Seeing how we left things the last time we spoke, I haven't tried to reach out to him. Maybe I should. "Do you know when he'll be back?"

"He'll be here tomorrow."

Tomorrow.

After a few minutes in my dressing room, I head

for home. At my apartment, silence greets me. The spacious duplex is professionally furnished but lacks any personal touches, a soulless monument to my wish that one day, I might return to live in this city.

That's unlikely now.

Who and what would I return for?

Aidan.

He wants to be with you, a voice whispers in my head. What does it matter if it's out of pity and compassion? It's what you want. You want to be with him.

You need to accept that there won't be any happy ending to our story.

We will never work.

The sooner you accept that and go back to your life, the better it will be for both of us.

He'd meant every single word, and as soon as his tender feelings arising from my loss recede, he'll remember just how much he hates me.

Then what?

Then I'll be right back where I started.

Desperate to escape my muddled thoughts, I open a bottle of wine and pour a full glass, before walking over to the windows to look at the view.

My phone trills from the kitchen counter, startling me. I hurry over, and a glance at the screen tells me it's Aidan calling.

I reach for the phone. "Hey."

"Liz." There's a pause after he says my name, and an aching tenderness fills my chest. "Where are you?"

My eyes sweep the apartment. "At my place."

There's another pause. "I'm coming over."

A memory of his anger from our last confrontation flashes in my mind. He doesn't sound angry anymore, just resigned. I pull in a breath. "Okay."

While I wait for him, I down the rest of the wine in my glass.

Is he still mad at me?

Is he going to try to convince me I'm wrong about him?

Am I?

I rinse out the glass and push all thoughts out of my mind. The only thing that matters is how much I want to see him.

By the time Aidan arrives, I'm nearly convinced that I imagined his call. When I open the door and see him on the other side, I almost burst into tears.

He steps into the apartment and closes the door behind him. His eyes sweep the sparse living room, then he turns back to look at me, his gaze dark with an intensity that reaches deep inside me. My eyes roam his face, waiting.

He takes a deep breath. "I want to be with you," he says quietly.

"Aidan..."

He cuts me off. "No. I know you plan to leave. I know this is all temporary for you. But for now, even though I'm angry, and confused, I can't keep pretending that I haven't dreamed of being with you like this again, all these years."

Why am I so disappointed? I feel like deep inside, I had been hoping for a grand declaration, a laying of his heart at my feet, no matter what.

"You're not going to ask me to stay?"

His eyes flare. "That's up to you, Liz. Stay or leave if you want. Do what makes you happy." His chest rises. "What I want is to be with you, for as long as I can. And if it's only for two minutes or two days, then I plan to make the most of it."

I swallow, wishing I had another glass of wine. "And here I thought you planned to convince me of how much I mean to you. How much you want us to work this time."

He cocks his head to one side. "Is that what you want? For me to beg? Why? Will it give you some vicarious pleasure to crush me all over again?"

I shake my head. "No."

He strokes a finger along my cheek and brushes his thumb across my lower lip, his eyes igniting when I let out a sigh of pleasure at the small touch. "Let's not pretend that you ever intended to make us work," he murmurs. "There's a lot more we can do instead."

"Like sex."

His response is a smile, then he draws me close, bringing my face to his, and covering my lips with his own.

His kiss is tender and sweet. He teases my lips apart with an expertise that's almost diabolical. I close my eyes, losing myself to sensations. If this is all I can get, then I'll take it, for now.

"Where's your bedroom?" he asks when he releases my lips.

Almost too eagerly, I lead him to my room. It's as soulless as the rest of the apartment. Aidan takes in the bare walls, the expensive but impersonal furniture.

"You don't live here much."

I shrug, a little defensive. "I hardly ever came to New York, and I stayed over at my dad's most of the time anyway. This place was just an excuse to tell myself that I still lived here.

He looks at me. "Why?"

"I wasn't ready to let go."

His eyes pierce mine, searching, the silent question in them urging me to tell him again that I never wanted us to end, that I still don't.

What's the point? He didn't believe me before. He won't believe me now.

"Come here, Liz." His voice is low.

I go into his arms and he captures my lips again. His body is warm and hard. I let my hands drift over his chest, feeling his muscles bunch underneath my touch. I unbutton his shirt and slide it off. He tugs off his white undershirt, revealing the smooth and perfect expanse of his chest. Sighing, I place a kiss on one hard slab of muscle.

He groans softly and reaches for my dress, pulling it over my head. My bra and panties soon follow. His hands move over my skin, caressing, stroking every single inch.

"I can't stop wanting you." His voice is a low murmur.

It hurts to know that he has tried. I close my eyes, focusing on how good it feels to be in his arms. For now, it has to be enough that he wants me enough to forget how much he hates me. "Show me."

He pushes me back onto the bed and as I land, the soft mattress bounces beneath me.

He grins, then covers my body with his. His lips meet mine, then his tongue is exploring my mouth, leaving me breathless. Impatient, I move beneath him. He grabs my hands and clasps them together over my head, holding them in place so I can't move. He lowers his head to my breasts, rolling his tongue around one peaked nipple then the other.

His tongue is delicious torture. "Aidan..."

"Hmmm." He lifts his eyes to mine, his tongue still teasing my nipple. "Your breasts," he says with a crooning softness in his voice. "So perfect." He licks the soft curve around a swollen nipple, and I sigh.

"If you keep doing that, I'll come from you playing with my breasts."

He laughs. "I can live with that."

I wriggle under him. "I don't think I have the patience."

Ignoring me, he keeps paying attention to my breasts, only moving lower when my whole body starts to tremble. He releases my hands, kissing his way over my stomach and down to the mound between my legs. He places a soft kiss there, causing a soft fluttering that travels from my core to low in my belly. Then he nudges my legs apart and traces my outer lips with his tongue.

"Aidan..." I'm wet and aching for him. I tangle my fingers in his hair and urge him back up. "I want you inside me."

One eyebrow quirks, and then he's surging above me, using one leg to part my thighs. I feel him, hard and insistent, probing at the juncture of my thighs, and then unhurriedly, he slides inside me.

I let out a long moan as he fills me. My lips curve around his name. I take his face in my hands and cover it with kisses, moving my hips in time to his slow, sweet thrusts. He fucks me slowly, teasing me as he rolls his hips, driving me over the edge with a maddening desire.

"I love you," I whisper, tears stinging at my eyes.

His eyes are dark, but even through my pleasure, I can see that he thinks I'm lying. He surges hard into me and I cry out again, my whole body arching. His lips seize mine, silencing me, while with his body, he pushes me past my limits of pleasure. A delicious heat builds between my legs as he moves faster, each new stroke sending me closer to the edge.

I wrap my legs around him, and pleasure explodes like fireworks in my brain.

"Fuck, Liz." He groans, his body jerks powerfully, and I feel the warm rush of his climax inside me. He wraps his arms around me, shuddering slightly, the only sound in the room, that of our breaths mingling in the silence.

"You're mine," he whispers into my hair. "Wherever you go. You'll always be mine."

"Even though you despise me?"

He rolls to his side, facing me. "I don't despise you."

I shrug and settle in his arms. "Where did you go?" I ask after a while. "Your cabin?"

"No." He shakes his head. "I sold that a while ago."

"Oh." I study his face. "You also got a new apartment," I say softly. "You wanted to forget me very badly."

He looks sad. "Do you blame me?"

"No, I tried to forget too."

He's quiet. "I went to Windbreakers. I planned to bury myself in a few drinks, but my family has a way of showing up and pulling me out of my misery."

"You're lucky to have them."

"I know."

We're both quiet. He strokes my hair, and the intimacy of the moment belies everything we are, a temporary couple, nothing more.

You can stay with him, a voice whispers in my head. Stay for as long as he'll have you until he starts to resent you again.

It's shameful how tempting it is. How little I would settle for, just to be with him.

"I wish I'd never left. I wish I'd never left you."

He takes my face in his hands. "You can't change the past, Liz. You work in the present to make the future you want."

"Is that what we're doing?"

He chuckles. "No. We're living in the now. Since it's all we have."

All we have.

He doesn't leave me time to think about it. He slides his lips over mine, and desire chases all my thoughts away.

CHAPTER THIRTY THREE

AIDAN

I'm fooling myself.

Pretending this will be enough.

That the moment she leaves I won't be a wreck.

But those are the things I never say. We go to rehearsals, then end up at Liz's or my place. We make love, eat, watch TV, and we don't talk about what we both know is coming.

Now, I watch as she finishes her makeup. It's the first night of previews and she had already transformed into a beautiful suburban housewife from the mid-eighties.

Her eyes meet mine in the mirror. "What are you thinking?"

How much I want you to stay with me.

"How beautiful you look." I give her a smile. "Are you nervous?"

She looks at me like I'm crazy. "Of course I am."

"You have no reason to be."

"I wish I had your confidence." She comes over and plants a kiss on my lips. My hands linger on her back, reluctant to let her go.

There's a question in her eyes, all the things we're avoiding.

"You'll be great," I tell her, releasing her. "I'll see you after."

"I can't wait." Her voice is soft, then she laughs. "I keep thinking I'll need the consolation."

"You won't, Liz." I blow her a kiss. "Break a leg."

In the auditorium, there are critics, people from the production company, and investors. It's more packed than most previews, but that has a lot to do with Liz and how hungry her public is to see her.

I know the night will be perfect.

I know Liz's performance will be extraordinary, even more so than during rehearsals.

I see Landon and Rachel take their places in the audience. They can't see me. *Look inside your heart,* Rachel had said.

In my heart, I can see that I don't want to be without Liz, but what does that change if she's just going to leave me again?

Reed waves at me from across the stage. I wave back and he gives me two thumbs up.

The orchestra starts to play. Reed calls places as

the actors arrived backstage. The curtain opens and I wait for Liz to take over the stage.

Like she has taken over my heart.

"THERE ARE A FEW ARTICLES ONLINE," LIZ announces the next morning, sipping from a glass of orange juice. "My assistant sent me a few links."

"What do they say?"

She responds with a nonchalant shrug. "The usual."

I burst out laughing. Most of the critics won't publish their thoughts on the play till opening night, but a few hints and teasers have made their way to the pages of most of the widely read publications, and the effusive praise is far from *the usual*.

"I can't believe how modest you are." I scroll through my phone and read from one article.

Liz McKay left a vacuum when she left the stage, a vacuum it seemed only she could fill. Her return to Broadway meets our expectations and then some. Catch her sublime performance in The Break of Day at the Shermann Theater from September Seventeenth.

She smiles happily. "A vacuum."

"The city has missed you, it seems."

"And I missed it," she sighs. "Being on that stage, Aidan, it felt like coming home."

Not enough to make you stay.

"Landon and Rachel want us to spend the day with them on Saturday. At Windbreakers. Do you want to come?"

Suddenly, she looks vulnerable. "Do you want me to come?"

"Yes, I want you to come, and the children will erupt with joy, and Rachel and Landon will appreciate it very much as will Wilson and Betsy. So... Will you come?"

She nods. "I will."

Landon sends a town car for us on Saturday morning. Since I'm too exhausted to drive anyway, I don't mind. Liz is wearing loose pants and a flowery top that exposes her shoulders, with a thick cashmere sweater over one hand.

"You're wearing too many clothes," I tell her in the car. "What am I supposed to do throughout this long drive?"

She giggles. "What were you planning to do?"

"Get in your pants."

She turns a shocked glance at the driver, who can't hear a word we're saying because he has earplugs in.

"What? We'll be quiet."

"No way," she laughs. "You're crazy."

I grin unrepentantly. "You're irresistible."

"I know." She leans over and plants a long kiss on my lips. "I love you, Aidan Court."

My eyes close and I expel a breath.

I love you more than life, Liz McKay.

She owns me.

She always will.

Don't leave me, Liz.

I want to beg.

I want to give her everything again, even though I don't know how long it will be before she throws it back in my face.

WHEN WE ARRIVE AT THE HOUSE, THE KIDS ARE excited to see a new face. They demand Liz's attention, and she ends up on the beach, playing fetch with the boys and the dog.

I watch Damien jumping around Liz's legs, looking up at her with an adoring expression.

"I think you have competition," Landon teases, handing me a drink with ice floating at the top. "Damien is definitely more attractive than you are."

"I'm not arguing that." I watch Preston throw the ball to Damien who catches it and hands it to Liz. "He's got it as bad as his uncle."

"So," Landon gives me a serious look. "Is she still leaving?"

I nod, trying to ignore the pain. "She hasn't said anything about staying."

Landon sighs. "It doesn't have to be the end if she leaves."

"I know that," I reply, "Or at least I think I do. But if I can't make it work while we're here together, how am I going to make it work when we're miles apart?"

Rachel emerges from the house and takes in the scene on the beach.

"Awww," she croons. "This is sweet." She takes a few pictures then comes to sit with us. "Why the sad faces?" she declares. "Come on, Penny's finally asleep. Let's all go for a walk."

THE BOYS LOVE IT. WE WALK ALONG THE BEACH while they run after Scribbles, who barks joyously at all the activity.

"It's so beautiful out here," Liz says.

"More so in the summer," Rachel smiles at her. "Are you nervous about opening night?"

Liz makes a face. "A little."

"Well, judging from that preview, you'll blow them away."

Liz looks at me and I shrug. "I told you."

She smiles softly, and in that moment, it feels like we're the only two people in the world. "You did."

Why do I feel like my heart is tearing?

Don't leave, Liz.
I love you.

CHAPTER THIRTY FOUR

LIZ

*W*e're still walking along the beach when Damien runs back to join us and Rachel scoops him up. He's a sweet little kid, more like his mother than his father and uncle, unlike Preston who is a little copy of Landon.

Damien gives me a shy smile. "Liz, are you Uncle Aidan's girlfriend?"

I turn to look at Aidan and he chuckles. "Yes, she is."

I'm almost too happy to notice the cute glare Damien shoots at his uncle. "Ohkay. I guess I'll marry someone else, then." He wriggles down from his mother's arms and runs back to Preston, who has the knowing expression of the big brother who guessed right.

"Awww." I watch Damien take his brother's comforting hand. "Did I just turn down his proposal?"

"Broke his little heart too," Aidan says, shaking his head. "How could you?"

"He'll get over it." Landon laughs. "Aidan used to fall in love with his nannies and propose in the first week, then when they scolded him, he'd go, *I don't want to marry you anymore.*"

I can't help chortling with amusement. "I don't believe it."

Aidan glares at Landon. "Because it's not true."

"It is," Landon continues, still laughing. "Of course, that was before..." he stops and gives Aidan an apologetic look.

Before their mother died, and he stopped speaking.

Nobody says it, but the tragedy hangs in the air like the ghost of an albatross, even so many years later. Rachel squeezes Landon's hand and they exchange a smile. Aidan turns to gaze at the water.

"Why don't we go back?" he suggests. "I think we walked far enough. Boys!" he calls out. "Race you to the house."

They shout in glee and start running. Aidan runs slowly enough so they can catch up and run past him.

❧

After lunch out on the terrace with the Hayes, the old couple who're like parents to Landon and Aidan, the children go to bed for a nap and Landon and Rachel disappear too.

"They won't be back for a while," Aidan tells me, a dirty grin lighting up his face.

I try to keep myself from giggling. "You have such a dirty mind."

"I didn't say anything." He holds up his hands and tries to look innocent. "You assumed. Who has a dirty mind now?"

I cock my head. "I still have sand between my toes. I'm sure you do too. Maybe we should take a shower or something."

His eyes narrow. "Is that an invitation?"

I rise and head inside the house. "What do you think?" I say over my shoulder.

Aidan is already behind me. "I accept your invitation."

He scoops me up and throws me over his shoulder like a caveman. I'm still laughing when he takes me to his room and sets me down in the bathroom. Then he undresses me, and laughter is the last thing on my mind.

∾

WE LEAVE IN THE EVENING. LANDON, RACHEL AND the children wave from the front of the house as the same driver takes us back to the city.

Aidan dismisses the driver after he drops us off in the underground garage of my building. He follows me up to my apartment, but at the door he makes no move to enter.

Running my hand down the front of his shirt, I watch his eyes darken. "Aren't you coming in?"

Smiling, he shakes his head. "You need to rest, and you won't if I spend the night."

I give him a look. "That sounds like an idea I want to test out."

He laughs. "Seriously though, I need you to forget about everything tonight, just the play. Don't think about me, or anybody's expectations. Can you do that?"

I nod. "I think so."

"Right." He gives me a light kiss on my lips. "Tomorrow Liz."

I sigh. "Tomorrow."

I watch him walk to the elevator, then I try to do as he asked, taking a long bath and sighing with satisfaction as hot water soaks through my limbs, warming the parts of me that still ache from his lovemaking.

How am I going to live without him?

And why?

Think about the play, Liz. Not Aidan, Not tonight.

I close my eyes and try to stop thinking. I bury my thoughts in my character, and it works for a while, but when I go to sleep, I'm thinking about Aidan.

THE PLAY RUNS FOR TWO HOURS AND THIRTY minutes. When the final curtain comes down, there's a moment of silence, a silence so deep that it's possible to hear a pin drop, then the audience erupts in thunderous applause.

The curtain comes up again and Aidan joins us on stage. He sweeps me up in his arms and kisses me deeply.

Like he doesn't care who is watching.

I don't care either.

"You were spectacular," he exclaims, holding on to me as we walk to the front of the stage with the rest of the cast. We bow amidst the applause and a few people throw flowers. We stand there waving for a few minutes before the curtain comes down for the final time and we go backstage.

People are hugging each other and laughing. It's pandemonium. All the people with a backstage pass, eager to chat, to congratulate me, to ask me questions. I find Aidan's eyes in the crowd and when he sees how tired I am, he comes to my side, helping me shut down most of the conversations.

After the last of the critics and fans and investors have gone on to the after party, I go to my dressing room to change. I wonder what I'll do now, after I leave the play. I don't think I'll work. I'd like to travel. I could go to France or Switzerland and work on my French.

Without Aidan.

Without him, nothing seems attractive.

There are flowers on all the surfaces in my room. On my dressing mirror a huge bouquet of white lilies occupies center space. From Aidan.

I touch a soft petal and sigh at the velvety texture.

There's a knock on my door. I open it expecting Aidan, but it's Lucy, my recently hired assistant for the production.

"Your car is here to take you to the party," she informs me.

When I get to the ballroom at the Concord, the venue for the party, a cheer erupts in the crowd, I return the smiles, wondering where Aidan is. He enters the room a few moments behind me and when I turn around our gazes meet.

I love him so much.

He smiles at me, making something ache in my

chest, then comes over to kiss me again. Lots of pictures and toasts follow, and I drink so much champagne I stop feeling tired.

After a while, the reviews start to come in, and as Aidan predicted, they are overwhelmingly positive. Each new one that goes online cause a cheer to go through the room. It's beautiful.

A few hours into the party, Aidan comes up behind me and I turn to face him. "Congratulations," I tell him.

He pulls me close. "It was all you."

"You know that's not true."

"Are we going to dodge each other's compliments all night or are we going to get out of here, together?"

I place my hand in his. "Let's go."

We sneak out of the hotel through a side entrance. Aidan gives me his coat and we walk along the sidewalk. I let my hair fall into my face and it works. Nobody recognizes me.

At my apartment, there are no paparazzi, they're all waiting at the hotel thinking I'm still at the party.

We enter the building, kissing. In my apartment, I offer him a drink, watching as he unbuttons his dress shirt and undoes his cuffs before taking a sip. I drink mine, still watching him.

"What are you looking at?" he asks, after a while.

"You. Every sexy inch of you."

He takes my drink from me and sets it on a table along with his. "Come here."

I walk into his arms. He runs his hands over my shoulders and arms, then turns me around and removes my jewelry before undoing the zipper of my dress. His fingers graze my back and I tremble.

He kisses the back of my neck, his lips making a sweet trail along my skin before he turns me to face him. "You will ruin me, Liz. If I lose you now, I don't think I'll ever recover."

I don't know what to say.

"Don't you see?" His voice is low. "You've made me your slave again. All I do is think of you. You're intoxicating, and I can't bear to imagine not having you."

I bury my face in his chest. Allowing myself to hope, to fantasize, to imagine that future I've dreamed about. Me and him together. His arms tighten around me and I melt and moan his name.

"You're temptation, and punishment...and I'm helpless to resist." He kisses me again, and there's a frantic intensity in his kiss, a hunger that makes me forget everything but how it feels to be in his arms.

"I need you." The words fall out of my lips with an urgency I can't mask. "I need you so much."

My dress falls to the ground. His clothes follow and then he carries me to my bedroom. He covers my body with his and covers every inch of my skin with kisses, bringing me to a fever pitch with his touch.

By the time he pushes my legs apart and plunges into me, my body is almost fluid with pleasure and heat. He makes love to me, fast, and then slow, bringing me to a climax again and again until I fall into an exhausted sleep in his arms.

CHAPTER THIRTY FIVE

AIDAN

I stay all night. The next morning when I wake up, Liz is not in bed. For one frantic moment I'm convinced she is gone, just like the last time, but then I see her standing at the door to the balcony, wearing a cream silk robe that reaches down to her knees.

"Good morning."

I stretch and notice I'd tossed the covers off sometime before waking. I'm naked, with the sheets tangled around my legs. "How long have you been ogling me Liz?"

She laughs. "Longer than I care to admit."

I leave the bed and walk over to her, still naked. I grab her waist and press her body against mine, covering her face with kisses.

She giggles and dodges my kisses. "Get dressed."

"Are you sure?" I untie her robe. Underneath, she's wearing just a wisp of silk panties.

"Yes." Her voice sounds breathless. She escapes from my embrace, her face pink as she gestures toward the food laid out on a low table on the balcony. "Let's eat. I don't know about you, but I need food every once in a while."

I raise an eyebrow. "You mean feasting on me isn't enough?"

She tries not to laugh but doesn't succeed. With a smile, I steal another kiss before heading to the bathroom.

I join her later, wearing my briefs and a bathrobe I found in her bathroom. She reads the reviews from the night before, grinning in delight at every little word of praise for the play.

In the afternoon, I leave for the theater, and in the evening, once again, Liz kills it with her spectacular performance.

This time we go to my place, I fix her dinner, and we eat, make love and fall asleep. Hours later, I wake up and watch her sleep by the light filtering in from the windows.

She looks more beautiful asleep than she does when she's awake. Her skin is alabaster smooth, her lips soft and parted as she breathes softly.

Who am I without you?

I don't say the words out loud, but I think them.

Those seven years without Liz, I was an empty shell, if she leaves again, I won't even have my resentment or my supposed hatred.

Who would I be then?

She stirs, then opens her eyes and catches me watching her. "Apparently, I'm not the only one who likes to ogle," she murmurs sleepily, stretching like a cat.

"Perfection should be admired."

"It means the world that you think I'm perfect."

"The whole world thinks you're perfect."

Her eyes soften. "But I only care about your opinion."

I reach up and stroke her hair, then place a soft kiss on her lips. Just then, her phone beeps.

"Sorry." She gives me an apologetic smile and reaches for the phone. "I set an alert for when the Steven Dash review goes online."

Another critic. It's amusing to see how excited she is. "You already know what it's going to say."

"Even more reason to read it. I always read the positive reviews. It's the negative ones I've learned to avoid."

She scrolls through her phone, then stops. She frowns and taps on something. A page opens, casting electronic light on her face. She turns worried eyes in my direction.

I know it's impossible that the noted theatre

critic would have anything negative to say about her performance. How can he? It's the performance of a decade. "What is it? What did he say?"

She hands me the phone and I see a headline screaming in lurid red lettering.

Lkay gets her groove back! Liz McKay and director Aidan Court enjoy opening night tryst.

There's a picture of us on her balcony, kissing. My hand is inside Liz's robe and I'm naked. There are a few other pictures of us having breakfast together and even entering the building together. Obviously, a lucky photographer has been watching her apartment from one of the other buildings on the street.

"Assholes," I mutter under my breath.

"I'm sorry," Liz says.

I look from the phone to her apprehensive expression. "It's not your fault."

"Yes, but...it's my reality, and now I've dragged you into it."

The chaos of her celebrity life is the least of the things I'd brave to be with her.

Then tell her.

I can't

Because it won't matter. She'll leave and rip my heart out when she does.

"I don't mind. I don't have any qualms about being seen with you, Liz. I don't know if you've noticed, but you're one of the most desirable women in the country. In the world, even."

She inhales sharply and reaches for the phone. "You didn't even read the article."

I shrug. "I have zero interest in what people at a gossip site have to say."

It's partly true. In a few weeks, I'll care again. When the rumors are about her and another man. I'll torture myself with images of how things could have been different. I'll torture myself with how, once again, I've been left behind, holding the pieces of my heart.

"It won't matter in a few days," I hold her gaze, hating the regret I can see in her eyes, because it changes nothing. "Once you're back in L.A., there'll be new rumors, a new love interest."

The sheets rustle as she turns away. "Stop it."

"It's true."

"And you're okay with that?"

I shrug. "Are you okay with that?"

She pulls in a breath. "What do you want me to do, Aidan?"

I want you to stay! I want us to be together. To rebuild the life we could have had. I want you to know that I love you desperately. That I'll never be able to love anyone else, only you.

Out loud, I say nothing, because whatever she needs, it's not the words that communicate the feelings she already knew seven years ago. Feelings that didn't stop her from leaving then and won't stop her now.

She will take your soul and crush it without a thought.

I stroke my thumb over her bottom lip. Under my touch, it quivers. "Come here," I murmur, pulling her to me. "We might as well make the most of the time we have left."

We make love, and it's only later, when she's asleep in my arms, that I notice the tears on her cheeks.

CHAPTER THIRTY SIX

LIZ

"*Liz, are you sleeping with your director?*"

"*Liz, when are you returning to L. A.?*"

"*Liz, why are you leaving the play?*"

"*Liz, are you having an affair with Aidan Court?*"

The questions batter me as soon as Percy opens the door. I climb out of the car and let him shield me with his body as we hurry to the stage door. Rope barricades line the path to the door to protect me, but as the reporters hurl the words across like missiles, each new one makes me flinch.

The door closes behind me and I breathe in the relative peace and silence inside the theater. The security guard touches his cap in a silent greeting and goes back to the book he's reading.

"You're all right?" Percy asks.

I nod.

He heads back outside. It's been like this for days. Ever since the pictures came out. The frenzy is draining. The paparazzi follow me from my apartment to the theater and back, taking pictures and screaming questions at me.

On TV, it's no better, the entertainment networks show the pictures of me and Aidan on the balcony over and over again, and we have to listen to suggestive comments about his *perfect* ass. Aidan isn't fazed, apart from arranging for extra security at both our buildings and at the theater, he ignores the frenzy and the paparazzi like they don't exist.

I hurry toward my dressing room to prepare for my last performance. After the press release went out two days ago about my departure, there were protests on the website and on my social media accounts, and a flurry of returned tickets. I'm almost too ashamed to face anyone on the production, but I have to leave, for my sanity.

Natalia is waiting outside my dressing room.

"Here you are," she says drily. She's mad at me too, but she understands a lot more than the people outside.

"Here I am." I give her a tight smile and unlock my door.

She follows me inside. "When are you leaving?"

I frown. "You already know my last performance is tonight."

"I'm not talking about the play." She waves a dismissive hand. "When are you leaving New York?"

I shrug. "In a few days...maybe sooner."

"What about Aidan?"

I swallow. "What about him?"

She gives me an impatient look. "Is he okay with it?"

I sigh. "I don't know. He hasn't asked me to stay... And you know how he was before. He could barely stand to be in the same room with me until my dad died..." I take a deep breath. "Now, he's...I have no idea what he feels."

"You're such a fool," Natalia rolls her eyes. "We're all fools though, when it comes to love."

"I'm trying not to be a fool. I love him, but what happens in a week, a month, when he's no longer overcome with guilt, or pity or whatever he's feeling for me right now?"

"Jesus, Liz."

"You know what my dad said to me in the last moments I spent with him at the hospital? He said, don't settle, Liz. Don't settle for less than you want..."

"And you think he meant Aidan?"

"Yes! He knew more than anyone how easily I could be tempted to stay with Aidan, even when I can't be sure how he feels. What else could he have meant?"

"Your father didn't want you to spend the rest of

your life unhappy, trying to make the most of a career that has long ceased to inspire you, just because you're too afraid to fight for the love you always wanted." Her eyes soften. "Aidan is what you want. You love him. He loves you..."

"He doesn't...I don't..."

Natalia barks out a bitter laugh. "Liz," she says with a pitying smile. "I thought it was obvious, even to you, that he never stopped loving you. Isn't that the reason you came back and tried so hard to change his mind about you? He was angry, Liz. He has been angry for seven years."

"But..."

"Death makes us question our convictions. At least, it's made me question mine. For years, I focused on all the reasons I couldn't be with your father the way I wanted, instead of all the great things about what we had. Now, it's too late for us, but it's not too late for you."

"Nat..."

"Don't walk away from him again."

I pull in a breath. I wish it was that easy. He expects me to leave, and he hasn't asked me to stay. Natalia has tears in her eyes, and I don't want to distress her any further with this subject.

"You sure you're not mad about the play?"

"Oh, I am." She smiles. "Very mad. Once again,

you're costing this company a chance at the best actress award."

"I'm sorry."

"I understand. The first time, you were rash and immature. This time, you lost your father." She sighs. "It's not all sentiment for me, however. I love you, but our lawyers have made sure it'll cost you a lot of money to leave. Money that will compensate McKay Theater Productions for ticket refunds and that award." She pauses. "Your manager is the one who'll be furious with you."

"He's half furious and half hopeful I'll do the movie with Devlin Coates."

She shrugs. "He's a good manager." After a pause, she gives me an encouraging smile. "I wish you the best, Liz. No matter what you do."

"Thanks."

"We're arranging a press conference with your people to clear all the crazy rumors flying around."

"Yes, I know."

After she leaves, I close my eyes, and my mind drifts to Aidan.

Aidan is what you want.

My heart longs for him with a raw aching hunger. I've wanted him for so long, ached for him for so long…that I believed I'd be willing to take almost anything he offered.

Even if he was offering nothing at all.

But I can't. I can't choose the uncertainty of not knowing when his resentment and anger would rise to the surface again. I'm not strong enough to bear his inevitable rejection when the sex and pity is no longer enough.

An announcement comes over the loudspeakers and I undress. It's time to let go of my thoughts, my hopes, myself, and to prepare for that one last performance, my last curtain, which sadly, feels like it's also a curtain closing on my life.

"WE'RE SAD TO ANNOUNCE AND CONFIRM THAT this will be the last curtain call for Liz McKay on the Break of Day."

I bow again and the audience applauds and makes sounds of regret. The orchestra plays loudly from the pit. The applause grows to a crescendo. Beside me my co-stars clap as I walk downstage and bow again to the audience.

Aidan is not onstage with us. In fact, I haven't seen him all day.

Is he keeping his distance now that the end is in sight? Maybe he has decided there's no point in sticking around for a painful goodbye?

Backstage, the mood is bittersweet. I say farewells until my mouth is dry. I leave my set assistant to pack up my dressing room and call Percy. Then I go to the stage door and spend an hour signing autographs until my wrists are aching.

Still no Aidan.

At home, I let the sound of the TV distract me from my thoughts. I pour myself a glass of wine and run a bath. I read my messages, the censorious one from my manager, the understanding but confused one from Fiona. She wants us to hang out tomorrow after the press conference. I agree, even though I'm sure I'll be too heartsick to be anything but a drag.

There's nothing from Aidan. Not a message. Not a call.

He loves you.

Or maybe not.

Maybe he crossed the thin line a long time ago, and now, there's no crossing back.

I finish my wine and get into bed, trying not to cry as I drift into sleep.

CHAPTER THIRTY SEVEN

AIDAN

"I never knew you to be a coward." Cruz gives me a judgey look and turns back to watch the basketball game on the court.

"Why is everyone making this about me? She's the one who decided to leave...again."

"It is about you," he says. "You're the one who's choosing to let her go."

I try for levity, even though I'm dying inside. In a few hours, Liz will give a press conference to discuss her decision to leave the play and talk about her next project. I won't be there, and if she leaves immediately, then I won't see her again. I sigh. "Modern woman. Mature woman. Makes her own choices."

Cruz snorts. "And you, what choice have you made? To hide until she leaves?"

"I'm spending time with you, my friend. Watching an intensely competitive game in good weather. Who's hiding?"

"You are."

I close my eyes and cover my face with my hands. "It doesn't matter what I do or say. She'll leave anyway."

"You won't know that until you do and say something." He tears his eyes away from the game and faces me. "She came back. She told you she never stopped loving you. You pushed her and pushed her, and she didn't give up. Now, that she has, maybe it's time for you to pull."

"And if I come up empty?"

"Then at least you tried."

IN THE UBER ON THE WAY TO LIZ'S APARTMENT, MY mind churns with all the unspoken words from the past seven years, from the past months.

I love you.

Those are the most important words of all. The words of surrender.

And I am ready to surrender. No matter what happens. I'll let her know that I'll be here, loving her, for the rest of my life.

She doesn't answer her phone when I try to call, and no one answers her doorbell when I ring. Desperate, I call Natalia.

"Aidan." She sounds distracted.

"I'm sorry to bother you, but do you know where I can find Liz?"

She is quiet for a moment. "Her people moved the press thing up by an hour. It's starting around now."

I swallow. "Okay. Thanks."

I know the venue of the press conference, and I start to request another ride to take me there, then when I reach the sidewalk and the ride isn't there yet, I cancel it and break into a run.

I need to speak to her.

Outside the hotel, there's the usual gaggle of paparazzi. Inside the lobby, signs point out the direction of the conference room. I follow the signs, stopping just outside the double doors that lead inside.

I can hear a voice speaking into a microphone, the clicks of cameras, the rustle of tens of bodies hoping to be the first to break an interesting titbit, to take the picture all the celeb magazines will want to buy.

And then Liz. There's her voice through speakers. Even through the doors, though I can't hear what she's saying, I can hear her, and I can feel the preview of my loss of her, and it's something I cannot bear.

"You going to stand there, mate, or are you going to go in?"

A surly man with a camera and press credentials is glaring at me, and shaking his head, he pushes the door open.

Sound envelopes me, the cacophony of questions. At the far side of the room. Liz is seated at a table, her manager and agent beside her, her face serene as she watches the clamor of cameras, notes and recorders.

I love you.

"Are you returning to L.A.?"

"Not for now." She smiles at the reporter. "I think I deserve a few weeks of rest."

Noise.

"You're going on a vacation?"

"Yes."

Noise.

"Will you be returning to film your movie with Devlin Coates?"

"Not right now. No."

Noise.

It's news to me that she's not returning to the film. She's leaving everything behind, and for a moment, all I feel is pride, for her. Because she's doing this for herself.

Her manager's face is stony, but I barely notice. I can hardly take my eyes off Liz. My legs move me toward the front of the room.

"Are you leaving the production of the Break of Day because you have a bad working relationship with Aidan Court, the director?"

Liz smiles and shakes her head. "Working with Aidan has been the high point of doing this play. I have a great relationship with him, and he's a very talented director, and a professional."

"Yet, you're leaving."

"As I said, I need some time to rest."

"Is there anything that would make you stay?"

She turns in my direction, looking as shocked as I am by the sound of my voice on the speakers. I wasn't even conscious of grabbing the mic from a passing intern. "Is there anything that would make you stay?" I ask again.

Liz stares at me, wordless. Around us, the room is silent, but I barely notice. She's the only one I see. "I don't..."

"What if I told you I love you? That I've always loved you, that I never stopped loving you...that no matter what happens here, I'll always be waiting, unable to love anyone else? What if I admit you've captured and enslaved me, and I'm helplessly yours, and even if you choose not to stay, I'll be happy, grateful, delirious even, if you consider forgiving me for my rudeness, resentment, anger...enough to bear my presence in your life...as anything you want...Your companion, friend, lover, your willing slave?

She chuckles, and it lights up her face. "Aidan...I..."

"I love you," I say again, letting her see the truth on my face.

Always, Liz.

Her eyes close, and when she opens them and looks at me again, the whole room disappears and it's just me and her. She rises from her seat and rounds the table, stepping down from the raised area and approaching me. I go to meet her, closing the distance in a few strides. In the background, I can hear the clamor. I can hear her manager making an announcement, but I don't hear the words.

I only have eyes for Liz. When I'm right in front of her, I stop walking and reach for her. She turns up her gaze to mine, and there's a small smile on her lips.

"What took you so long, Aidan?"

I release a breath, weak with relief, weak with the realization that everything has changed.

"I have no idea."

She sighs. "Say it again."

I don't hesitate. "I love you."

"And I love you, Aidan. Always."

I cup her face in my hands and claim her lips in a tender kiss.

Mine.

Always and Forever.

EPILOGUE

LIZ

 *ive years later...*
"Cut."

I turn a glance toward the director's chair, and he grins at me, clasping his hands together in unconcealed ecstasy. "That's it, folks."

I let out a tired sigh. "Thank God!"

"It's your last scene, right?"

"Yup." My co-star is one of the newest screen gods stealing hearts from the UK to Australia. His British accent is crisp and delightful. The women on the set can't seem to get enough of it.

"You want to hang out tonight? Get a drink, celebrate?"

I shake my head. "I'll be celebrating," I tell him, grinning. Just not with him.

Outside, the air is sharp and cold. Around us, the Swiss countryside is different shades of green, and in the distance, the blue of far-off mountain ranges are topped with white, like the mountains in a Christmas card. I take a deep breath, then head for my trailer, pulling my phone out of my jacket pocket at the same time.

The last message from Aidan is from about an hour ago.

Plane landed. Heading to you. I have a surprise.

What surprise? My heart is skipping as I type a quick reply.

Where are you?

No answer.

I hear running footsteps behind me. It's my set assistant, a multilingual Swiss angel called Gigi.

"You haven't said if you'll be needing a ride to town," she says in French-accented English. "or when. The hotel is on standby waiting for confirmation..."

I shake my head. "I'm fine, Gigi. You've been great."

She smiles. "Thank you. Working for you has been a dream come true."

I make my way to my trailer. I've already said my goodbyes to the others on set. Hair and makeup, the lighting people. Another job done. Another success, and now, back to what really matters.

I open the door.

Aidan is standing just inside, his tall frame dwarfing the warm, spacious interior. It's a luxurious trailer, the best...for the best. He turns around when the door opens, his perfection breathtaking, from the wavy hair that frames his head to his long legs, his heartbreakingly beautiful face, his sensuous mouth... it takes every bit of self control to keep me from launching myself at him like a child.

"You're here already!"

"I am."

"I thought you'd be another hour at least."

He grins and my heart somersaults in my chest. Five years of him being mine, and I still can't get enough of him. We never go more than a few weeks without seeing each other, no matter what we're working on, and still sometimes, I want to toss all my work out of the window and focus only on being the woman by his side.

"Are you going to stand there ogling me and letting the cold in, or am I going to get to kiss you at some point?" he teases.

I close the door and walk into his arms. He wraps them around me, and I sigh contentedly. "I'm hoping for more than kisses."

He claims my mouth in a warm, tender melding of our lips, and it feels like heaven. More than heaven. I moan into his mouth. The journey to the chateau he has rented for the next week can wait. I want him now.

"Mommy!"

The piping voice from the rear of the trailer interrupts us, and I tear my lips from Aidan's just before the three and a half foot tall projectile of perfection launches into my arms.

"My angel." I scatter kisses all over her face and hair. "My darling angel."

"I told you I had a surprise," Aidan is smiling in satisfaction. "Rachel wanted her for a week. Penny, apparently was looking forward to having her cousin around, but guess who just had to see her mommy or nothing?"

"Me!" Ella pipes up. My three-year-old miracle who's a perfect mixture of Aidan and me.

"And guess who is so happy to see you?" I croon.

"You!" She answers, giggling.

I look over her head at Aidan. "Thank you," I mouth.

He grins, then looks at his watch. "The plane is waiting. Why don't we get started, and maybe in a few hours, we can do something about the hope you expressed earlier?"

I give him a curious look. "What hope?"

One devilishly perfect eyebrow quirks. "For more than kisses."

"Ah..." I return his smile. "I can hardly wait."

The End.

AUTHOR'S NOTE

Thank you so much for reading this book. Writing it was a truly delightful experience. Aidan is one of my favorite characters, and I hope you enjoyed reading his story.

BECAUSE OF YOU is the fifth book in the Swanson Court series. Thank you for staying with these characters, loving them, and challenging me to keep them alive.

I wish you all the best of life and love.

Serena.

ABOUT SERENA GREY

I'm obsessed with books and read whenever I can—romance, fantasy, mystery, history—anything I can lay my hands on. I grew up reading Danielle Steel, Nora Roberts and many other romance authors. These days, I read Whitney Garcia Williams, Laurelin Paige, E.L James and Sylvia Day, though you're as likely to find me reading Brandon Sanderson and George R R Martin.

I'm an older millennial—made in 1985. I have a husband I love and a baby son I adore. I love wine, coffee with lots of cream, chocolate chip cookies, and my superpower is knowing how to live on the bright side of life.

To be the first to find out about my new releases, sign up for my Mailing List at www.serenagrey.com/alerts

For more information, go to www.serenagrey.com

BOOKS BY SERENA GREY

A DANGEROUS MAN SERIES

Awakening: A Dangerous Man #1

Rebellion: A Dangerous Man #2

Claim: A Dangerous Man #3

Surrender: A Dangerous Man #4

UNDENIABLE

SWANSON COURT SERIES

Drawn to You

Addicted to You

Lost in You

Landon

Because of You

WILD SEXY SERIES

Wild Sexy Thing

Wild Sexy Fix

Wild Sexy Hurt

Wild Sexy Love

MORE THAN ANYTHING: A CHRISTMAS
ROMANCE

Find at www.serenagrey.com/books

CONNECT WITH SERENA

Facebook: www.facebook.com/authorserenagrey

Twitter: @s_greyauthor

Goodreads: www.goodreads.com/serenagrey

Website: www.serenagrey.com